ONE NIGHT BRIDE

NICOLE SNOW

ICE LIPS PRESS

DESCRIPTION

JUST ENGAGED. WHO SAID ANYTHING ABOUT LOVE?

The plan was simple: find the perfect girl, wife her for a few months, and save my parents from a stinging case of heartbreak.

That was before I got my first taste of Skye's whip-sharp tongue.

Before she woke up wearing my ring and a hundred questions.

Before I found out it takes more than a million dollars to put the sun back in her smile.

She needs a friend. A protector. A relentless caveman who won't quit until her haunted, uptight good girl act is history.

One glaring problem: Cade doesn't do serious.

I built my name on fast money, vicious good looks, and a rebel charm that never beguiles the same woman twice.

I expected this one night bride thing to be complicated. I didn't know how wrong I could be.

She's scandalized my very soul.

Every secret, every touch, every smoldering glance is fresh insanity. We're on a collision course.

There's no hiding the truth when Skye, my delicious little lie, has me asking the unthinkable.

What if the woman I'm about to pretend marry is chaos incarnate? What if her kiss is an obsession? And what if I can't let our sweet madness end?

I: DUTY BOUND (SKYE)

A man brings a woman to her knees three times in a lifetime: once with his passion, once with his promise, and once when he shows her his heart.

Our love just trashed the cardinal rule. I think it hurts because he's not the one to blame.

It's my own fault I'm on my knees crying, knowing it's too late. There won't be a fifth time to fall down and let him save me.

I don't even recognize my own reflection in the spotless mirrors. I'm on my hands and knees, crawling the university's polished marble floors, suffering the earthquake left in his wake.

Tremors are all I have since he walked out. It shouldn't be such a surprise.

Oh, I knew there'd be heartbreak.

That was in the cards since the night we met, and branded in the morning after, when he thrust this stupid ring on my hand that's become emotional corrosion. It's a tiny diamond paradox worth more than this building. Hell and happiness in equal balance.

1

Snatching it off my finger, I hold it up, asking for the hundredth time how it's possible to love and hate an object this much.

I need to start seeing it differently. It's an absurd, teasing remnant of something we never had.

Something I was foolish to ever hope for.

"Ridiculous," I whisper, voice trembling.

Ridiculous and beautiful.

Somehow, it's more priceless than the heavy Roman bust laying against my hand. I knocked it off the table in my fit after he stormed off. Thank God it didn't break. I don't need to cause more grief for a school I've already cheated.

I sigh, gently holding the artifact, looking for cracks through my tears. One day, the end will come for this eighteen hundred year old statue, just like it does for everything, but not today.

Staring is a mistake. The longer I do, the worse the pain twists my intestines.

If I deserve this – and after the anger and disappointment in his eyes I *certainly do* – I still don't like it.

It just isn't fair.

The dead things I've devoted my life to get off easy. They stay dead, inert and timeless as the Marcus Aurelius face I didn't break, thank God again. Their existence is abstract, casual, painless.

Everything I wish I had when I remember my last words, before I put the look on his face that destroyed me. *"Stop making me your problem. I don't need you, and neither does Vinnie. We'll handle it like we always have. I'll pay back the money and move on. I don't want your damn job or your money, Cade. It's over. I'm sorry."*

I don't know how he held my gaze without exploding. The sadness in his soft blue eyes was enough to drown any woman with a conscience – even a shrinking one like mine.

His last words were brutal. *"And what about love, Skittle? You want to stand here and tell me you don't need that, too?"*

I shook my head. I turned my back. I didn't answer.

Coward me didn't look back. Just watched him in the mirror on my desk, one more tool we use to help clean the museum pieces.

The same thoughts looped in the space of ten seconds, over and over, shaken to a core I was so sure no man would ever break. Everything I desperately wanted to, but wouldn't let myself say.

Damn it, Cade, can't you see I have to do this?

Don't you know it's for our own good?

Can't you fucking see what you've done to me?

He doesn't. I didn't give him the chance. And so I'm on my knees alone, gently wiping grit off this ancient bust with my shirt, surrounded by a wealth of history, art, and learning that feels like poverty after his blazing blue eyes.

Cade is nothing now. Just another needle in my heart. Toxic venom, denial, and loss.

I'm not cut out for this hero thing, especially when I can't tell him the real reason we'll never work.

It's for my good, and for his, and for Vinnie's. If I could make him understand, then maybe it wouldn't hurt so bad to lose it all.

There were no second options.

I'm a smart young woman. I don't need another PhD to know pursuing this...this *thing* with a man who promised me the world would be the end. The consequences, the danger, just keeping him around wouldn't end our love. It could easily cost us our lives. Apocalyptic, guaranteed.

Loving him already is.

And that part, I can't control, when a man this rare poached my heart.

Cade is the unthinkable, the one I didn't plan for.

Scary, sexy perfection in lightning blue eyes and a five o'clock shadow. Muscle and depth. Jagged smirks and piercing smiles.

He's everything I secretly craved. Everything I never should've tasted. Everything guaranteed to ruin me if I let Mr. Relentless seep into the screwed up, imperfect chasm called the life of Skye.

The grief will come, but I'll get over it. There isn't another choice.

I cut him lose because I swore I'd fix the nightmare staring me in the face.

I'm not doing this for me. It's for my little brother, my sins against my school, and the asshole who still owns a piece of my soul. The very same asshole I don't need Cade's help with because he's done more for me than I deserve.

You can live without his help, I tell myself, with no confidence whatsoever it's true.

But without his love? I'm almost as ruined as the moments when I thought I had it.

Cade and I never had chemistry.

We had alchemy. The scariest, best, most heart-binding kind that's meant to burn nuclear and then wink out.

The time is now, even though it hurts. There's no more to waste sacrificing my heart.

In just a couple seconds, I'll get off this glossy floor and tell myself one more time I'm doing right.

I'll repeat it until it loses its meaning because then I won't know it's a blatant lie.

I'm in too deep to pinpoint whenever the truth stopped mattering.

What we had, ridiculous and beautiful, was real.

And it still is. It's overwhelmingly real in the steady hurtful throb in my temples, which tells me I haven't seen the last of Cade Turnbladt, as insane as that seems.

Fresh ache pools in my knees. So does fear.

It's not the crazy, impossible thing I have to figure out over the next few days.

It's because I have a sick feeling they haven't begun to kneel for this man, and if I do it a fifth time, none of us might stand again in one piece.

* * *

Four Months Ago

"Cough drop, sug?" Adele throws the bag down next to me, spilling a few cherry red drops bleeding through their white wrappers across the bathroom counter.

I shake my head, never taking my eyes off the mirror. Doesn't she know I was just clearing my throat in case someone requests a song? I'm not sick. I wouldn't dare perform for the clients with a bug, but I guess some of the other girls who go all the way don't share my concerns.

"Suit yourself," she snaps, stepping over to Ruby. Her frown deepens when she swats the girl on the butt. "What did I tell you last time? An inch higher up the thigh and lower at the top. They need to see you to figure out whether you're worth their time and money, dearie."

"Yeah, okay. Understood." Ruby adjusts her cocktail dress.

"And you, again," Adele says, returning her jade huntress eyes to mine. "I'd *better* see some proof those lessons are paying off. Last time, a couple of the older guys said you were off key. Remember you're getting off lightly, Skye, considering you don't do the after-shows. Now, I don't care if you're Harry's niece or whatever. But I do have a business to run, and I expect improvements."

5

I don't say anything. Silence pisses her off even more, but not enough to keep her berating me.

Waiting until I hear her heels click across the bathroom floor and the door swing open, I release my sigh, casting it into the mirror.

I look good tonight. At least half-human. The expensive creams I really can't afford on this salary took out the bags under my eyes. That always goes far with the kind of men I'm starting to get used to entertaining.

They love to look me in the eyes when I sing, hunched over the piano, a strangely intimate gesture I never expected at the start of this.

They say I have beautiful eyes, like a full storm drifting in. I'm not sure if it's a blessing, or a curse.

Certainly, they're the only thing mom left behind, and that could easily make them either.

"That was close. You got off easy," Ruby says, flashing a messy smile as she does her lipstick. "She's losing out big keeping you from the after-shows, ya know. You have a clue how many men want to take you home most nights?"

Of course I do. I'm the one they can't have, at least not in full, and it makes me top prize. I watch my eyes narrow in the reflection, trying to control the loathing in the pit of my stomach.

I'm not like her, this desperate whore, selling herself after every performance to the man with the shiniest platinum watch. I'm not like any of the other girls, who work for Adele *willingly.*

I'm one degree removed. On the right side of the thin, dark line that involves teasing strangers, without actually sharing their beds.

This isn't some high horse. I was knocked off whatever stallion used to show me right and wrong a long time ago.

I close my eyes, ignoring the pop tune Ruby starts humming to herself.

Just another night. Nothing special. I remember why I'm here. I think about the debt I'm paying, the only thing that's keeping Vinnie and me fed, sheltered, and alive.

This is a job. It's desperation. It's temporary.

I've done it for the better part of a year. Three, sometimes four 'performances' every month, as Uncle Harry calls them. It should be easy money for a grad student in a subject that should give a bright future flipping burgers.

Then I remember how I almost had it all, how easily I could've taken myself around the world and paid for Vinnie's treatments, if only that stupid fucking box hadn't gotten lost in the mail. I'm reminded what I did to get it, how I thought nothing about breaching laws and ethics, if only it would've meant money for my dreams, my family.

If only, is a demon no matter how many times it beats me over the head.

If only I'd been able to ship the thousand year old jewelry I took from under the university's nose.

If only I'd gotten it into my uncle's dirty hands to sell on the black market.

If only he'd paid my cut, I wouldn't be here tonight, shaking my ass like one more of Adele's girls for the oh-so-rich, oh-so-handsome men of Seattle's upper crust, who totally aren't investing in their latest pump and dump side candy, many cheating on their wives by showing up for our 'performances.'

That's the cold truth. Maybe never had a high horse. My moral compass always pointed toward desperation.

Sometimes I wonder if I deserve this. Uncle Harry let me keep the loan, after all, the down payment he gave us for tuition and a part-time caretaker for my bratty little brother.

Ruby leaves with the other girl, both of them laughing, leaving me alone.

I look into the mirror one more time, drawing a breath.

"It's not forever. Be in the now. Get this over with," I whisper to myself in the quiet.

It doesn't help because I'm lying so hard about the last part. There's no end in sight.

I owe Uncle Harry *a lot* of money, and what little I have left is running out.

* * *

"My, what a crowd! Any special requests tonight? It's nice to see so many handsome gentlemen who know a good song. What are you boys hungry for? Jazz...classical...contemporary...or just me?" I smile, staring across the ballroom, ending my words with a cringe-worthy wink.

No matter how many times I do this, it never feels normal.

We're thirty floors above downtown Seattle in a ritzy ballroom that's half glass. I'm sitting at a piano that probably costs more than the stupid jewelry that put me here, trying not to scream.

The men in their suits lost interest as soon as Adele told them I was off limits. This is an older, hornier crowd. They're hunkered around Ruby and another girl, Ambrosia, running several hands up their legs while they sway to my gentle background score.

"I'll bite. I'm a sucker for Sinatra." I look up, and see a man far younger than I expect considering his request.

"You play beautifully," he says. Almost like it's a real rehearsal, and not a flimsy excuse for a high end peep show.

I smile, embarrassed by the blush lighting up my cheeks. He looks older than me, but not by much, five or six years, maybe. Late twenties, if not early thirties, and dangerously handsome.

He sits on the edge of my bench. Very bold.

I'm expecting him to get grabby and this to get creepy, probably in the next few seconds.

I clear my throat loudly, hoping it'll keep his hands away a while longer. "Sorry. I'm a little rusty with this stuff. Any particular song?"

"Surprise me," he says, a rich warmth in his deep voice. It sends an instinctive chill up my spine.

This better not be insta-lust. I've never been a big believer.

But I can't deny the goosebumps painting my skin. My fingers push the keys, trying to find their focus. I try to make it obvious I'm not watching his every move out the corner of my eye.

I'm halfway through *Fly Me to the Moon,* the only thing I'm able to reconstruct by memory, before I start relaxing.

He isn't moving closer. He isn't doing anything he shouldn't. He's just staring, admiring, and it's not just my nipples beginning to pucker.

This man is *too* well behaved. What the hell is he hiding?

His blue eyes glisten. If I could step outside myself for a second, I'm sure I'd actually look beautiful reflected in his eyes. Not at all like the stuffy, desperate creature I become every time I perform, and never this bad because he's the first client who's easy on the eyes.

"Sing," he whispers, leaning in, his gaze intensifying. "Sing for me. You know the words?"

"Vaguely." It's better to be honest. Especially when my body is betraying more than it should.

I don't know this stranger. I don't trust his eyes, however kind. If he's here, he's come to get his rocks off, whatever his face says to the contrary.

And it's not just his baby blues doing the talking. We

share a look while we sing, his deep voice mouthing each line perfectly, refreshing my memory as we go.

His looks are napalm, a gradual burn destined to sink beneath my skin the longer I'm trapped in his gaze. I spend as much time studying his six foot something godliness tucked into the suit as I do his face. Every gorgeous angle tells me something new.

His sandy blonde hair frames his brow, the lower dusting on his powerful jaw another accent.

His broad shoulders look more like they belong to a Viking groomed into a crisp suit than tech CEO number one hundred in this sleepless, greedy city.

His eyes are kind, like I mentioned, but there's a harsher understanding in their layers. A warning. *Do not fuck with me,* they say.

Ironic, I guess, considering he's the first man I've encountered at these wretched events who makes me wonder what it'd be like to do the unthinkable. To leave the room with him just like the other girls.

You've lost it, I tell myself, catching the crazy thought. But I don't know how the hell to stop.

I just play on, finishing the song, going out with a low, long note.

"Lovely," he says, once my hands are off the keys. My turn to pull my eyes off him. I do it slowly, reluctantly, even. "You're pretty well put together for a woman playing the piano buck naked."

My cheeks go to a hundred and twenty degrees. I knew the asshole had to emerge sooner or later, but I didn't need to be reminded how exposed I really am.

"Topless. I'm still wearing heels and a thong." A minor correction. Not that I want to give him incentive to check. "And yeah, I try. It's kinda my job."

"Is it? I wonder. You didn't fool me for a second with that

pretty, but empty smile, Skittle," he says, sliding across the bench. I don't move while he reaches up my neck. His fingers trace its curve and stop in my hair, flicking the blue and pink alternating highlights. "You're a sore fucking thumb. Too indie, too colorful, too authentic to be like the rest. You remind me of my favorite candy. Tell me, do you actually like this? Or are you just here for the tips?"

I shrug. I don't tell him I could care less. The ballers who always show up at our performances rarely leave more than a few hundred dollars behind after finding out I'm not getting in their car later. A paltry dent in my seven figure debt slavery.

"Aw, come on," he says, smiling through my silence. "I'm just making talk. Your business isn't mine beyond naming your price. How much for the night?"

"Sorry, not for sale," I snap, standing up, folding my arms across my very bare chest. "Neither am I. I'm musical entertainment *only*. If you want a night cap service, the others here are more than happy to –"

"Dreadfully sorry for any disappointment or frustration, sir." Adele cuts me off, appearing out of nowhere behind us. She grabs at the stranger's shoulder, digging her emerald green nails in. They match her jungle eyes. "I should really start putting a disclaimer next to this one on the entertainment listing."

Or remove me altogether, I think, holding my words, aiming a dirty look at the madam.

"Bull. How much for the night?" He repeats the same question, reaching into his pocket, keeping his eyes glued to me, rather than the woman trying to negotiate.

My heart sticks in my throat. Adele doesn't give me another look, just flicks her hair over her shoulder, and repeats the line I've heard a hundred times. "You'll have to accept my apologies, sir. Again, she doesn't work overtime outside tonight's venue. No private shows. If you'd like, I'd be more than happy to introduce you to our other girls, who are free to be far more accommodating than –"

"I'll ask you again since you didn't hear it the first time – *how much?*" He's opening a small leather folio and taking out a pen. I realize it's his checkbook a second later. Adele frowns sourly, unused to clients putting up a fight.

"I'm sorry, sir. This one, she's special. I'm afraid I can't allow you..." She drifts off when he turns the checkbook toward her.

"Do I need another zero in there, or what? Tell you what, I'll keep writing, and you just say when we're good."

His pen moves for another second. Adele clears her throat, whips her head around, and gives me a look I've never seen before.

Panic.

It's infectious, too. My heart drums so heavy in my chest blood roars into my ears, deafening for a few rough seconds.

"Let's go over here a minute, shall we?" Her arm is around me. Like she seriously wants me to hear her out, and forget the guarantee from my uncle, her boss' boss.

"I'm *not* going home with him," I say, once we're alone in a corner across the ballroom. An autumn rain pelts the windows, this city hellbent on reminding us how bone-chilling it can be as we drift toward the holidays.

"I can't make you, obviously. I'm asking you to *consider* it. He's offering a considerable sum for a night. At least ten times more than any of my girls normally average. Plenty left over after my cut, when we're talking *that* much money."

"Oh, joy. A crumb of my debt, maybe. Pop the champagne," I say, motioning toward the endless bottles of Dom being replenished near the snack bar.

Anger curls lines through Adele's face. Pretty impressive

because I'm sure she's on her third face lift. "Skye, let me ask you something...are you stubborn, or just stupid?"

I blink, surprised to see her soulless cool falling apart. "You're kidding, right? I said from the very beginning what I'd do, and what I wouldn't when I took this job."

"Yes, yes. Mr. Coyle was *very* clear." She shakes her head, preening her lips like she's bitten something sour. "Still...just between you and me, you're a foolish, selfish girl not to consider it. That man over there isn't offering money. He's offering time. Do you *know* how many nights you won't have to do this if you'll just get in his bed for one night?"

Dozens. A hundred, maybe, considering how little I usually earn doing this. Sighing, I lower my eyes, and think about my misery waiting at home.

Vinnie's latest application for medical aid hasn't gone through yet. I'm skeptical the state even covers what he needs. The stuff that works best is too experimental. I've been lucky to keep him on it this long, but next month...the seizures could come back any time.

I bite my bottom lip. Adele jabs a long painted fingernail into my skin, just above my right boob and under my throat. "Think carefully, is all I'm saying, Skye. Please. Nobody wants to drag this out any longer than we need to. Not me, not my boss, and certainly not –"

"I'm not saying yes." I take a wide step back, batting her hand away. "But...I guess...I'm not saying no, either."

Adele's eyes go wide. I'm not looking at her anymore, though.

I'm staring past to the sculpted enigma still waiting patiently on the bench, his eyes never moving off mine. I don't know anything about him beyond the fact that he's here, he likes Sinatra, and he's a good deal younger than the other vain, horny men crowding Ruby and Ambrosia like flies.

He could be anyone. Anything. I don't even have a name.

There's no telling whether he's classy, or just crude. And what's he escaping chasing high end escorts – a wife who's clueless about his antics when he's 'just working late?'

An addiction to beautiful women who won't say no?

Hell, maybe he's into stuff no ordinary woman would ever do without him paying through the nose for it.

I'm blind, deaf, and dumb about what I'm getting into if my answer, my risk, is anything except a resounding *no*.

I look at him again. Normally, I'd say his looks, his money, and his obvious ambition wouldn't make selling my virginity so bad. If he isn't a total demon under the Adonis exterior, it still might not be terrible, especially when I think about what happens if Vince's latest medication runs out.

I can't watch him have another seizure. *Jesus, and what happens if he has one while the nurse who checks in on him while I'm working isn't there?*

"We don't have all night. Make up your mind so I can tell the client, one way or another," Adele says, tapping her tall black heel.

"Let me talk to him privately, please." I don't wait for her approval. Before Adele has time to take a step, I'm walking toward the sly, demanding wolf on the bench.

It's a miracle my legs work when my stomach is nothing but knots.

* * *

"Three ground rules if you want me," I tell him, as soon as we're alone. "You won't take my phone. You won't walk away without giving Adele your check tonight, and it damn sure better not bounce."

"That's two," he says, a smirk creeping across his face.

14

He's too good at making me blush, and want to look anywhere except his endless blue pools.

I do a quick look around to make sure no one hears us. Then I lean in, so close I get a lungful of his cologne. I'm not sure if it's intoxicating by itself, like the ritzy brands are, or if it's only when it's mingling with his masculine scent. "We have to use protection."

There's no excuse for mumbling it in his ear like a clueless school girl. None, maybe, except for the fact he grabs my wrist, and locks his hand around it.

"Fuck, Skittle. You must really need it bad. I never brought up sex – you did."

What the hell does that mean? My eyes flick to his. I wonder if I'm being gamed.

It doesn't make sense. No man in his class would come out for an evening like this, with Adele's women, if they weren't looking for the obvious.

"I don't understand," I whisper, trying not to let his stern gaze paint my face red a third time.

"You shouldn't. This isn't the time or place to talk details."

"Okay, can you stop the riddles and tell me what you really want?"

The smirk lining his handsome face gets wider. "Don't know. Can you get dressed and follow me out to my car?"

My saner instincts are in full rebellion. I should stand, walk away, and cut this weird evening short, even if it means less pay.

But then I think about Vinnie's prescription. The pills will be gone in two weeks, maybe less.

Anything could happen if he doesn't have a refill.

Last time he went without, he collapsed in my arms while he was playing a video game, twitching and choking, making every button I tapped on my phone to dial 9-11 feel like a rosary. *He's counting on me, damn it.*

The stranger stands and tugs my arm once. "You coming, or what?" he asks.

I am.

I have to take this risk.

* * *

I'M in his sleek black sedan ten minutes later, riding in the passenger seat, a burgundy camisole that goes past my knees wrapped tight for protection.

I'm no closer to knowing if I'm doing the right thing, or making my biggest mistake.

He doesn't say a word, just gives me that smug, self-assured smile, taking us through the Seattle night.

"How can you be so cool at a time like this? The run up to...you know." I'm hoping provoking him brings some answers.

"How are you so nervous when you walk around flaunting that sugarplum hair, Skittle? These colors scream courage. Don't fuck with me." His blue eyes glow, so much confidence shining through it puts the moon to shame. "Not yet, anyway," he adds, looking up my body, before he puts his eyes on the rain spattered streets again.

"So, we *are* doing this? You and me? Tonight?" *Oh, God.* It's starting to hit me. *What have I done?*

"You're spending the night with me, yeah. That's why I popped that fat check in your madam's hand. Haven't decided yet if it means naked or not."

I stare through him while he isn't looking my way. I try, and fail, tenderly biting into my bottom lip, annoyed and intrigued all at once. If he's putting on a show, it's a good one.

"Do you have a name? Or do you just want to keep the Mr. X shit going through sunup?"

He laughs. It's a rich, resonate tone starting in his chest and ending in the dark, giving it more life than it deserves. "Cade. I'd tell you my last name, but you'd butcher it like everybody else. It's a fit for these Icelandic good looks."

"Try me," I say, folding my arms. His car does a sharp turn, and we roll into Edgewater Park, the exclusive city quarter that seems to house half the rich perverts who attend Adele's shows. "I was a language student, once."

I don't tell him I'm still in grad school. He could be a demented stalker freak, for all I know, and the last thing I want is a maniac in my ordinary life, the one where I'm still an archeology student with a perfect GPA and international accolades.

"Turnbladt," he says, giving me another quick glance. I repeat the name without skipping a beat. His smile wants to spread to my lips, and I hate it. I'm not here to impress him for anything that isn't covered in that check. "Very good. You've heard of me, then."

"Nope. What, you're a Senator, or something? You look a little young. I don't follow politics."

Again, his infuriating, sexy chuckle rings in my ears. "Too sane for that shit-show. There are easier ways to make money without getting on my knees for shady pricks all day. No offense."

Ass. I bat my eyes, unsure whether I should grind it into him that I don't normally go home with strange men.

I just serenade them in the buff, let them ogle me, and stir the disappointment in their eyes when they find out they can't do more. Totally no big deal.

"You look offended," he says, almost like he's surprised. I turn my head, staring out the window, beguiled by the lights illuminating the big houses on the coast. "Sorry, Skittle. Didn't know you were serious about that good girl act. Figured it was just a sales tactic."

"Enough with the suspense. Who are you?" I look at him again, convinced I'll give this one more chance before I fling the door open, step out, and get my far too easily offended ass an Uber home.

"The Turnbladt in Randolph-Emerson-Turnbladt. Biggest financial firm on the West Coast. We make money for the guys who already live, breathe, eat, and shit diamonds, and we're damn good at it."

I frown. The name is familiar, surprisingly. I try to remember why.

I don't read business journals, but I do like true crime. "You mean the place with the kid who killed that other kid years ago?"

Cade's temples bulge, clenching his jaw. "Yeah, and that was a long time ago, Skittle. That *kid* is a good man now. He just so happens to be my best friend. Watch your mouth if all you've got is gossip from guys looking for their next blog click."

"It's not like I went to Maynard Academy to find out," I say, shrugging. Whatever went down there years ago, it was all over the local press when I was just a teen. I'm glad I wasn't part of it. "I went to a normal school."

"Am I supposed to be impressed?" his car slows, turning up a long, winding driveway.

"Excuse me?" I'm not sure whether to be more alarmed by the sudden bitter note in his voice, or shocked to my core by the elaborate castle we're approaching. His place is down-right palatial, a mega-mansion glowing in front of the dark waters. He must not have a wife or live-in girlfriend to screw around on, I guess, or else he's rich enough to afford several places this grand.

"Don't look so wounded. I didn't mean it to sting. I'm not impressed by the mundane, Skittle. Wouldn't have picked you tonight if I wanted the same crap I get everywhere else –

a girl who jumps to my beck and call the second I wave money in her face. You had me at hard-to-get."

So, it's a game to him after all. He wants me because I'll make him work for me. Does he do this constantly?

Does it even matter?

There's another barb growing on my tongue when I see my brother again. I can't screw this up when it hasn't gone completely off the rails. I need to make the most of it. I *need* that money, and maybe it's worth a few bruises to my ego.

"Show me inside," I say, motioning to the fancy double doors hiding his Pacific castle.

"You recover fast. I like that," he says, pulling the car to the curb.

He kills the engine, steps out, and rounds his way to my door. I draw a deep breath before taking his hand, and let him help me out.

If there was ever a time I wanted an out of body experience, it's now.

Whatever comes next, it's for Vincent. It's for the debt on my Uncle's ledger, and the poison karma in my soul. It's so I'm better than mom before she took herself out of this horrible world.

Mostly, I think, it's to prove to myself that I can shut up, play along, and dig myself out of this pit just for one night.

* * *

THE WINE BOTTLE's cork blows like a gunshot. I jump, turn, and see him filling two crystal glasses.

Deep red liquid sloshes high near the rim. Apparently, moderation isn't his style.

Stepping into the room, he slides one glass over. I take it, and can't hide how quickly I gulp it down my throat.

There's no point. I'm seeking courage, and the liquid kind

will do tonight.

I'll need it to face the mess I've gotten myself into. Not to mention the thought of his hard Viking body pressed against mine, wedged between my legs, taking what I always thought I'd give a man who deserves it.

"You got a name, or should I keep calling you Skittle?"

I hesitate. At least he's named me after a candy I actually like – that's worth something, isn't it? It takes another heavy pull of wine before I answer. "Skye," I say softly.

"Skye." It rolls off his tongue like the shallow sip he takes a second later. I watch his throat force it down, eyes locked on his muscles, powerful and elegant when they're just acting out their nature. "Pretty name. Not what I'd expect from one of Adele's girls. Hell, I'm starting to believe you're honest about the stuck up virgin act."

"Whatever," I say, turning my back. His eyes are still fixed, staring through me. Why is it so easy for him to see what I've tried so hard to hide?

Why doesn't it bother me like it should?

Crap. I can't be so smitten, so soon.

"Have a seat," he says, pulling me toward a large ivory sectional against the massive windows. It must be gorgeous during the day, but even at night I can see the tinsel gold warmth bathing the marinas around the bay, every dock and boathouse as magnificent as his.

"Let's cut the bullshit," he says, running one hand up my thigh.

Double crap. I stop, lungs full of cement, bracing for the inevitable. *This is it. The beginning and the end of me.*

"Tell me what you were really doing working for Adele, if you're not here to fuck your way to riches?" I open my eyes, and see his narrowed, locked on mine, demanding answers.

I expected seduction. Not an interrogation.

"It's a living. My business. You don't see me asking about

yours." I shrug, rolling my shoulders. "Do you seriously want to know?"

He's silent. "Yeah, now who's putting who on?" I whisper.

I don't expect his hand on my cheek, pulling me closer, controlling my neck with a swift, but gentle precision. There's no denying his experience, or the thousand new goosebumps it kisses on my skin. "I like to know who, or what, I'm dealing with, beautiful," he growls. "You're in my house, less than an hour from my bed. You could be anything: thief, druggie, serial killer."

It's my turn to laugh. Maybe it's just the wine tickling my brain, but there's almost something innocent in this sudden doubt, this concern dripping out of Mr. Tall, Dark, and Relentless.

Where the hell was it before he decided to throw down six figures for one night?

"You promised we'd use protection. Don't know what you're worried about. Something tells me you enjoy a good mystery," I say, bold fingers braced against his chest, teasing and exploring. He's even harder than I thought. I feel through his shirt. I can't believe a man who must have spent his life in an office clicking keys developed a body like *this.*

"Mystery, yeah. Not a fucking ambush. I look before I leap, Skittle. Had a perfect view of the first fiery hoops I jumped through like a damn poodle to get you here. How many more are you hiding?"

Holy shit, he's serious. I pull away, settling onto the sofa next to him, staring into the night.

It's weirdly cold without his embrace, those thick, heavy hands surrounding me only seconds ago.

"I don't know what to tell you. You're the one who paid to bring me here...right? I thought you'd do whatever risk assessment you needed before you plunked down the cash."

"That only happens when you talk to me, Skittle. Sing.

Crisp and clear and beautiful as you did when I asked for Ol' Blue Eyes. What's in this for you, if money isn't your angle? I've seen enough to know it isn't. Never seen anybody treat a check for a hundred-K like a trip to the fucking dentist."

I'm desperate, but I'm not stupid. I can't tell him the truth. "Sex is the angle, isn't it? I mean, *really?* You need my life's story to cleanse your conscience or something? Before we run off to bed and..."

I can't even say it. Tears sting my eyes. Maybe they'd come anyway after I slept with him, but this warm up, this bitter probing in my heart...

It shouldn't be happening. It's almost like I'm not the only one who's only here because I'm at my wit's end.

"You want to know? Fine. You tell me first, what the hell's going on? If you don't want my body, then what? What is it you're really after?"

"Skittle..." He whispers it long and slow. There's a smolder in his eyes, a warning, and also a shortcut to melting everything below my waist. "I hired you to do a job. Entertain me. You can interpret that however you want, but first I want answers."

I stiffen, knocking back the rest of the wine in my glass. Maybe I shouldn't hide it. After all, isn't he seeing a secret side of me already?

Screw it. Here goes...

"I'm sure you're a smart man to have all this," I say, waving my hand across the Turkish rug underneath us, beneath the sparkling chandelier overhead. "Use your brain. Do you think I'd be here if my life were roses? If I didn't *have* to be? If I had a trust fund from my dead father to put myself through grad school, or knew the right people to get a better job with a dress code fancier than naked, or maybe if my little brother wasn't a few missed pills away from fucking dying?"

Damn it. I regret the last part instantly. I regret all of it, spilling my spaghetti like this, more than the ice cold tear of honesty pouring down one cheek.

Then Cade gives me the look I don't expect.

Sympathy. Exactly what I didn't want tonight after the lengths I've gone to keep this a cold, emotionless transaction.

And yet, the cracks are there. It's falling apart, and so am I. I don't even fight when his arms go around me, and he pulls me in, running his fingers through my hair with a goosebump-inducing murmur. "Shhhhhh."

"Sorry. I didn't mean to lose it like this. I never –"

"Skye, stop. Just let me hold you. I wanted answers, but I'll wait if it means souring you like this. I'm not a *total* asshole."

No, just a sneaky one. His face sinks down to mine while I'm on his lap, staring up at him, trembling like an unsure kitten. We touch foreheads. Heat bristles through me where our skin connects, and then it rips up my spine.

I can't stop crying.

Not when I see so many faces in my mind. Adele, Vince, Uncle Harry, mom...

Judgment. Dependence. Evil. Fear.

Yes, in that order.

This can't be what he paid for. It certainly isn't what I wanted to deliver. I don't think I'm in any condition to deliver what he's after. Not sex, or anything else. Not after breaking down in front of him like this.

But his lips don't seem to care. They brush mine once before they come in hard.

I can't remember the last time I kissed a boy, but it was never like this.

They were boys at their worst: messy, inexperienced, incomplete.

This is a man with hungry lips. This is a kiss that consoles even when it commands. This is respect, domination, and the sweetest tongue I've ever tasted, laid against mine like he owns it.

It quiets the sadness for a few merciful seconds.

There's nothing silent about the moan that boils up, though. Not when he grips my face tighter, pulling me into him, tasting me deeper, fiercer, fully.

Sweet Jesus. It's too much, too fast.

I'm grateful when he lets me up for air. But I'm also torn, wondering why it feels so good and so natural. *Blame it on the wine,* I decide. It's a hell of a drug when it's mixed with raw, seething emotions.

I know I've failed him. But it's a disappointment I think I can live with after that kiss, that heat and heart I've been missing for God knows how long.

"Cade, look, I'm sorry for all this, again. I'm a mess. There's your truth. Just let me up, I'll take my things and go. I'll make sure Adele knows to give you back every penny, and –"

"You're drunk, Skittle. You're not going anywhere except straight to bed," he growls, running his hands under my shoulders, drawing me to his lap. "Don't fight me. Please."

Please. It echoes in my ears because I'm definitely intoxicated. What little fight I have when I try to stand, slip out of his grip, and fall back against him when he mirrors my movement fades in a few slurred words I can't believe I'm oozing. "Nah, nah, I'll be fine, Cade. I'll be...outta your hair...right after we..."

After I make an utter ass of myself, apparently.

Because that's what I'm sure I do in the minutes between standing up, secure in his arms, and when I slump against his guardian chest.

Darkness, regret, and shame consume me, but they don't destroy.

He won't let them.

Tonight, I know I'm his. Not in any way I imagined before I let this stranger buy my soul, but *his* nonetheless.

* * *

THERE'S a strange warmth around me all night long. Weird because his place is comfortable, but I'm never able to sleep this easy without a blanket, not even when I'm drained.

I realize somewhere in the middle of the night it's him. He hasn't let go since he carried me to bed. We're on his vast mattress, soft as a cloud and just as dreamy, still fully clothed.

Vaguely, I remember him waking me up a couple hours after the first time I passed out, dropping several Tylenol in my hand. He lifts a glass of water to my lips and I take several sips.

"Drink this and go back to sleep, beautiful. You're okay. You're safe. You're mine," he whispers.

Such confidence in those words I believe them, and fall asleep again the instant my head hits the pillow.

He keeps the angel act going until morning. That's when I wake up from the calmest, darkest sleep I can remember, without the usual worries putting nightmares in my head.

"Cade?" I whisper his name once, searching, studying his outline.

He's sitting at the edge of the bed, tall and straight. Almost like he's waiting for me.

"Mornin'," he says, doing a slow turn. There's a smile on my face, merging with the early sunrise. I want to reach over, grasp his hand, and thank him for taking care of me. So many lesser men wouldn't have put up with this crap. They would've thrown me out or worse.

Then I notice the thing on my hand that wasn't there last night, and the hell I've expected breaks open.

II: THE GOOD SON (CADE)

Minutes Earlier

I CAN'T BELIEVE Spence put me up to this after the vile fake engagement shit that went down with our buddy, Cal.

He didn't even know it at the time, almost a month ago in that bar, pouring my heart out over the bomb dad dropped on my head. Hell, he warned me *against* getting too involved, a smile like venom hanging on his lips when he leaned over, and whispered where Cal couldn't hear.

"Screw you with a rusty wrench if you fuck this up, bro. Last thing we need is another one of us shacked up with a chick he'd never swipe on Tinder in a million years."

But that's *exactly* what I needed to straighten out this inheritance bullshit. It's what I needed a month ago, and what I still needed the instant I saw her, sitting at the piano with tits way too perky for any high class whore.

It's what I need today when I take her hand. She's passed out, sleeping so sweetly. I'm extra quiet, opening my nightstand drawer. The little black box has sat in there for two weeks, taunting me like a dormant wasp.

It came all the way from New York City. My last trip there, where I swallowed my pride and asked the billionaire jeweler's daughter I fucked a few months ago to show me her best. Normally, I would've smirked at the bitter disappointment in her eyes when she undid the top button on her blouse, and I let her down gently.

My one night stands always want more.

This angel sleeping halfway off her pillow is the only time I've ever wanted it with any woman in my bed.

It's a sadistic irony we haven't had a proper first.

Congratulations, Skye. You're the one, I think to myself.

Hell, I believe it, because she's got it going on for miles in ways I'm still trying to comprehend.

How does she do it? What is it about this woman? *Honestly?*

Maybe it's how her long legs run up to those baby making hips, perched below two perfectly palm-sized tits teasing my inner Neanderthal.

Maybe it's the blue streaks in her brassy gold hair, dark as the swaying waters lining this city, a vicious compliment to the cotton candy pink that fluffs my cock at every glance.

Damn, maybe it's the pink on her tongue, the pink inside that smart mouth, calling some freak spark lost inside me to explore. Conquer. Tame.

And last, but certainly not least, maybe it's the words coming out of that mouth. They've got a bite like she's been through Hades without losing her modesty, a trial by fire I want to believe makes her the perfect candidate for the unbelievable side show I'm trying to recruit her for.

That's what I'm trying to do here this very second, isn't it? And shit, I haven't made much progress.

"This is the most fucked up way in the world to ask, but I

need a favor, Skittle," I whisper, pushing my lips against her sleeping ear, hoping the fire in my blood doesn't make me wake her before she's good and ready. I'm serious about her rest after the meltdown earlier, even if I can't hold the big secret in forever. "Marry me."

Just like that, it's pinched between my fingers.

Just like that, I slide it on her hand.

Just like that, a woman I've only spent a few hours with – who's in my bed with her *clothes still on* – is the wife I never thought I'd ever have.

I'm Cade Turnbladt, damn it. The man who's never been in a bind like this. The asshole who practically had his stomach turned at the thought of paying any of those whores for sex – every last one of Adele's girls except *her.*

Hell, a few times, women have paid *me* for the privilege. Sure, I turned them down every time, except for the odd chick who bought me a cup of coffee before I dropped her off, deleted her from my phone, and swore I'd start draining my balls in better pussy next time.

Only, next time never came.

And now, I think, it never will.

Skittle moans so sweetly, a fraction of what she gave me last night when I calmed her with my lips. Assuming *calm* is the right word. Nothing felt remotely placid about how our tongues collided, but I kept a short leash on my cock for this, the crazy, desperate shit I just did rolling that million dollar rock up her finger.

"Cade?" She's awake.

Fuck. I'm on the edge of the bed, the shirt from last night clinging heavier than it should. It's a second skin, a shroud I'm way too conscious of, probably to protect my sanity from the next sixty seconds.

Smile, dickhead, I remind myself.

Before I look at her, I reach into my guts, pulling out the warmest, strongest, friendliest curl of the lips I can muster.

"Mornin'," I whisper. I wonder how long it'll take her to realize I left the 'good' part off it for a reason.

I hope to hell she's not hungover. Should've known she'd be a lightweight before I opened that wine last night.

It's not like I make escorts a habit.

I pull so much prime tail on an ordinary night, every high end club in this city has a harem for my choosing. And if I wasn't worried about gold diggers and emotional atom bombs waiting behind their pencil skirts and pretty lipstick, I'd have picked a club girl for this job – not a down-on-her-luck thing like Skye.

Even though she's so desperate, she might humor the ring, instead of hurling her shoe at my head.

I count ten seconds before I hear the words that stop my heart. "Cade, what's...what's this?" It comes out slow, soft, like she isn't sure if she's still asleep.

My eyes glide up her hand, stopping on the ring, gold and diamonds glittering like the Seattle sun struggling through the morning clouds outside my window. "Oh, that? What does it look like?"

She isn't saying anything. Guess I'll have to do the talking, like always.

"Hope it's your style. If you really hate it, or it isn't the right size, just say so, and we'll find you something better. I went with the law of averages on this one. Looks like it's a good fit, at least. Lucky me. Lucky *you*. Should fool everybody into thinking we're serious for the next few months."

"Engagement?!" She's wide awake now. Anger follows shock in her eyes, and it's growing when she springs out of bed, searching for her clothes, stumbling as she claws at her hand. "Holy shit. I knew it. You're *crazy*."

"Hey, hey, hey," I say, rushing forward. I feel like I'm

cornering a loose cat, one more low blow to a screwy situation. "It's not like that at all. Back up. I *know* what this looks like..."

Absolute insanity.

It couldn't be anything less.

And what does that make me, despite my frantic denials? If it wasn't for mother, and my stupid cousin, and the castle – yes, *castle,* as in medieval fortress with spires, a draw bridge, million dollar gardens, the works – if I wasn't the good fucking son, trying to do right, I wouldn't be standing here making this poor woman's life a misery she never could've imagined.

"Please," I say, taking a deep breath, approaching her. "Give me a chance to explain."

"Explain what? That I spent all night in bed with a psycho who wants to get engaged less than twenty-four hours after we've met?"

Guilty. I can't deny it, but it isn't what it seems.

If she'd shut her smart mouth for a second and listen to reason...

"I'm offering you a job, Skittle. Screwed up way to do interviews, yeah, but how the hell else was I supposed to find the right one? I went to Adele's thing shopping. Found what I was looking for when I found you. Let's not mince words – I need a favor, and so do you. Wouldn't have come home with me last night if you weren't desperate."

"*Not* desperate enough for this!" She brushes past me before I can grab her, the quick little minx, pulling the ring off her hand. When she's gotten a safe distance away, she turns, hellfire and confusion in her storm grey eyes.

"Skittle..." I watch her hand fly into her purse, and when it comes out, she's clutching her phone. She presses it to her ear, tapping her foot.

"Damn, where is she?" Skye means Adele. I hear the

madam's voice when it goes to voicemail, curdling the look on her face.

Slow the fuck down.

Think.

How can I put this into words she'll understand?

I'm trying to talk like it's business, and it isn't working. Maybe if I show her the human side I let out last night, it'll keep her feet planted to my posh Brazilian floor for the sixty seconds I need to sell her on this madness.

"Don't go. You're free to keep looking at me like that if you want – hell, I deserve it for ambushing you like this – but just give me a chance." I put my hands out in front of me, low to my waist, resisting the urge to place them on her hips. "At least hear me out."

"Already did. There's no sane reason you'd want to marry me. We barely know each other, Cade. Jesus!" She pauses, running a hand across her face, wiping the nervous sweat beading on her brow. "I was so wrong. I thought it would be easy. Thought I'd spend the night with you, earn the check you gave me, and walk away without having to see you again. I was so ready to sell sex. But this? *This?* Find someone else. I'm not the right one for the job – whatever the hell it is."

"Wrong. You've got the spark, the chemistry, and the fire under your ass to do what I'm looking for. Plus you're ten times more adorable when you're pissed."

"Done. I'm out of here," she says, turning to the door.

"Whoa," I growl, rushing up, throwing my arms around her waist. I pull her to me for a second, until she stops fighting, settling in my arms. My hand covers her little fist, the one that's still holding my ring. "Okay, too soon. My bad. I'm not done yet, Skittle. It's not like I *want* to do this anymore than you do."

"No? Then why take me prisoner? Why keep me here,

trying to convince me to do...what, exactly? Why the hell do you even need a wife?"

"Fake wife." I'm quick to correct her. "We'll make sure that part gets spelled out by my lawyer. Iron clad pre-nup, NDA, the works. For you, a handsome fucking salary. More money than you've ever laid eyes on. Everybody walks away happy."

She doesn't look convinced. Guess she wants me to read her the fine print. That's where the devil always is. "Shit, I know it's crazy. Desperate. Wrong on so many levels. You want to know why? Really?"

Her eyes dig in, seeking answers, and won't let go. "There's this castle in Iceland," I say, already wanting to face-palm at how ridiculous it sounds. "It's my mother's favorite place. Been in our family for generations. She goes there every summer to get away. It's her happy place, sacred ground, whatever you want to call it, the works."

She's studying my face like she doesn't believe me. And then the hammer falls off her tongue. "You can't be serious. Castle? Who *are* you, Prince Silas?"

"Nah, but supposedly he's in the family tree somewhere. Very, very distant relative. I'm third generation, Icelandic blood, pure blooded American. Never been to Sealesland," I say, name dropping the kingdom not far from the old country, with its bad boy king and royal baby drama making several tabloid writers millionaires.

"You're *nuts*," she says, turning to the door again, one hand on the knob.

If she goes, this time I can't stop her. *Fuck.*

"Wait. I didn't finish. This castle, it's in limbo. I've got a cousin who gets it according to an ancient fucking trust and its dumb ideas. All because he's married now to some French girl he knocked up. We're equals, but my mother's blood always took priority. Until his wife and kid came into play. Cousin Jonas doesn't give a shit about the old place. Wants to turn it into an amusement park and put a damn parking lot over ma's favorite reading spot in the gardens." Is anything making sense? The words are flying from my mouth, desperate to convince her, before she walks out and leaves me holding my dick with zilch. "That's where you come in, Skye. If I can settle down, too, or at least fake out the bastards overseeing the inheritance, mom keeps her favorite place. That's all I care about. Last night, you talked about family..."

The skeptical spark in her eyes fogs over. Sadness dims their glow.

I'm in too deep, damn it. I have to keep going. "You mentioned a brother. You'd do anything to help him, wouldn't you? It's the same with my mother. I'm her only son. She's got a heart condition. Fuck, she doesn't even know what's coming down the pipe...if she finds out her special place is lost, turning into a goddamned carnival..."

I can't say the rest. It's already too much.

"What I want, or need, is none of your business. Forget explaining, Cade. I'm not the one you're looking for. You don't know anything about me, and I wish I'd never learned so much about you. Keep the ring and your money. I can't help."

The rest is a blur. She sets the ring on the table next to the door, turns, and yanks it open. She disappears in a final vanishing shake of her sweet ass and candy colored hair I dreamed about holding in my fist.

The sweetest lips I've ever tasted are gone, and so is my obvious choice to save mother from a heart attack.

"Shit!" I whisper, leaning against the wall. Both my fists slap the hand crafted wooden panels.

I was a fool to think it'd be so easy.

Ms. Hard-to-Fucking-Get is going to be far harder to nail down than I thought.

* * *

"FUCKING FINALLY. Decided to grace the office with your presence, Your Majesty?" Spence pokes his head into my office. "You know I've been putting out fires with the board all day, right? This hack, investors getting compromised, they're pissed off and they've got every right to be."

"I'll deal with it, Spencer. Already told you I've got a meeting set up with IT, first thing tomorrow. We'll find the source and make sure our teams stay on notice. RET doesn't fuck around with people's money, or their information. Anybody who's been with us for years knows that."

"Okay. Tell that to the assholes in the newsrooms. It's already hitting the media. Cal got hounded on his way out. Couple guys pressed him over whether or not it's related to the asshole we put in prison."

"Shit." I run my hand over my face. This is bad.

I doubt what's happening now is due to the corrupt city councilman we helped lock up just a few months ago. But the prick used foreign hackers to blackmail the board, back when he knew Cal was onto him, and when he pulled out all stops to prevent him from taking his rightful place at the top of the company alongside Spence and me.

"We've got to handle this ourselves. Cal doesn't need this crap when he's just gotten back from China."

"Yeah, Einstein. Why do you think I'm beating down your door?" Spence flops into the chair next to my desk in his usual fuck-the-world way. "This place is too big for you. Always liked Stefan's décor better, too."

"Well, it's my office now. Dad's off enjoying retirement, leaving us to shovel shit for this firm. He did it for years. You ever hear how the guys in the eighties survived the bad bond market?"

"Yeah. Wish I had half their balls sometimes. We were

lucky we barely missed 2008. The guys camped outside with pitchforks wanted us to work miracles when the whole market was busy shitting itself. The ones who stayed in made mega-profits in the next two years."

"And the guys who pulled their cash and went home fucked themselves, and us. We had to beg for a loan with Grant Shaw's boys in New York. I don't want that to happen again. We can't have another exodus because some hackers make our clients piss their pants." I'm drumming my fingers on the desk.

Spence's dirty look stays glued to me for a minute, before he gets up and walks behind my desk, fishing in the liquor cabinet. He pulls out a tall bottle of imported vodka, one of the last dad brought back from his last Baltic cruise.

We knock back a shot, but I cut myself off when he offers a second one. His gaze narrows. "Getting your courage somewhere else these days?"

I wish.

I re-live the insanity with Skittle over the next three seconds. Christ, was it just this morning?

Makes me want him to get the hell out so I can return to the important business of finding out where she is.

I'll close this deal, one way or another.

"Just learning to fill my old man's shoes," I say, standing up. We walk to the massive window overlooking the Puget Sound together. "I take this job very seriously."

On one side, the sea glistens beneath the sunlight, vast and unchanging. Nearby, downtown Seattle bustles, sleepless in its new constructions, awe-struck tourists, and steady traffic. A clear sky shows us Mount Rainier in the distant, huge and immortal. Bigger and older than the pitiful concerns knocking around in my head.

"If anyone's got a chance at building on his work, it's you, Mr. Marketing CEO." I do a slow turn while Spence sips his vodka. My old friend might be a jackass sometimes, but he means well, and I appreciate it. More than he even knows.

"Thanks. I'll be sure to give your best to dad next time we chat."

"Please do. I've had the break I need. Now it's time to roll up my sleeves and make sure everything doesn't go to shit," he says, setting the empty shot glass on my desk.

We bang fists before he heads out.

I almost feel bad keeping so much from him. Especially when he put the idea in my head to do it in the first place.

This make believe bride crap, the bitter truth that dad isn't enjoying his retirement in the slightest...

He closes the door. I sink down in my chair, still turned toward the sun sinking below the horizon. It'll be nighttime soon.

Another dark Seattle night not much different from my father's retirement party, when I thought everything was right with the world. Then I noticed I hadn't seen him since he made the obligatory rounds, taking his sweet time to compliment Cal and Maddie on what a lovely couple they were.

I'll never forget the look on his face when I stepped into his office. He'd been trampled, soaked in a bourbon barrel, and blinded on top of it.

It's a fucked up thing to see your sixty year old father in tears. *"Dad? What the hell's happened?"*

"Your cousin, Jonas," he whispers, wiping his eyes furiously.

It takes me several seconds to remember I even have a cousin Jonas. I've met him twice, both times when we were just kids at a family reunion in Montreal. "Huh? You mean that kid from Iceland? He isn't dead?"

"Of course not! He's married. He's getting the Turnbladt castle, according to the law," he says sadly. It takes his explanation a minute to hit me, and when it does, I'm at his side, slumping

against the wall. "It's your mother I'm worried about...her heart can't take this abuse. Not after – "

"Jesus, dad, don't say anything. I've got this." I walk behind him, and my hands come down on his shoulders hard.

I'm trying to reassure him as much as myself. He looks up, a bitter glint in his eye.

"What're you saying, son? There's nothing you can do. Nothing for anyone. The law is different over there. It's based on ridiculous bloodlines and property rights going back to times when families traded rams and swords for wives. One thing it's not is mud. It's clear as stone, I'm sorry to say. Oh God, it'll kill her when we break the news."

The worst part is, he isn't exaggerating. Mom had two heart attacks over the last five years. The last one put her in the ER, and when she got out, the first place she wanted to go was...

"Turnbladt," I say, finishing my thought, whispering our family name that's still attached to that place like a curse. "We'll keep the castle in the family somehow. We have to."

Dad laughs. It's the kind of raw, sad chuckle a person hears at funerals. Just bitter finality. "You're a good boy, Cade, but don't get my hopes up. Unless you're secretly engaged and you've been keeping it from us, there's nothing we can do. I'll figure out a time. We'll sit down with your mother one evening, both of us, and break the news as gently as possible."

"Dad, no. I've got more connections in legal than you do. Give me time. At least let me see if there's something we've missed, a loophole or two to keep it up in the air, give us time before it's transferred and – "

"You know he's serious about turning it over to the public, right? Jonas and his metal band." Dad shakes his head, chewing every word like it's the most bitter thing he's ever tasted. "He told your Uncle Barge he'll turn it into an amusement park. Needs all the money he can get to keep touring with that stupid band, and keep the little groupie he knocked up on one of his tours in new *heels, I suppose. The family strong-armed him into the wedding, I heard. It's gone. Lost."*

"Fuck, dad, why're you giving up so easy? It can't be!" I'm not one to back down.

But when I see the sadness swept aside by rage in my father's ice blue eyes, I know it's not that simple. It never, ever is.

"Cade," he says my name, wagging a finger. "A man just has to accept some things. Take a bite of the shit sandwich, as the Wall Street boys like to say so often. The last thing we're getting into is a legal fight. It'll break what's left of your mother's heart. If she can't have her castle, then at least let her stay on good terms with the family."

"Family? Bullshit. They send us a Christmas card once a year and mom falls all over herself to prove she's not just a foreigner with a silver spoon in her mouth."

Those were my last words before I walked the hell out. When he came out to join us for drinks later, Dad had his happy face on, eager to fool the crowd into thinking he was ready to sail off into the sunset.

But our eyes knew the truth across the room, behind the laughter, under the congratulations and well wishes sharper on the tongue than the lime soaked octopus ceviche our personal chef rolls around the room for the guests.

What seems like a stupid, made up fairy tale to Skittle has the highest stakes I've ever known.

I won't risk my mother's life on a heartbreak. And I'm damn sure not letting my distant cousin pimp her slice of heaven out so he can light a few more torches to Molech at his death metal concerts.

I'm not backing down.

I'll find a wife, and keep her for however long it takes to nullify Jonas' claim to the place.

Call it duty. My folks have given me everything, and if that stupid castle is the key to my mother's smile and the retirement dad deserves, I'll break my back keeping it in the family.

Come hell, come grief, come heartbreak, I'll take it in my soul like shards of glass and suffer the consequences. That's what good sons do.

I haven't given up.

I'll convince her yet. If I'm able to fix Skye's problems, and put a real smile on her face for a few months, then that's a bonus. But she'll be marrying me one fucking way or another.

This one night stand I haven't even sunk my dick into *will* be my bride. I just have to hunt her down, put my ring back on her rightful finger, show her our date with destiny is as real as the siren hues in her soft gold hair.

III: THE THINGS WE DO (SKYE)

"Yes, Adele. Yes. I said return it all. Add your cut to my debt, whatever fees, I don't care. Yes, I know the next performance won't be until next week. I'll turn over every penny to you first. It's my decision." I'm not sure who hangs up first: me, or the furious woman who can't believe I'm making her void a six figure check.

At least the worst part of the day is over. *Hopefully.*

I'm halfway home, and I've already given the other people on the bus for their evening commute an earful they didn't ask for. Truth is, I'm happy the commute takes awhile. I needed some time alone after I walked out of his swanky house this morning. It wasn't far from my favorite parks by Union Bay, where I got coffee and sat, clutching my camisole tight in the seaside breeze.

I spent the last few hours trying to contemplate how I'm breaking the news to Vince that we might not be able to refill his meds in time. *Especially* if I'm giving Adele an even heftier cut from my paycheck.

Jesus. Even with a history major's math skills, I know I'm up shit creek with just my hands to paddle.

This isn't fair to my little brother, or myself.

I need money. I need his medicine. I need a damn break.

The only person who can help is the one I'd rather talk to least.

Harry.

I've been dreading it all day. But now that I'm close to home, there's no more putting off the call.

Halfway between the bus stop and our ratty one bedroom apartment, I stop in the alley behind the noisy biker bar, and flip through my contacts. I don't expect him to pick up. That's why I've been rehearsing the sad, sticky sweet voice-mail I'll leave for him to find, but nothing ever goes according to plan for a girl whose luck ran out sometime a decade ago.

"Yeah? Skye? What the fuck do you want?"

"Uncle Harry!" *What a surprise.*

"How are you?" No, I don't even care if these fake pleas-antries hide my surprise. They're ash in my mouth before the brutal silence between us, when he waits for me to get straight to the point. If he's ever had the slightest patience for small talk, I've never seen it. "Listen, I need a favor."

"Another handout? Christ. Like I haven't given you enough, letting you shake tail without putting out, feeding off my nasty girls who work for what they do."

His harsh words wrinkle my nose. It's a cringe-worthy, ugly reminder my uncle isn't shy about being a pimp. Just one of the many mysterious, disgusting hats he wears after a long career in Seattle's gritty underworld.

"Not for me. It's for Vinnie," I snap, ten seconds into the conversation and already completely sick of this crap.

"Vinnie? What's the matter? He's a good kid." My heart starts beating again after my uncle says those words. He's always had a soft spot for his only nephew. He's more than happy to pin the blame on me, and honestly, if it helps my

41

little brother, I'll let him. "Shit, is he in trouble? Start talking. What is it you need?"

"Just a break, Uncle Harry. This month only. I'll put in more hours with Adele, obviously, and I'm not asking for money. I just need to...keep what I've earned this month. Otherwise, we won't be able to afford his medications."

"Tell you what, little screamer, it's your lucky day. I'm in a giving kinda mood. Got some new business happening in Portland that's making *mad* coin." Harry pauses just long enough to chuckle, pushing frost up my spine. "Forget the debt these next two weeks. Buy Vinnie his meds. I'll give you one more chance to take care of him right since I was sweet on your ma, and I know she'd want to keep you two kids together."

A glass bottle bangs against the window next to me, and I almost jump out of my skin. I turn, brow furrowed, and give the drunken asshole behind the glass the dirty confusion reserved for my Uncle.

"One more chance? What do you mean?"

Frustration grunts through my receiver. "Ain't it obvious? Vinnie deserves better than being cooped up in that ratty fuckin' apartment while you wrap up that useless degree instead of getting a real job. If you can't give him what he needs, I will."

The ground falls out under me. I start speed walking through the alley, trying to suck the air from my lungs, before rage creeps into my voice and makes a bad situation worse. "We're fine, Uncle Harry. Really. I don't need you to come get him."

"Yeah, that's the thing – I don't want to neither. That's a last resort. Plan B, if you're not up to snuff. Besides, I love the kid to death, but I'm not exactly the fathering type. Hell, I've got you stripping for the next ten years, or however long it takes to repay that mill or so you owe. Generous, right? Just like the good guy I am. You promised a lot of goodies on that treasure hunt, screamer. They never showed up."

"I know. I was there," I say bitterly. "We don't need to rehash –"

"Oh, fuck yes, we do, screamer. Every month you're on the horn whining about how bad you've got it, we very much *need* to remember why we've got ourselves this pretty little deal. We need to remember how your fuckup cost me *big*. Also how you really don't give a shit how nice I've been about it."

"Uncle –"

"Shut up. Sure, maybe you don't say it point-blank to my face because you know better, but I ain't stupid. I can read between the lines. You think I'm a creep for making you do this. You think it's hard, even though I could have you toting drugs instead, and then you'd find out what real work is. And just between us, I know it wasn't a fuckin' boo-boo, that Roman shit disappearing in the mail, or whatever. You took my money without delivering squat. Probably your way of getting back at me for laying the moves on your sweet mom before she threw herself off the bridge. Everybody needs their scapegoat and a little sweet revenge, screamer. I get it."

He didn't...he didn't just go there, did he?

Jesus, yes, he did.

I stop just short of throwing my phone in the road, but I can't do anything about the hot, angry tears rolling down my cheeks. Mission accomplished. Harry laughs quietly to himself when he hears me crying, just like the other times it's happened.

"Aw, there, there, screamer. Don't you worry your pretty tie-dyed head. You're still wearing that shit just like a weepy Emo chick who had a one night stand with a rainbow, right? Just like I saw you last?" I'm silent, shaking, standing under a tree next to the bar while a couple beat up bikes tear down the road. I never answer his stupid questions – it's the only thing I don't have to give him. "I'm glad we had this talk, Skye. Now pucker the fuck up and thank your Uncle for being such a stand up guy. I'm waiting."

"Thanks." That word is a nuclear tipped barb on my tongue, harsher than any curse I've ever uttered in my life.

"I gotta go, sweetness. Call back anytime. I'll be seeing you and Vinnie real soon if things keep going sideways on you." He pauses just long enough to let me imagine his gross smile while he walks my little brother down to his car, never to be seen again. "Make sure it doesn't for everybody's sake. Yours, Vinnie's and most of all, mine."

It's over. My arm slumps at my side, clutching the phone.

It takes me another thirty minutes before I'm able to walk the last few blocks home.

Every black day of my life is this poison. It spreads to Vinnie far too easily if he knows I've been crying. I make sure to wipe my face on my sleeve, apply a quick dash of makeup, and then stop at the gas station across from our place for a couple cheap tea drinks.

* * *

"Vinnie, come on, what did I tell you about the heat?" I send a mom's nagging look his way, turning the old thermostat, wagging my finger.

It's amazing how much heat a fifteen year old kid needs to feel warm when he's cocooned in like three blankets, eyes glued to the screen with an Xbox controller in his hand. "Yeah, yeah, turn it up. I hear you."

"*Down*, Vinnie. Sixty five degrees is plenty comfortable with a blanket or two. We're going to be in trouble this winter if we waste too much money on utilities."

"K, Skye, I hear you loud and clear. What's for dinner?"

Rolling my eyes, I stomp back into the kitchen without a reply. I stir our canned spaghetti sauce, wondering how it's possible to love the kid so much when he's so ridiculous.

But I was that way, once.

Mom tried her best to give me a normal adolescence. Money was tight, except when Uncle Harry sent us his 'vacation fund.' He'd tell us we deserved a family vacation, the least he could do to look after the people his brother left behind.

I think we used it for a trip to Oregon once. Every other time, it went toward bills, paying down debt, mom trying to keep our family together, and make sure I'd stay her straight A pride and joy.

All until she couldn't cope anymore.

I still wonder if the last letters Harry sent drove her off the deep end. She'd been spending more time away from us, taking these late nights and trips to God knows where. It wasn't long after the letters and calls became a weekly thing that she rode the ferry to Bremerton, found a bridge, and –

No. You can't think about that right now. Not when it's been a fucked up day.

I throw some garlic toast into the oven and set a timer before I rejoin Vinnie in the living room. Surprisingly, he's standing by the door with his coat on. He flicks the TV off and sets the remote down on our messy table by the door. A long lost ChapStick I forgot there rolls off the edge, bouncing to the floor. One of several from a multi-pack.

Ignoring it, I cross my arms. "Where do you think you're going, Mister? I just slaved over this four star dinner. Even picked up a Parmesan shaker at the drug store."

"Ben says there's this awesome midnight movie playing down the street." He lowers his eyes sheepishly. "Uh, you know I was gonna ask your permission, Skye. I'll have a little spaghetti," he says cheerfully, as if stuffing his face with pasta will solve the world's problems.

I frown. "You mean you'll ask for a few bucks after I'm good and stuffed, too tired to say no. Come on, Vincent, we both know the game."

I'm not sure why I bother. There's little sense scorning him over normal teen wanderlust. But I'm serious about him eating. I don't like how he's underweight for his age, too nauseated some days to keep much down. A side effect of the anti-seizure meds breaking the bank.

"Look, there's no sense in hiding it – this is going to be a tough month. Probably a rough winter, too." I watch his eyes hit the floor, the life sucked out of his young face. *Damn it.* I sigh. "I know you don't want a lecture. I'm just laying out the facts. If your homework is done, and I see you clean your plate, then maybe I'll dig around in my purse and see if I've got a spare five or –"

"That's my saucy sis! Knew you'd be cool with it!" He runs forward, throws his arms around me, grinning like a fool. "Thanks a million. I sent Mrs. LeMay my geology paper right before you got home. I promise I won't be out too late after the movie ends."

A blatant lie. Still, he's a good kid, overall. I don't think he's out doing anything much worse than I did at his age. "One o'clock curfew, kiddo. I'll be up, and waiting. You won't like what happens if you're not up here and brushing your teeth for bed. Now, get your butt over to the table and eat."

It's rare to see him this pleased, and it takes so little.

I'm able to eat a plate of spaghetti and some toast without throwing up. No small miracle. Vinnie's grin turns my stomach before he plucks the last crumpled ten from my hand.

I smile back, but I'm secretly crying.

Why can't I make you this happy all the time?

* * *

IT'S past midnight and I'm slumped on the couch, a stack of freshly graded papers for Professor Olivers on my lap. A little too early for Vinnie to come home. Too far past my bedtime on the nights I get to stay in.

So, who the hell is pounding at the door?

It takes a second to realize it's not just a dream. There's a steady, incessant banging.

I get up, cautious because it's so late. When I see the familiar face through the tiny spyhole, I freeze.

"Holy hell. I'm dreaming..."

I'm not even joking this time. It *can't* be him.

I'm expecting my disorganized apartment and the man at the door to disappear in a puff of smoke the instant I jerk it open. But life is never so easy or merciful.

Cade Turnbladt stands in front of me in all his tall, broad shouldered, wicked smirking glory.

He's not *coming in.* I don't dare take the chain off the door.

"Had a feeling this was the place," he whispers, voice as nosy and self-sure as ever. Smiling, he pokes his face toward mine, peering through the tiny crack in the door I'm allowing.

"What the hell are you doing here?" I whisper, eyes drilling his. I hope I look angry. It'll be easier not to lose myself in his pearly blues if my obvious annoyance keeps him extra guarded.

"Couldn't leave off after how we finished the morning, Skittle. Let me in."

He isn't asking. His hand reaches through the door.

Hell no! I don't even hesitate. He roars, cursing when I slam his hand in the door, and immediately regret it.

Not because I'm sorry for teaching this cocky ass some much needed humility, or bruising his fingers. His swearing is loud enough to wake half the building. We really don't need another warning from the landlord this month – not after Vinnie's left his stupid shooter games cranked up, prompting the old lady down the hall to squeal a couple weeks ago. And in a city where there's plenty of tenants to go around, I'm scared to give our owner any eviction excuses.

"Hey, keep it down!" I fling open the door, hissing through my teeth. I do a quick look around, and then motion him in. I'm annoyed he's really here. I'm even more annoyed there's a pang of empathy when I see him rubbing his wounded hand. "Stay there and make it quick. I'll get you a bag of ice."

He follows, disobeying me again, the fury in his eyes melting in rogue amusement. "If I'd known a little pain was the key to your heart, I'd have done things a whole lot differently last night."

He's in the kitchen. So close it's hard to hide my blush, cooling my cheeks in the freezer. I reach inside for an ice pack and linger, totally trying to pretend his eyes aren't locked on my ass. My cheeks are so hot, even when I'm face-deep in frost.

I don't think I'm into the whole dominant spanking thing, but how would I really know?

"Here's your damn ice," I say, shoving a small baggie into his hand while I retrieve a paper towel to catch the condensation. "Start talking. You've got five minutes."

"Must be my lucky day," he says, that damnable smirk I've tried to forget hanging on his lips as he pushes his hand into the ice pack. "That's a lot more time than you gave me this morning."

"You're reading way too much into this, Cade. If you're here about the same offer, sorry. Still not interested." *Why does it come out so weak?*

I want to kick myself a second later. The wildcat glint in

his eye tells me he senses it just like I do. It's hesitation. With a man like this, it could be fatal.

"Tell me what you need," he growls, grabbing my wrist with his good hand. "Everybody has a price. Name yours, beautiful. Do I need to put another zero on that check I told Adele to keep this morning? How much so you'll never have to work for her again? It's obvious you don't want to."

Arrow, meet heart. His aim is way too good. Or else cupid is one twisted little SOB.

I glance at the clock, hoping that stupid movie isn't one of those short anime things Vinnie watches with his geeky friends. For once, I don't want him home early. I cringe at the thought of him seeing me with this strange man, contemplating a deal with the devil.

"A million even, after tax, would go a long way toward making us comfortable. If you really want to know..."

"Us?" he echoes.

"Me and my little brother. He has a condition, and medicine isn't cheap."

Cade smiles, stroking his jaw. I hear his stubble scratching his thumb. "You mentioned that when you slipped last night. I'm a charitable man, Skittle. Saving a sick kid just sweetens the deal for my fucked up sense of karma. How 'bout yours?"

I don't answer, looking away. Hot shame tans my cheeks, and he's the sun. "I don't have one. I told you what I want."

"Yeah, finally. Consider it done. You want the check in your account, or sent straight to Adele? If you've got a normal bank account, we'll probably have to give them a heads up. It's not everyday some random walks in with seven figures."

Holy hell. He isn't even joking.

My eyes are so wide it takes a minute to catch myself, and

I remember I'd better look normal. It's business, after all. Nothing more.

But Jesus, apparently, there's no amount that makes him think twice. I should have said a hundred million, a billion, some unfathomable sum. There has to be a number to convince him I'm not really worth it.

And if he just offered me a million bucks, didn't I imply I'd take it? *So much for ending this swiftly.*

"Back up. It's not that easy, Cade. I'm a busy woman. Money is only half of it," I say. I'm as desperate to talk myself out of this as I am to convince him to buzz off. "There's time to consider. I can't give up my life and be your doting, stay-at-home wife baking you cookies in nothing but an apron, or whatever it is you think I'll be for a million bucks."

"I was hoping you'd say that, Skittle. If I kept you on your knees with a leash, mirroring my every move – although that would be fucking hot – it wouldn't convince my cousin's people we're the real deal, man and wife. And they *will* come checking, one way or another. Asshole won't let his meal ticket go so easy. He can rent our place out for *a lot* of cash."

Cade comes closer. His hand flies out, slaps the wall next to me. The more I try to look away, the harder he stares. Ice and magma war in my blood.

"Skittle..." His hand reaches out, tipping his fingers to my chin, lifting it until I can't avoid his world ending glare for anything. "You worry too much about specifics. Take the damn deal and be happy. We'll iron out the fine print later. I *know* you want to. You need this as bad as I do, Skye."

There's something I never noticed before around his neckline. A black flare creeping up his skin like flame. It's the edge of some dark, wonderful tapestry no doubt stamped on his chest. I shudder helplessly.

It's bad enough to have this strange, mysterious, demanding bastard in my home, a total hovel compared to his Edgewater palace. It's worse every time my eyes caress his body. I see a hint of the freak underneath that button down shirt, painted like a canvass, the same one winking at me every time the dull light catches his eyes.

But I'm not afraid of his darkness, his secrets, everything I still don't know about Mr. Relentless.

It's my own. My darkness, my unknowns, my hellish predicament. They can't trap him, too, when it's already spun a web around me and Vinnie.

"This is crazy. Why don't we just quit while we're ahead? I'm serious, Cade," I whisper, breaking his grip, turning away. "How many times do I have to say 'no?'"

"As many as it takes, Skittle. I'm not backing down. I'll be back tomorrow if you shoot me down tonight. I'll show up next in the middle of your class, and book the fucking keynote when you're handed the PhD. I'll hire a guy to write Skye *in* the damn sky, next clear day, and I *will* make sure it's an engagement announcement. You're perfect for this gig. That's crazy, yeah, but that doesn't mean it isn't true. I want you. So much I'm wasting precious time hunting your sweet ass over anybody else. Let's get this straight, from my stalker lips to your lovely little ears: I'm not going anywhere until you come to your senses, Skye. You've got plenty of those hiding behind that pretty face."

I'm lost. I don't know how to get him out of here. For a second, I contemplate calling the police, but what will I tell them, exactly? A billionaire finance tycoon broke in and demanded to pay me a million to become his make-believe wife?

There's only one person who'd get hauled to the loony bin, and it won't be Stubborn Blue Eyes.

"If I say I'll *think* about it, will that get you the hell out of here so I can have a decent night's sleep?"

He smiles like I've just reached through the window and

handed him the moon. "We'll see. In the meantime, think about this."

He stands, walking slowly to the door, a new beat in his step I really regret putting there. Cade reaches into his pocket, digs around, and then pulls out the irrational diamond ring that's worth so much more than everything else in this building, it might warp time and space. Or at least a few pocketbooks.

"This is all you've got to think on," he says, parking it gently on the end table's only bare spot. He tucks a thin scrap of paper underneath, which I see has his number on it from across his room. "Call me tomorrow, or I'll be back. I need a yes."

The door swings open. I pad over, gritting my teeth, embarrassed to have these oversized diamonds sitting next to my ChapStick, collection notices, and junk mail with notes I no longer cared about scrawled on their corners. It's in my palm when the door swings open, and Vinnie steps in, a couple laughing boys behind him.

"Crap." He freezes as soon as he sees me. "Sorry, sis, I thought you'd be asleep. Just wanted to bring the guys in for a minute or two, and show them –"

He trails off. I'm the one who looks guilty. I close my palm, but it's too late. The hundred pinpricks of light reflecting off this crazy ring draw every eyeball in the room.

"You're early, and when did I ever say you could bring company?" I summon my best mom voice, trying my damnedest to pretend nothing happened. "Go home, boys. It's late. James, your dad's even more of a worry-wart than me."

"Sorry, Skye!" The kids say it in unison, then head for the door. Vinnie whispers a few quick phrases after them about meeting up tomorrow evening, how he thought I'd be asleep, and – oh – of course he's found new ways to kill zombies on the screen he simply has to show them.

"You're in trouble, Mister," I say, gently yanking him inside as soon as we can't hear his friends footsteps plodding down the hall. "Next time you bring friends over this late, without asking, the X-box is coming with me to campus. You'd be surprised how much grads like blasting zombies between classes."

"Jesus, sis. Settle down. I knew you'd be pissed if you found out, but you're not usually this defensive. Where'd you jack that?"

My heart skips a beat. He's staring straight at my hand, his young eyes dark and curious, eager to brand me the hypocrite like every fifteen year old kid railing against authority.

"It's..." I try, but the words won't come. I'm caught red handed, or at least red faced.

Half a dozen possibilities roll over in my mind, sticking in my throat. None of them sensible.

It's...what, exactly?

A fake? An artifact on loan from the university? Something I found, and yes, of course I've already posted on Craigslist to help find whoever lost it?

None of it sounds right. It just makes me look guilty as hell.

There's only one possibility.

"Well, I was going to wait a while longer to break the news, but since you're so nosy..." I draw out the last part, wondering if I'm really ready for this. "I'm engaged, Vincent. Our lives will be very different soon."

"Engaged...what?!" He blinks, his cynical little tongue struck quiet. "Who? When?"

"Someone I've been seeing between classes. His name is Cade, and he's really wonderful. We're in love."

Lies, lies, lies! If it's a sin to tell these whoppers to my clueless little brother and my own messed up heart, then I must be headed for circles of hell even Dante never charted.

I'd let myself feel bad if I wasn't so panicked. The shame will have to wait, and there'll be *plenty* tomorrow, when I go crawling to my blue eyed savior on hands and knees, when he knows I'm willing to be his – *Oh, God* – his wife.

"It's a shock, I know. I'm sorry, Vinnie. I didn't mean to break the news this way. You just caught me at a bad time. We only made it official tonight. I'm probably still processing." At least there's one truth in there. "I really meant to take it off my finger, tuck it away, and sit down and explain all this. Hey, don't look at me like that."

"It was that guy in the hall, wasn't it? We saw him coming in. Nice shoes, great smile, not a care in the world...he stepped into a freaking Maserati out front! Wow. I never thought you'd be the gold digger type."

"I'm *not* marrying him for money." Oh, but I am. "Vinnie, please. You're getting carried away. You don't understand –"

"I understand plenty, sis. You know what else? Screw you."

"Vincent!"

"No. This is bullshit," he says, racing halfway to his room before I call after him again, and he whips around. "You chastise me night and day for stepping out of line, trying to fill mom's shoes, thinking I don't know how to look after myself."

"That's different!" It's got to be, right? If it isn't, none of this is making sense. "You're fifteen. You have a medical condition..."

"Like I don't know?" Pain lines his face. His fingers brush through his sandy brown hair, so quick and careless they twist his glasses crooked on the bridge of his nose. "I have to live with it everyday. I take care of myself when you're not here. You think you're so grown up since we got into this mess, trying to make the best of all this crap. Well, I've grown up, too."

"I know you have, Vinnie. Look..." I pinch my eyes shut, disgusted because I know I'm not the only one tearing up. "This is coming out *wrong.* Let's sleep on it tonight, okay? I promise, in the morning, we'll hash it out over breakfast. I'll explain everything, and why. No more secrets."

Just the huge, glaring fact that I'm about to wipe our debts clean by pretending to be a billionaire's bride to save a castle. If my heart weren't stinging from the stitches, I'd be laughing my ass off.

"Whatever, sis," he says, turning. "Good night."

His door bangs shut, scraping its frame. It's always a little uneven thanks to the shoddy job our landlord did hanging it. I crash on the couch again, and accidentally knock my half-empty tea bottle onto the coffee table. Sweet smelling brown liquid soaks through the folder with the undergrad papers.

I'm too fucked up to care. Too tired. Too confused.

Right now, I have to clear my head. It's the only way I'll figure out how I make this work without demolishing my sanity, and everybody else's.

* * *

VINNIE IS GONE before I'm awake the next day. I'm alone in our apartment, ample opportunity to take the world's slowest shower. I use the few minutes I have beneath our jerky, hissing shower head to meditate. Afterward, I stand in front of the mirror, massaging my temples.

Am I really going to make a deal with the devil I don't know?

"Yes," I whisper, trying to pump myself up. It doesn't help. "What else do I have to lose?"

The facts couldn't speak more clearly if they punched me in the face. I don't know the rock in this situation, but the hard place, I know brutally well.

Dealing with the devil I know – Uncle Harry – hasn't gotten me anywhere. There's no doubt what more limping along with him means.

The bastard turns my stomach. He's a karma dealing monster. He's the serpent and the apple that's left me cursed, once by my own desperate judgment, and again with the invisible strings he's strangled us with for the past six months.

Bender of my morals. False hope. Possible murderer.

If there'd been another way, *hell no,* I wouldn't have put up with him this long.

Now, maybe I don't have to. I'd gotten so used to the idea of being his slave, stripping for Adele and her soulless clients, that I've forgotten what it's like to even contemplate freedom.

That's over. Whatever else Cade is, he's an escape.

I'm halfway through blow drying my hair when I realize the soft, shrill noise isn't coming from the dryer. I'm singing. Something that hasn't happened since before mom's suicide.

When I'm on the sofa with the phone perched in my palm a couple minutes later, I remind myself how stupid I'm being, trying to practice the best words before I make the call. But only for a second. This dumb, desperate glee coursing through my heart gives me the courage to dial the number Cade left, and find the words when I hear his gruff voice pick up.

"Skittle? What's the good word?"

"I'll do it," I say. My head feels lighter the instant it's out. "With a few conditions, but we can talk about those later. When do you want to meet?"

"How about now?" he says. "I'm at my place. I usually

work Saturday mornings, but I took this one off just to hear your voice. Come over."

"I'll need the address, I guess. I wasn't really paying attention when I stormed out the other night."

"No need. My driver's been outside your place all morning. Even had him give your kid brother a ride to his friend's house."

I'm bristling. Vinnie should've texted me, should've known better than to take rides from strangers...but it's my fault. I'm the one who lied last night. Why the hell would he pass up a chance to ride with my new fiancé's fancy chauffeur?

"Maybe terms can't wait," I whisper, sharpening the edge in my voice. "Cade, whatever happens next, it's between you and me. Leave Vinnie out of this. I don't want him getting any crazy ideas, especially when it's not going to last."

"He's, what, sixteen? Let him enjoy the ride. What's mine is his while we're together. You want him to have his own place, or move into mine, just say the word. I'll leave that to you."

"Hell yes, you will. I *don't* want to drag him into this anymore than I already am. Don't spoil him." I can't figure out what's worse: the guilt curdling my stomach, or the anger dousing my veins. Both due to the kindest favor anyone's ever done for my little brother.

I have to bite my tongue before I blow this. It's good practice. I'm sure there'll be a lot more tongue chewing happening in the future.

"I'm a businessman, Skittle. Obviously, I'll respect your wishes when it comes to family. No need to say it again." He sounds almost offended.

I stifle a laugh, rolling my eyes. "Whatever. Let me get my things. I'll meet you in an hour or two. Just need to get in touch with Vinnie first and tell him what's happening."

I'm also secretly hoping my kid brother won't throw a total fit after he finds out it's moving day, without warning. Not that I expect he'll put up much fuss when he sees the view from Cade's place. We've lived in this city our entire lives, and I don't think either of us have seen Seattle from *that* angle. Not since the scarce times mom brought us up on the Space Needle when we were little.

"Got it. I'll let you tell me when you want me to send the car around for the kid. He can have my whole basement until we're situated. Never do anything down there except lift."

There's no goodbye. I'm left with a flashing screen, silence, and a vision I really don't need in my head of Mr. Relentless pumping iron in whatever private gym he has in his house.

* * *

PREDICTABLY, Vinnie doesn't answer any of the four texts I send him while I'm riding across the city in millionaire style. Nate, Cade's older, genteel chauffeur treats me like a total princess. I could get used to a guy opening the door for me when I step outside the apartment, ushering me into the backseat. There's a TV screen, a built in tablet, chargers galore, and a freaking cooler stocked with mineral water, cold brewed coffee, organic juices.

Maybe I shouldn't worry so much about Vinnie getting spoiled. There's plenty of that to go around.

I raise the privacy visor, too much out of my element for small talk. The shiny new ring on my finger is an easy distraction, strange and beautiful. I've decided I'll wear it when we meet as a token of good faith.

When we get to his place, he's standing outside the double-door entrance, between the tall Greek columns. It's an even prettier approach through the gate in the daytime, meandering up the long driveway, a slow descent into paradise. It even makes me forget how out of place I feel here in jeans and a cardigan, which I'm grateful for when I step out, and the crisp Pacific breeze nips at my shoulders.

I came ready for the wind. His first insane words, on the other hand...

"Welcome home, Skittle," he says, grasping my hand. "Let's step in my office. Unless, of course, you'd like to review the paperwork on the master balcony?"

The glint in his eye threatens my cheeks with another blush. "Whatever feels like business," I tell him. "That's all we're doing. Plain and simple."

"No pleasure? Fuck me. That's like walking out on dessert wine after a hell of a dinner. Suit yourself, then, Skye. Follow me."

I do, hanging close to him, trying to keep my eyes off the muscular shoulders calling to my baser senses while he leads me inside.

He's dressed more casually today, sexier than any man should be in a sweater and trousers. He's even wearing high end sneakers, which makes me feel slightly more at ease.

It's easy to forget men as rich as Midas don't dress to the nines every single day. His home office is just as neat and regal as the rest of the mansion. A huge desk sits in front of tall windows, perfectly positioned for the landscape behind it, empty except for a monitor, a platinum pen on its stand, and a slim stack of paperwork. He slides it over. "Read and sign, please."

"Jesus," I say, lifting it closer. "You already had time to see a lawyer?"

His smirk disappears. "Not exactly. I'd been planning this for weeks, before you dropped into my life, singing the best rendition of *Fly Me to the Moon* I ever heard from a naked chick."

"You've heard others?" I raise an eyebrow, skimming the language, putting on the critical lens I've developed over a hundred research papers. Except it's too late to be saved by being a smart ass.

"I've lived a full life, Skittle. You're not doing a deal with an angel, in case you wondered. We're here for whatever feels like business, plain and simple. Remember?"

I try not to bristle when he throws my words back at me. "Obviously, I don't expect anything else."

Yes, obviously. It's an elaborate quid pro quo, I tell myself for the hundredth time. We wouldn't even know each other if we weren't both in a bind.

He needs his castle, his illusion, peace of mind for mother dearest. I need money, a fresh start for me and Vinnie. If it's a miracle we're together, about to put our names on a messed up wedding contract I never thought I'd sign, then it's the strangest kind ever.

The terms are sensible, at least. Typical legalese. They spell out our obligations, the six month term he wants locked in, carrying us early into next year. Payment is more generous than he said – a quarter million beyond what it takes to cover my debt. I've already told Adele to send a million right to Harry's account, and take whatever cut she thinks I owe.

My naked nights in front of the piano are through. But the extra pay he's doling out doesn't sit right with my wonky moral compass. "Go ahead and strike out the salary part. I'll take fifty thousand beyond what we talked about, a normal year of pay, and that's it. I'm perfectly capable of supporting myself for anything beyond that, thank you very much. *Really?* You're rolling your eyes?"

He's insufferable. Cade picks up the contract, yanks his pen out of its holder, and runs a thick black line through the section like a dagger. "Done. Modesty intact, beautiful.

Would you like me to pretend we met over a lush French dinner, instead of that party for horny old fucks with their dicks hanging out?"

I'm rolling my eyes this time. "Sure, why not? This whole thing *is* pretend, isn't it?" I use my sharpest tone, dripping oily sarcasm. "We'll have to come up with a story for Vinnie, though. It won't be easy, convincing him we're serious."

"Leave that to me," he says. "And don't bother worrying about it until after we're done here. Read the rest. Make your amendments. I'm sending this off tomorrow. We've got a few weeks turn around for the wedding."

I do a double take. His eyes are flaming blue mischief. "What? I mean, I knew you wanted to get this going...I just didn't know it'd come together so fast."

"The quicker, the better. If my friends and family are blitzed out, hit by the shock and awe, it'll give them less time to bombard us with stupid questions. Should slam the door in my cousin's face, too. Then we'll be on maintenance kisses. Easy peasy."

"Maintenance kisses?" I'm trying not to laugh. He's so casual about marrying a complete stranger it's almost absurd.

"Yeah, the kind where we just do a quick peck in public for appearances. Not the ones where we'll be attached at the face over dinner for my family and friends."

"You're disgusting!" I hiss. More at myself because I utterly despise the heat imagining his tongue on mine brings.

The rest of the contract is thankfully sane. There's nothing else I want to quarrel over.

It's not like I have the time or money to consult my own attorney, anyway. I tap the cheap, flimsy pen from my school I've pulled from my purse against the contract, frowning when I hit the end.

"What's wrong?" he says, laying his hand on my neck. I never knew a touch so gentle could bathe me in fire.

"Your hand," I say, shrugging him off. I don't like the coolness replacing his warmth after his skin is off mine. It's sudden, empty, and annoyingly noticeable. "Obviously, we'll be touching if we want to make this look convincing. I realize that. I'll do maintenance kisses, or whatever else. But when it's just you and me, living our little secret, with nobody except this lawyer aware..."

"Say no more. You're afraid I'll bite, and you should be. Hell, maybe I'd use my teeth to yank down your panties if I'm in the right mood, Ms. Hard-to-Fucking-Get. You're right about me." He stands up straighter, taller, staring right through me.

Stop making this so damn difficult, I warn him with my eyes, wishing I could telepathically beat it into his head across the empty space between us.

"We're not sleeping together, Cade. We can't. Yeah, we met under...unusual circumstances. But I'm taking this job seriously. I'm trusting you. Deep down, I'm assuming you're a decent man. You won't take anything that isn't yours, or force me to –"

"Stop right there, woman. If you had any clue how many girls have *begged* to have every inch of me inside them, you'd know force isn't my style. There's no fun in it. I leave my pussy shaken, quenched, and completely fucking soaked. Always aching for more." He steps closer, holding my eyes hostage, a vicious tone on his tongue like I've hit his faith or politics. "If you really want a binding legal promise, fine. I'm game. Just know I'm not the desperate, slimy fuck I'm sure I look like because I'm shopping for a wife who won't even last a year. And in case it isn't clear, I fully intend to keep getting my dick wet when nobody else is looking, and you're spending long nights hunkered over papyrus, or whatever the fuck you study chasing that fancy degree."

"Deal." I keep it to one word, hiding a disappointment that shouldn't even be there.

Of course, he's entitled to see other women. This isn't even real.

Hell, I can do the same, I'm guessing. Not that I have plans to get my V-card punched by a guy I'll have to explain a fake marriage for money to.

No fuss. No muss. No jealousy.

I wish I could suck that last green feeling from my veins.

"Good. In the meantime, as long as we're keeping this professional, you need to get used to these hands," he says, laying them on me again. "I won't do anything I shouldn't, you have my word. But if you're coming apart in my office, shaking like a damn leaf every time I run these fingers through your rainbow hair..."

I stiffen when he does it. I hate his heat, I hate his precision, I hate how his words give me goosebumps, a lightning rush beneath the skin. I hate that he makes me want to forget everything I just said, and put myself in a terrible position guaranteed to make this stupid bride job a hundred times more complicated.

"Don't say it," I whimper. The cap pops off my pen too hard, and I lean over the desk, eager to just sign this and get it over with.

"How the hell do you expect to hug and kiss in public? How am I supposed to show the world I'm happier than a cowboy in the world's best brothel because I just married the hottest woman on the face of this fucking planet?" He grabs my wrist, lifting my hand away, warm breath teasing the back of my neck. "And Skittle?"

I'm so, so screwed. "Use my pen. Cheap ass purple ink from your Professor's office probably isn't legally binding."

He shoves his pen through my fingers, mirroring my

every movement while I move it over the blank line with my name printed neatly above.

I sign, date, and quietly say my last words. I see my epitaph in the tiny ink smudge lingering on my finger. My end is in the evil words that come to mind while his fingers hug mine to the silver pen, imagining everything else he could do with those powerful hands of his.

Liar. Imposter bride. Virgin.

That's who I am now. The old Skye Coyle is gone.

The new one doesn't have any idea how screwed she's about to be.

IV: SOMETHING TO TELL (CADE)

*S*ome promises are easy to keep.

Others make a man want to hit the ground and punch his way clear to China.

I know which kind of vow I've made the second I take my hands off Skittle, a whiff of the ink she just put on the paper still in my nostrils, mingling with her bargain bin perfume. I turn quicker than I should, hiding the raging hard-on I've had the whole time in my trousers.

"Anything else?" she whispers. I try to ignore her, marching across the room and stuffing the documents into a manila envelope. It'll be heading for my lawyer's office tomorrow.

Don't fucking tempt me, woman. I haven't had my dick pricked up like this for years.

Something about the ones who're off limits, I suppose. Also seems like a savage injustice that I just agreed not to bed the woman I'm going to marry, especially when she looks like a painted up song asking me to make every note scream.

I see the challenge I'm dealing with the second I'm facing her again.

Cotton candy hair begging to be tamed like it did the night I first saw her, body naked and tight, fingers moving beautifully on the keys.

Hourglass hips begging harder.

Lips so pensive I've got to believe they're hiding a few sins. Big ones, perhaps.

Soft grey eyes that can be pretty if they want to. Right now they're too mellow, too numb, too sad.

They need my fire, damn it, and if it weren't for the terms I just shackled myself to, I'd be hauling her upstairs right now for the evening and discovering how fast I'd turn them into stars.

"We're done," I say, wondering how long I've been choking back the words with my tongue hanging out. "I'll have my man, Fields, show you to your room. Make sure the kid doesn't think you're sleeping anywhere except with me, and tell me when he shows up. I've got work to catch up on."

I press the button for the intercom on the wall and call my butler. Fields knocks at the door a minute later. He's genteel, restrained, and far too proper as always when he shows up in his vest, giving the new lady of the house a bow.

It's hard not to snort every time he does that shit, like something out of a fifties movie. He does his job well enough, though, managing this place on the many occasions I'm either gone or too distracted to do it myself. "Grab her bags and take her upstairs, please," I tell him.

It's a weight off my shoulders when they're finally gone. My cock finally deflates while I pour myself a drink, mulling my options.

I've never been too proud to admit when I'm in over my head. That's definitely the case here, considering I don't know the first thing about engagements, even one that comes with a built-in expiration date.

I need advice. I pick up my phone and sit at my desk,

sifting through my contacts. When I dial her number, I'm hoping like hell Cal isn't around.

"Cade? Is that you? What's wrong?" A strained, soft voice chirps in my ear when she picks up.

"Aw, come on, Madds. You really think it's the end of the world every time you see my number on your caller ID?"

"Well, considering the last few times...what's up? Something happening for Cal's birthday?"

Shit. I almost forgot my best friend turns a year older soon. Fine, I'll use the opportunity to slip into the call more naturally.

"Good guess. I wanted your say before Spence and I haul him away to Alaska that week. We've been talking about it for years, and it just so happens our business buddy, Ty Sterner, runs a private retreat up there. We'd love to bring him up, with your blessing, Madds. Assuming it isn't interrupting any celebrations on your end, of course."

She laughs. "Whatever. You just want to drink and screw off like old times. Of course. I'm not his ball and chain, Cade. Let me know when you're thinking, and I'll be sure to clear the weekend."

"Will do. Say, speaking of marriage, I had something else I wanted to run by you." I exhale slowly, wondering how the hell I get the next part out without the news trickling down to my friends before it should.

"Oh, what's on your mind?" She's waiting. *Damn it all.*

"There's this girl. We're...kind of engaged." It just falls out. Heavier words were never spoken by this tongue. I hear her gasp. "Anyway, it's a weird situation. Lots of drama. A bit like when you hit it off with Cal, except not quite so fucking crazy. We're not in any trouble. I'm just looking for advice, but before we get too deep, for the love of God, please say you'll keep this between you and me."

"Jesus." It takes a few seconds to recover. I can't blame her. "Your secret's safe with me, Cade. How can I help?"

"Need to know how you two navigated things with your parents. Cal said plenty about how it all came down, and we were in the middle of it at the craziest, but I didn't hear much about the rest. How did your folks take it? They couldn't have been too happy at first, I mean, knowing how much trouble you were in."

"My little sister fought the hardest, actually. But she came around. Everybody did. Trust is earned. I don't know who the lucky lady is, but if you're wondering how to win her parents over, just be yourself. Reassure them. Make everybody in the room *know* she's where you start and end. Never let them doubt how much you mean it. Oh my God, Cade. I'm so happy for you! When's the –"

"We haven't set a date for anything yet, but it'll be very soon. You'll be the first to know," I say, heading off her praise. There'll be plenty of that to go around soon, and I'll have to pretend to enjoy it. Just not today. "Thanks for the advice, Madds. Give my best to my blood brother when he gets home. I'll be seeing you both soon. Glad you're back from Asia for a few weeks."

"Take care!" It takes a couple more seconds before I see the call disconnect.

She wanted more. I haven't heard her this amused since their wedding day, when I saw them making the rounds, slowly winning over her family. I wish like hell I'd paid more attention. It might help me introduce Skye without stepping on landmines.

For her and Cal, it was a battle. Her folks barely gave their blessing after the storm blew over, before Cal decided he couldn't wait a second longer to make it official.

I never told Maddie it's not Skye's folks I'm worried about – *hell, does she even have any?*

It's mine. If I want to save my mother's heart and soul, she's got to believe her only son is really getting married, and that goes double for dad.

If I'm pulling this off, I need to become a first class liar, and fast.

* * *

"You must be Vinnie. Go ahead, touch the clock, it's all real." Skye's kid brother whirls around when he hears me, hand perched on the grandfather clock towering over us. "Used to belong to my grandfather. Brought it over from Iceland, and it cost a small fortune to ship. Totally worth it, though. They had a way with tracking time, don't you think? Put the Swiss to shame two or three hundred years ago."

"Oh, yeah. Wow." The kid lets out a nervous laugh as I give his shoulder a friendly squeeze.

He might as well get comfortable with me since I'm the asshole pretending to marry his sister. Nothing says male bonding like staring at a three hundred year old clock with accents straight out of Revelation. Angels, demons, reapers, and warriors lock swords around the grand face, the gold hands neatly touching six o'clock sharp.

"Just in time," I say, smiling. I love the hell out of this part.

Gears turn, perking up his ears. The figures begin moving, dancing, locking swords, spinning around the face. They're re-enacting a celestial battle fought thousands of times as the chimes kick in, louder by the second. The music runs its course, ending in a clash of symbols.

The full show only happens four times a day, ornate background music I've lived with since I was a boy.

Vinnie looks impressed. So am I, honestly.

I was half-expecting a snot-nosed punk, remembering how I used to be at his age. Any kid who can sit still long enough to appreciate some Old World bad-assery is okay by me. Maybe he'll settle in here just fine after all.

"Vinnie, what the hell? Keep your hands to yourself!" Skye rushes in, yanking him out of my grasp. She clucks her tongue, fresh redness lining her cheeks, sending me an apologetic look.

"Easy, babe. Already told him he could admire it as much as he wants. He can even touch it considering this isn't a damn museum." She's wearing an uptight historian's frown. I'm smiling like a fool. "I kept this thing to make this place cozy, spark conversations worth having. That's what old *Avi* used to say." I smile fondly, remembering the old man who raised me half the summer years ago. My grandfather was kinder than his princely, mysterious air would suggest every time he emerged from his study in the castle's depths.

Mom isn't the only one whose happy times are anchored to hallowed ground. No, I probably wouldn't be poaching a fake wife to save it if she weren't in the equation, but damn, thinking about asshole Jonas turning it into an amusement park makes me taste bile.

"Cade, I'm sorry, again." I don't know why she's still apologizing, or why she's clinging to the kid like he's eight, and not fifteen. "This is my little brother, of course. Vincent, say –"

"We've already met," Vinnie mumbles, rubbing his arm after he jerks himself out of his sister's clutches. "I'll be more careful in the future, mister. Thanks for the company."

"Save your worries for something that counts," I tell him, motioning for him to follow me toward the stairs. "You've got the best guest room on the lower floor. Come on, let me show you. We'll do the grand tour. I'll have Fields grab your suitcase later."

"Hey, hold up! I want to see, too." Skye runs after us.

My smile just got wider. She almost sounds jealous

because I'm giving her kid brother the full show, seeing how I glossed over it earlier with her.

Of course, she didn't understand how bad she was making me throb back in my office, hovering over her, sensing her pulse race through my fingers while I bent her over my desk and put her name on the paperwork that'll make us official soon.

It's easy to forget how huge this place is until I have to show somebody around. It takes the better part of a half hour. We wind through the upper level with its three sun rooms and wrap-around balconies, then the dining hall, the gourmet kitchen I only use when I'm entertaining or frying up breakfast to shake off a hangover, the lower deck on the main floor overlooking the manicured gardens that open to my small slice of pristine Seattle coast.

We walk through the library, stick our heads in all fifteen bathrooms. Two game rooms, a library, and a sculpture garden later, we're making our way back into the house, touring the basement which has my indoor tennis court, a sauna, and the place I have the biggest love-hate relationship in my house with.

The kid perks up when we get to my gym. I've got enough equipment for a football team, which is weird because I only played lacrosse in my Maynard Academy days, and then at university. I swear I pulled pussy easier than any quarterback. Don't need hulking steroid muscles – just good ones – when I flash my pearly blues and the Icelandic smile that's soaked every pair of panties I ever wanted gone.

I let Vinnie try the machine I call the Ass Kicker, a custom leg press with kettlebells suspended on pulleys. When his back is turned, I pull Skye close, flexing like a champ.

"I'm doing him a favor. A couple months on that thing, and he'll be well on his way to looking like this. Or did you think I got this body grooming kittens all day, Skittle?"

Her sour expression says she doesn't appreciate a damn thing. For shame.

"I'm glad he's settling in easy, honestly. It'll make this whole thing smoother. *He's* the one I'm really worried about. This is a huge change for us," she says, refusing to look at me.

"Oh? You're not worried for yourself? Not even a little bit?" The arm I've got around her tightens.

Fuck, if we weren't sharing the room with a boy I've just met, she'd be at serious risk of my palm impacting her lush little ass. My eyes keep drifting to it while we huddle, her squirming harder than she should, overcompensating to look like she doesn't want to be this close to me.

"What *are* you doing?" she whispers under her breath. "Did you forget what we just signed?"

I haven't forgotten anything. It's the only thing on my frustrated, horndog mind when I arc my hand up her back, seize her hair softly, and lay my lips on hers *hard*.

Goddammit, yes.

She tastes as sweet as the night we met. Sweeter, maybe, because she's confused. Feisty. Clueless about what's happening, except for the fact that I'm savoring her good and deep.

Vinnie sees us mid-way through the most maddening kiss of my life. I break it off just in time, giving him a wink, leading his breathless sis a little closer. "I'll give you time to explore the place and settle in, now that you know the basics. What's mine is yours, Vinnie. This is your home, too."

I almost feel bad he won't get to stay here forever. I'll make sure he's got a nice place to go home to when the time comes, and our fake marriage is done. What's a spare fifty grand to keep this young man happy and comfortable?

"If it's all right with you, I think I'd like to hang out in my room," he says, slipping past us.

"Anytime. If you need anything, just find me or call Fields. He'll be around, or else one of the night staff, always a button away." I rap my knuckles against the closest intercom mounted to the wall.

Vinnie smiles sheepishly, too awe-struck by the luxury I've learned to take for granted to try it out in front of us. Skye waits until he's gone before she lays into me.

"What the hell were you thinking? In front of my brother? Ew!" She doesn't even wipe her mouth. I'm not sure who she thinks she's fooling.

"Skittle, please. Was it really so bad? Besides, I thought we had an understanding..." She hesitates. My chance to step up, corral her in the corner, and hold her there until she puts those fuck-me eyes on mine. "This isn't a game. We have to *pretend* we're in love, remember? I had to kiss you, Skye. Call it testing the waters. I wanted to see how he'd react. I mean, hell, if we can't even sell this kid on our sham marriage, how do we get my parents to buy it?"

"That's completely –"

"Ridiculous?" I say, leaning into her, grabbing her waist. "Fuck yes, it is. That's the very definition of what we're doing, strangers shacking up so we can help each other out. In case you haven't figured it out yet, I half-ass nothing. We're all in, or we're nowhere. When you signed your name a few hours ago, I trusted you were on board. Don't make me think differently."

"You're so dramatic." Her face twists away. She can't stand looking at me longer than she needs. Not when we're this close. "It isn't like that, Cade. I'll do my best, everything we agreed. It's just, it's a lot to take in. Oh, and of course Vinnie didn't text me like I told him before he showed up. We had a little spat last night. I guess he's still getting over it."

I suppress a smile, noticing the red blush blazing on her cheeks is brighter. "Typical sibling stuff?"

"Yeah. Just stupid, really. He saw the ring after he dragged himself in late, and I had to lie to him on the spot. I'm not very good at it."

"Practice makes perfect," I say, pushing my fingers into the tender skin above her hips. "I'm an only child, thankfully. Mom couldn't handle another hell-spawn like me. I don't know much about the tit for tat crap that goes on between brothers and sisters, but I do know people. Had to work at it, believe it or not. My parents did a good job keeping me sheltered early on. I learned my tricks from the bottom up. When to gab, how to strong arm, what it takes to craft the perfect lie."

"Thanks for the life story. Did I ask?" she says.

No, but this minx is definitely begging for a spanking.

My blood is lava. Hellfire flowing through every inch of me, and there's one part that has a one-track mind when it gets that steady, teasing burn.

"Careful, Skye. You keep giving me a tongue lashing, you'll get one right back. We're only on day one." I yank my hands off her before it's too late.

Before the chorus building up inside me turns deafening, telling me I have to fuck this girl, override the civilized deal we just formalized hours ago.

"I know. Don't make me regret this already," she says quietly. "I'm turning in, unless you have dinner plans for us, or something."

"Nope. Your call. Tell Fields anytime you're hungry, and he'll handle it. Take out, oysters from the finest in Seattle, peanuts from the freaking gas station, you name it. I want you to rest this weekend, and help your brother settle in. Next week will be harder when we sell this to my parents."

I leave her with that, exiting the gym. I'm remembering what it's like to be grateful this place is as cavernous as it is. I'll need the distance, without any distractions, to figure out how I want to break this news. Probably to my old man first, and then mom.

I definitely don't need her sass putting us in dangerous territory, before we've figured out where the hell we really are.

* * *

It's Sunday afternoon when I clean up from an hour on the Ass Kicker, take a nice long shower in the spa, and then put on my business casual. I haven't seen her all day. The kid, he's already brought his friend over. They're both laughing it up in my sculpture garden, now that there's a break in the rain.

I'm glad he's settling in, honestly. Just wish I saw signs Skittle was taking to this place so easy, and to me, but maybe I'd better count my blessings she isn't.

Getting too friendly won't do us any favors.

My father's favorite coffee shop by Pike's Place is an easy drive when the weekend crowds are dying down. I leave my driver at the ready for Skye or Vinnie, and struggle to a parking spot, then rush the three blocks to our meeting spot.

I can't remember ever being this nervous to see my own father. He's already inside, stereotypically early, seated by the window with a steaming black espresso in hand. He rises when I join him, set my coffee on the table, and throws his arms around me.

"How's retirement?" I ask, returning the embrace before I sit. "You finally enjoying yourself?"

He flashes me a weak smile. "I looked at cruises last week. Naturally, your mother prefers something off the Norwegian coast, or possibly the Baltic. I'm trying to sell her on Alaska so she won't get any ideas about wanting to stop off in Iceland on the way home. Easier said than done, I'm afraid."

"She'll love it if you can get her to give it a chance. Might be taking a trip to Alaska soon with the boys. It's Cal's birthday soon, and he's been talking it up forever." I sip my coffee slowly, trying to build up to the bombshell I'm holding in.

"Yes, yes, but you know your mother. Stubborn as the day she was born. If it wasn't for Jonas and his plans for that damn place, we wouldn't waste so much time wringing hands over our fall trip, before the snow flies, and –"

"Actually, dad, I've got good news on that front." I set my coffee down and give him my best smile. Here it fucking comes. "This'll probably come as a shock, but you'll have to trust my judgment. It just so happens I've been seeing the perfect girl. I thought about telling you the usual way, merging her into my life slowly, doing introductions with you and mom over a nice long dinner at Elliot's, or whatever. But when we went out last week, I decided I couldn't wait. I had to put a ring on this one. Now."

"Ring?" His brow wrinkles behind his thick spectacles. It takes him a solid ten seconds before he processes the news, and I see his eyes light up. "Jesus, son! You mean you're getting married?"

"Finally. There's the genius we miss around the office." I really mean the last part. I haven't had as much time as I'd like to take over every single function since dad left his job and his corporate stake at RET to me.

I wait for the smile, the back slapping, the adulations. My heart sinks into my guts when it never comes, and my father shoots me the look I haven't seen since my sixteen year old idiot self dented his shiny new Bentley on a joy ride upstate. "Where the hell did you find her, Cade? Who is she? Tell me this isn't just a game to make me think there's some off chance at hanging onto Turnbladt."

"Whoa, whoa, game? Do you *really* think I'd put you through something like that over the castle?" I am, of course, and the rules in this screwed up game I've started couldn't be higher. My hand goes up defensively, brushing my coffee, causing the ceramic mug to clatter on its saucer. "I love her, dad. You know I hold my cards close to my chest, and I'm sorry you're finding out like this. I wasn't sure how else to break the news. Our engagement's on. I'd love for you to meet her soon."

"Cade." He says my name sternly, cradling his forehead in his palm. He rubs it like his head is two seconds away from exploding. "Fine. We'll do this your way. You deserve the benefit of the doubt, I think."

Christ. He sounds so...defeated. Wronged.

It puts venom in my blood, a vicious desperation. I want to sell this facade harder than I already am. If I make him believe I'm serious, then maybe I'll believe it, too.

"You think? With all due respect, what the hell? Do you think I'd ever do this if I weren't serious? If I didn't take mom's health and happiness just as seriously as you?" I'm growling by the time I push out the last words. "This isn't a stunt, dad. I'm not jerking you around, or trying to rush anything just to save the old place."

I'm amazed how convincing I sound. "I've found the right woman. I'm pumped like I've never been to make her my wife. You'll love Skye. I'll bet every penny of my trust on it. Because if you don't, if you think this is some stupid, reckless show I'm putting on for mom's benefit, if you're calling me a liar to my face – "

"Cade..." He says my name a second time, and I've barely slowed down.

Yeah, this is what I needed after all, to get worked up, dump my guts all over the table for my father to see. He's staring dumbfounded while I rattle it out, passion echoing through the whole coffee shop. We've got baristas staring at us, college girls peeping over their laptops to gauge the commotion.

"Cade!" My name leaves his lips with a sharper tone. "You need to get a grip."

I look around, stretching it out, pretending I'm embarrassed. Truthfully, I'm wondering where the hell to pick up my Emmy. I was never big on the performing arts. Didn't know I had it in me to give an all star performance.

But apparently, when there's this much hanging by a thread...

"You're right. I'm sorry. Didn't mean to let it get to me."

"No. I'm the one who should apologize," dad says, adjusting his glasses. It's the nervous tick he's had his entire life whenever he admits he's wrong. "It's been very stressful, this situation overseas. Still, that's no excuse. I shouldn't accuse you of the unthinkable, son. Your new fiancée deserves a chance. We'll meet her. If she's won you over, then I'm certain we'll have no problem welcoming her into the family. Let's talk time and place."

I smile, nodding slowly. I accidentally slurp my coffee when I raise it to my lips.

Deep down, I feel like an utter heel, coaxing an apology out of him after lying to his face. It's hard to remember why I'm doing this, but I do. There's also an evil sense of triumph.

Dad's peace of mind isn't even half the reason there's a hard road ahead. The rest is mother, and I'd better hope my convincing streak continues when it's time to bring her and Skittle face-to-face with a noble lie.

This is for her. For both my parents, really.

They've given me more than the average person could ever hope for. I'll pay it back, with interest.

This isn't the time to flinch, even if my turn at the karma wheel takes a sea of tears.

* * *

LATER, I'm on the edge of my seat when the phone rings. I've stopped by the office to catch up on some work. The hacker breach investigations haven't slowed for the weekend. I really need to sit down and catch up on the latest from security, without any distractions.

Life has other plans.

As soon as I see mom's number on my caller ID, I realize getting any work done is about as likely as roping Skittle into an ordinary chat without every part of me begging to be inside her.

"Mom?" My ear runs hot when I press the receiver close.

"Cade Sigmund Turnbladt! How *dare* you tell your father first and leave your poor mother out in the cold."

I smile. Predictably, she's pissed. "Hello to you, too. Look, mom, it isn't like that. I figured I'd feel him out first, considering this is a little...unconventional." I pause, stuck on the understatement of the year. If only she knew how true it is.

"If you mean your abject failure to mention the lovely girl you're engaged to, much less introduce us, then *yes.* You're a turd, son. Cosmopolitan in the ways I hoped you'd never be, but I love you anyway."

And she does. It's easy hanging onto your mother's heart when you're her only boy. I think I could take her car out to the strip club with Lucifer and crash it on the way home, and she'd still forgive me after a stern talking to.

"Love you, too. It wasn't easy holding this in, believe me. It all came together crazy fast. I always thought I'd jump through the usual hoops, book a day for her to meet the family...but all I'd be doing is delaying the inevitable. She's the one for me, mom. As unbelievable as it sounds, it's true."

"What's unbelievable, boy, is the fact that you think I want to get into wedding plans without even having tea with her! Do you have any clue how long I've waited for this day?"

Only my entire lifetime. My teeth pierce my smile, like

I'm sucking on a lemon, remembering how she used to tease me when I was just five on the long sleigh rides outside grandpa's place. She had my entire future mapped out for me, and she let me know it, too: straight A student, bringer of a daughter-in-law, father by thirty, Senator by forty.

Nothing went according to plan.

I hate the shit out of politics, my GPA took a beating so bad I came close to flunking business school after the academy before I buckled down, and kids? Fuck no.

This sudden bride thing is the only part of her master scheme that's gone right. I listen closely through her hurried breathing, wondering if I can't hear her jumping up and down because she's still in slippers from her evening nap.

"Name a time and place, mom. Your pick." I settle back into my seat, resigned to the cooing and shower of kisses we're certain to face when Skittle meets her.

"I'd love to bring her to the old place, honestly. It's too special for any old place around here. Pack your bags and make sure the jet has gas."

I sit up, almost knocking my coffee off my desk.

Old place? Iceland? *She can't be serious.*

"You're not talking about...Turnbladt? Jesus. That's quite a distance for a quick how-do-you-do, mom." I hope I've misheard her. But when was that ever the case?

"And there's nowhere more meaningful if you want her to be part of our family, Cade." Motherly wisdom is a bitch sometimes. I bite my tongue, wracking my brain for any excuse to dash this insane idea. "I've been trying to coax your father into an autumn trip there anyway. This is the perfect opportunity. She'll love it. Hiking, hot springs, medieval beauty, the rolling hills – oh, and my adorable little tea house!"

Like I could ever forget. It's only been her favorite place in the world to play diplomat and angelic hostess over the years. She must've sealed a dozen deals dad couldn't nail down for the firm alone. A piping hot cup of sweetness in a place that looks like it's been dropped into the world's prettiest fairy village schmoozes old money faster than all the promises in the world about triple digit ROIs.

"Cade? Don't tell me there's some objection on her end?" Her tone darkens. "Surely, son, you'd never marry a woman who can't appreciate our distinctive Old World Charm, yes?"

"Of course, mother. That's not an issue. It's just...we want the wedding to happen soon, and we want it in Seattle. We've got a lot of planning." I'm not ready to break it to her that our time horizon is about two weeks.

Hell, I don't think I could. My mind is stuck trying to fathom how I'll survive a trip to Iceland with mom and my fake wife. There's potential enough for nasty surprises when I have no idea how well Skye can act around my family. More if we're at ground zero, risking everything, especially if my asshole cousin gets wind of our visit, and my engagement.

Shit. What choice do I really have?

"I'll let her know tonight, and get back to you. She's a grad student, mom. Hope you understand she might have a few loose ends on her side to tie up, but we'll set a date to meet you and dad there as soon as we can."

"That's my baby boy," she whispers, practically purring into my ear. "Congratulations, Cade. I always knew you'd do the right thing. I simply can't wait to meet the love of your life."

The call is over. Doesn't do anything to calm my vicious pulse, or fix the thousand complications standing between me and making this trip happen.

These waters just got ten times harder to navigate. And the ice that's still there between me and my trick fiancée is the least of what could torpedo this entire thing.

What's that they say about good deeds again? Unpunished?

Seems like I'm about to pay for this one with half my soul.

V: WORLDS IN COLLISION (SKYE)

"*I*celand? Holy shit. You expect me to just...up and go?" I don't know why I even ask the question.

Cade's intense blue gaze says that's exactly what he wants. Yet another reminder I signed away my freedom to have my debt to a bigger monster wiped.

"I didn't tell her we'd jump to it this week, though I'd prefer to get it over with," he says, as if it's nothing more serious than a routine physical. "Talk it over with your professor, Skittle. Let me know. I'll work with your schedule."

Oh, I'd love to give him *something* to work with, all right.

But it's not like it's all bad. I've never been to Iceland. Hell, I haven't been anywhere for fun. The trips for archeology credit were always work. And compared to our last few interactions, when he backed me into a corner and stripped me with those relentless eyes, he's being downright genteel right now.

This is a job, I remind myself. Nothing else. I don't know why I'm so offended.

I'm afraid I don't want to dig too deep, and find out, if I'm being brutally honest. "I'll talk to Dr. Olivers. Maybe his other TA can fill in for me this week. I'm sure I'll find some way to make up credit on the trip."

"Fuck yeah, you will. The countryside outside our place is practically crawling with old ruins. You'll come home with a couple eggheads beating down your door to talk secrets with the hottest, youngest star in archeology."

"Jesus, Cade, I'm sold." What is this tone? *Excitement?* "Let me hash out the dates with my professor. You don't have to keep trying so hard." I sigh, realizing my inner bitch is off her chain. Maybe I'm counteracting the butterflies in my stomach. And she isn't going quietly without one more lashing. "Besides, I'm doing my PhD on Rome. They were never there. Not definitively, anyway, according to any mainstream sources."

"Vikings, Romans, what-the-hell ever. History was never my strong suit, Skittle. I did business." He talks like I don't know the half of it. "I barely remember old man Gregorson's Euro history class at Maynard. Must've spent every hour screwing off with Spence and Cal, whenever I wasn't trying to get a perfect angle to see up some cheerleader's skirt."

"Charming." *Ass.* I give him the dirty look he deserves, unsure why he thinks sharing these bawdy stories is a good idea.

His smirk disappears. "Sorry. Those were dumb, but happy times. Just wish they'd ended that way. When our buddy, Calv, got himself in deep shit, fighting with the resident bully we called Scourge, history class turned into a funeral parlor. Couldn't even pretend to care about dead kings and popes from five hundred years ago when life took a darker turn."

I raise my eyebrows. He takes his eyes off mine and looks away. He doesn't want to elaborate.

"Just figure out a time and let me know. I need to give my

flight crew at least a few hour's warning before we take off," he tells me. I do a double take, blinking as he smooths a crease in his sleeve like it's nothing. "What? You thought we'd be taking Delta or American? I *am* a billionaire, love. My private jet costs as much to operate in relative terms as renewing the insurance on your beat up Toyota. You might as well cancel that, by the way. I'll get you a car that doesn't drip oil all over my garage as soon as we're home from Reykjavik."

"I'm driving that car until it falls apart, thank you very much," I fold my arms, looking away with my haughtiest sniff. He just laughs. It's infuriating how much power he has over us. "If you want to give me a little privacy, I'll tell Vinnie about the trip and send an email to Dr. Olivers."

"Sure, whatever," he says, slowly backing out of my room, lingering by the door.

I don't understand what he wants. "Is there something else, or are we done?"

"Just thought tonight might be a good time to see if I can get you to pull your quills back in. Join me for dinner?"

My heart starts to race. Far more quickly than it really should.

"I don't know. Vinnie hasn't had much time to settle in, and we didn't exactly make the switch here under the best circumstances. I thought I'd take him out for a burger, or something, or maybe order in."

It's too soon to be alone with him again. Doubly dangerous when I see the sharp glint in his eye, the spark that tells me his idea of dinner probably has more to do with having it between my legs than on any tabletop.

"Fine. That's fair," he says, turning to go, but he grips the door with his palm at the last minute, aiming one last feral look over his shoulder. "You're gonna have to warm up to me sooner or later, Skittle. I'll melt that shell. Because if I can't, if we're stuck doing the bare minimum and we can't even be friends, then I don't know why we're doing this. We're wasting our time if we can't make this seem natural."

He's gone before I can say anything back, yanking my door shut gently. It clicks like an empty revolver.

Jesus. I expected more teasing, more smirking, another hot mess of a dinner invitation for tomorrow, where at least I'd have twenty-four hours to brace myself to fight off his delectable advances.

But he looked wounded. I wasn't expecting that.

Is it time to pull my mind out of the gutter and give him the benefit of the doubt? As hard as it is, he has a point, even though I'm not ready to admit it to his face anytime soon.

This isn't how it should be.

If it's not the sexual tension oozing off us with a sticky heat that makes me want to loose my clothes in the worst ways, it's nipping at each other's egos like strays in a catnip factory's alley. Love and hate. Vicious uncertainty.

This trip makes me nervous because it's clearly make or break.

We'll either learn to do this, without me clawing at his throat or fighting off his tongue, or we'll fail miserably. And no, I don't want to imagine what failure means.

Even if a million and a half is chump change to him, I can't walk away owing him if I blow this.

I'm done with debt.

I can handle my brat of a brother, and I think I can handle this beast I've agreed to marry, too. But I absolutely *cannot* take being under anyone's thumb. If I'm not a free woman by the end of this, who's earned it the hard way and learned from her many, many mistakes, then I'm nothing.

* * *

"PRIVATE JET? *Castle?* Holy crap, sis, I'd think you were making this up if we weren't already living a frigging fairy tale." Vinnie rubs his eyes for the third time since we sat down for a late night bite at our local bread and chowder place.

"Don't get too excited. You're only going if your tutor says it's okay."

His excitement fades. "Aw, I'm close to caught up. I swear. No worries. I'm on top of it."

"That's the news of the century, if true. She told me last week you had English to catch up on, at least three week's worth. Said you'd been blaming it on your health again."

Vinnie lowers his eyes. There's a break in the tension when our waiter shows up, laying two steaming white bowls of seafood bliss in front of us. I pick up my spoon, expecting him to start shoveling it in. I'm on my third bite when I realize he isn't moving.

"Vinnie, hey, I didn't mean to come down so hard on you. It's just been a little stressful lately, I'm sure you can imagine."

"Can I?" He lifts his face, the edge of his glasses slightly fogged from chowder steam. He picks up his spoon, shoveling an angry bite into his mouth. "Seems to me you've got it pretty good lately, sis. Landing us this mansion, a rich guy who looks like a movie star, trips to Europe. I thought we'd *never* get out of our crappy apartment barely a day ago. Excuse me if I thought maybe you'd want to...you know, share the wealth, without reminding me how fucked in the head I am."

My spoon hits the bowl and rattles. I hate when he swears in public. "I didn't mean it like that, and you *know it.* Your health matters to me, Vinnie." He'll never really know how much. I sigh. "Look, I just want you caught up on school-work before we go. I'd love to have you join us on the trip, really, if you're willing to behave and stop the guilt trip."

He slurps his soup loudly, giving me a glare, before reaching for his Mountain Dew. "I shouldn't go. You're right, I did feed Mrs. LeMay a story so I could skateboard with James and Mike." He pauses, shaking his head. "Do I ever win? I'm coming clean about the skateboarding, too, and you're still looking at me like I just stole your crackers."

He reaches over, pulling at the oyster crackers in their plastic baggie on the edge of my bowl. My little brother gets so dramatic it's hard to separate the usual prickly teen drama from the stuff I need to worry about.

"Please tell me you were wearing a helmet," I say, closing my eyes. It's hard to fight my natural instinct to chew him out for doing it at all. A sudden spill could make his condition a thousand times worse.

"Duh. I'm not a *total* irresponsible idiot, but I guess you already think I am, so..."

"So, stop. I never said that, Vinnie. Stop putting words in my mouth." I take another bite of soup. It's hot, savory, everything that should make my taste buds purr. Too bad every time I chew, I'm losing my appetite. I set my spoon down, pursing my lips. "I don't pretend to be perfect. This is a lot of change to swallow for both of us, and yeah, we're going to have friction. I'm ready for that. But it isn't exactly easy for me. None of it. Like raising you...do you think I ever asked for it?"

His eyes widen, but never brighten, even in the well lit bakery. "What are you –"

"I'm doing the best I can, Vinnie. I know it's hard to believe sometimes. I care. I want you to grow up, get on your own two feet, and be happy, damn it. Obviously, I'll never fill mom's shoes. I'm not exactly trying, either. I'm just making the best of a bad situation. Keeping you safe, housed, and loved. That's the reason for all of this." I'm careful not to spill the truth about my new fiancé, despite how it stings the tip of my tongue, begging to come out. Thankfully, there are times when being emotionally ruined are an asset. "There are days when I still can't stand to look at myself in the mirror. When I was in Turkey, at the dig, those people trusted me. They never even thought I could be the one who jacked a thousand year old Byzantine jewelry set and tried to sell it on the black market."

I'm careful to keep my voice down. Vinnie looks away, like a living embodiment of my shame. Nothing I'm saying to him is news. He's the *only* person on earth, other than Harry, who knows what I'd planned to do.

Deep down, I think he feels a little guilty, too, knowing I was doing it for him. For us.

My stomach twists a little, wondering how he'd feel if he knew Cade just entered the equation for the same reason.

It isn't love. It never is.

My life is survival.

"Sis, Jesus. We don't need to go there again," he says, stuffing more soup into his mouth, trying to ignore me.

My stomach growls. I try to eat the rest of my chowder in peace. It's been months since we've had more than a cheap frozen pizza. I don't want to ruin this.

Apparently, that's no longer a question when I see my brother blotting at his eyes with the tablecloth when he thinks I'm not looking, Vinnie pretends he's choked up on too much black pepper.

I know better.

I'm the reason our lives suck this much, even when they're getting better for the first time in ages.

He's only fifteen. Young, innocent, not ground down by hard deals and self-loathing.

I'm the one who wouldn't quit grad school when the writing was on the wall, and mom's meager savings bled out.

I'm the one who made the deal with Uncle Harry, just

months after her funeral, when he found out I was heading overseas. He may have put the devilish bug in my ear, sure, but I *acted* on it. I stole priceless history worth millions, violated my career before I had a doctorate to taint, and all for nothing when it disappeared, lost in the mail or intercepted by corrupt customs officials in one place or another.

I'm the one pretending I'm over grieving mom. Vinnie hates it when I hide my tears, so I've learned to keep them from showing whenever he's around. He wouldn't understand.

I stopped missing her months ago and feeling sad about it. Now, I'm just furious.

Every time I dwell on her suicide long enough, I'm afraid I'm starting to *hate* her for throwing herself off that stupid bridge. Whatever got to her, whatever Harry threatened her with, it was no excuse for leaving behind a twenty one year old starving student with a special needs brother to care for.

Her suicide was selfish, and I'm not sure I'll *ever* be over it.

"Sis? Look at me!" Vinnie reaches for my hand. That's what it takes for me to stop, and realize I'd been stabbing at my bowl, clinking the spoon harshly on the ceramic. "You okay? I'm sorry this got so serious."

I force a smile, pushing away the remnants of my chowder. I haven't touched half of it and it's like my stomach is full of cement. "Yeah. I'm sorry, too. Just put me in touch with your tutor and we'll see what we can do. Maybe LeMay can give you extra credit or something for the trip."

He grins, eyeballing the rest of my chowder. I push it across the table to him, wishing our fights always had a happy ending, but life rarely cooperates.

"Whatever it takes," he says, stuffing more soup into his growing mouth. "I promise I'll stay out of your hair. Man, I've never been on a private jet before."

* * *

IT'S MY FIRST TIME, too. Until mid-week, after I'm able to get time off and a makeup credit from my professor to review the local museums, I never imagined I'd ever fly in style.

It's beyond surreal the day we're dropped off at the airport. We roll right up to the private area with the sleek Gulfstream ready to carry us overseas. Cade waves bye to chauffeur Nate, and then we're off, without so much as a single tedious pat-down from security.

X-rays and claustrophobic lines are for the little people, it seems. Rich people travel differently. The pilot and several perky flight attendants greet us warmly the instant we're on board. Passing through the plane's door, I wonder if I've stepped into a five star hotel by accident.

The cabin is more like a lounge than any airline I've ever flown on. "I'll take it from here," Cade tells a stewardess. "Let me show you to your seat. Drink?"

"Maybe when we're in the air," I mutter, blinking the longer I look around. I'm also trying to keep track of Vinnie, of course, who runs to the back of the plane, looking for a charger.

"You look tired, Skittle. The kid can have my room, if you want some peace and quiet in the cabin. I'd rather have you rested. We'll get there near sunrise. Mom's very much a morning person, and she left with my father yesterday morning."

"No, you've been more than generous," I say. I don't even try to fight it when he lays a protective hand on my back, just as Vinnie glances our way.

"See that silver thing on the wall? Give it a good push and slide the doors apart, Vinnie. Nice big bed with a seventy-inch TV inside. Chargers galore. Knock yourself out, young man. Just stay out of the bar." He looks at me and winks.

Vinnie shoots me a sharp look, seeking approval. *Can I?*

"Fine, but behave," I tell him, rolling my eyes. It takes my brother exactly two seconds to disappear inside, and then the door slams shut. I turn to Cade again. "You're sure he'll be okay in there?"

"Perfectly. They built this thing pretty idiot proof. Plus there are buttons everywhere to call the attendants when he gets hungry." His hand slides lower, into the small of my back, grazing the top of my skirt.

I pull myself away later than I should, too flustered for a dirty look. Shameful heat races to my cheeks. My blood runs hot because we both know I started leaning into him when he had his hand there.

I'm saved from a more awkward confrontation by the pilot's announcement. I notice the door is up, and it's time to prepare for takeoff. I'm careful to put space between me and Mr. Relentless, who acts like nothing happened, his face tucked in a fancy travel magazine.

He can't hide everything. I see the smirk, how his eyes roam my legs when he thinks I'm not looking, glued to my phone until the plane is screaming down the runway.

At last, we're ascending in the wild blue yonder, soaring briefly over the Pacific. Ten minutes in, the plane starts its turn, charting a path through Canada and the great unknown north.

Next stop, Iceland. A capitol, a castle, and a country I've never seen.

If this weren't so forced, I might let the fairy tale magic pulse through my brain, drunk on the adrenaline high no matter how much I fight it. When I glance back from the window, and catch his eyes, I'm not even scowling anymore.

It's not so bad, maybe. I'm making peace with this screwed up marriage every second we're floating through the air.

I'll even live with his imaginary eye-fuck, without scolding him for it, if it means the rest of this trip goes just as smoothly.

* * *

"Breakfast in half an hour." His voice floats through my dreams. Fingers sift through my hair, soft and indulging. For a second I feel like I'm in a cloud. One with the plane's distant humming engines.

I sit up, rubbing my eyes, staring into his beautiful blue gaze. I'm slow to remember how dangerous it is to lose myself in this man for more than a second. But sweet Jesus, I want to.

"Any last words before you meet my mother?" His smile is infectious.

"No. I'm as ready as I'll ever be, I suppose," I tell him, looking out the window. We're already beginning our descent over the ocean.

If there was ever a land forged to perfection by the old Norse gods, it's here. A steaming volcano sits nestled between the rocky mountains, streams running through, tiny pastoral villages forming a green band separated from the sea. If this goes up in flames, at least it'll be in paradise.

"So, are you worried it'll get crazy? You mentioned your cousin," I say, facing my fake fiancé again.

"I'm expecting it. We're going right into the mouth of disaster, Skittle." The gentle smile on his lips never wavers. "Won't take long for cousin Jonas to find out I'm here with my betrothed. He'll throw a total shit-fit if he isn't too blasted out of his mind from another tour. My only goal is to keep him away from mom."

Cocking my head, I try to read his face. I can't figure out what he's really hiding, what he fears behind that smile.

"You sound numb," I whisper, just as a flight attendant hands me a bottle of water before the crew makes its final landing preparations.

"And you say that like it's a bad thing. I think you know plenty about coping, Skye. Finally, something we've got in common."

His eyes braise my skin so long I have to look away. "Where's Vinnie? It's been...what? Eight, maybe ten hours? I can't believe I slept so long. He should be up and about. Doesn't like to sit still longer than he has to."

"I had a lovely conversation with your brother a couple hours ago," he says cryptically. "Good kid. He's looking out for you, Skittle, even if you can't see it."

I grit my teeth, wondering how much of our lives Vinnie leaked to this man, smiling like a wolf in its prime. It's a sexy smile, too. It tames my worries, if only for a few precious seconds, pooling electric heat between my thighs.

"You should question anything he says," I say, turning my face back to the window, before I remember how his blue eyes glowed the night he saw me naked, shamefully tapping out Sinatra on the keys.

"That's fucking ironic, Skittle. Because I've been doing the same thing with you since the day we met. Must run in the family." He lifts a morning coffee to his lips and sucks caffeinated bliss through the plastic lid. Our stare-down hasn't ended when he pulls it away, stuffing it back into the cup holder next to him. "I wish I could figure you out. Pinpoint what it takes for you to relax, now that the weight of the world is off your shoulders. Your debt's gone. You're about to make progress with this gig, selling my mom and dad on us. When this thing is over, you're free and clear. I'll send you to Egypt for a year. Athens, Rome, wherever the hell you want to chase ghosts and get that tight body covered in dust."

"I don't remember that being in the contract." I wish like nothing else he'd stop offering these perks. It's *not* changing my no fraternizing policy, no matter how much my skin begs to be on his sometimes. "I'm a by-the-book kind of girl. I don't need any special allowances, Cade."

"Maybe so," he says, stroking his chin. "But can't you at least smile for me, babe?"

There's a sharp, barely perceptible sound when his fingers glide over his skin, slow and steady. It must be the five o'clock shadow grazing his fingertips, rough stubble that gives his handsome face an edge I'm scared to dwell on for too long.

I deepen my frown, refusing to give in. His eyes are asking too much. "I'll think about reeling the bitch back in for your parents, at least."

"Not what I'm asking. I mean when we're alone." His hand falls to the armrest, and he taps it with his fingers. "You know what I'm after, Skittle. Let's not mince words."

"No, let's not. I have a pretty good idea what you want, and we said we're not going there," I tell him, tensing up, just waiting for him to slide across the long seat and make me dangerously wet.

But he isn't moving. Cade stays on his side, patiently watching me, slowly drumming his fingers against the silver end of his armrest. The plane's engines chirp, cutting through the silence, bringing us closer to Reykjavik.

"What? Why are you still staring?" It comes out sharply when I can't hold it in anymore, after I've had his rogue eyes fixed on me for close to sixty seconds.

"Because I love a fucking challenge, Skye Coyle. I love that the real you is pent up, hidden, behind the heavy walls you're practically begging somebody to knock down. We'll be here about a week if I don't have to rush home to Seattle to put out any fires at the firm. Long enough to see the real you, and when I do, I'll be sure those spitfire lips glow brighter than your wild hair."

I turn my face to the window, refusing to dignify his smug, skirt-chasing confidence with a response.

It isn't easy.

If I'm brutally honest with myself, and I consider the possibility he isn't just teasing, I'm afraid. Terrified he might be right.

It's not fair, damn it. Wanting sex is no surprise. It's something I can handle, even if rebuffing his steady advances isn't easy. His looks make my heart race. The blue flames set in his face lash my body every time they're pointed my way, forcing me to imagine what he can do with that gaze, those hands, and those perfectly Icelandic muscles as rough, dark, and unrelenting as the medieval landscape we're about to touch down in.

Sex, I can deal with. But his other advances...wanting to know the real me? I've never had the luxury of finding myself.

I don't know what he'll find if he starts to chip away. This isn't archeology. There's no happy history waiting under this self. Just disappointment, shame, regret. All the ugliness I've wanted to seal away forever.

Too bad the questions I've tried to ignore are already ringing in my brain in an evil chorus on repeat.

What now? What next?

Because if Cade chips away at the ice, the only thing that's kept me alive and Vinnie out of hell for my whole adult life, what will he truly find?

Or, rather, *who?*

* * *

I'M able to ignore the identity demons stomping around

inside me long enough to get off the plane, clean up in the bathroom before we disembark, and make sure Vinnie gets his butt up.

Cade and my brother share a grin before we see him off. A separate car is taking him to his guest house on the castle grounds, and we're off to meet the Turnbladts. A small mercy, really, because making sure my brother doesn't make an ass out of us both isn't something I relish.

I haven't had time to feel nervous before. It doesn't hit me until our car takes the long, winding highway into the mountains, and I see what has to be our destination in the distance, catching the sunlight in its medieval glory.

"Holy crap," I whisper, catching Cade's smile.

"What? You thought I was joking when I said castle?"

I shake my head, eyes roaming the high watchtowers. It's like something out of a greeting card, an inverted Dracula lair in soft grey, protected by angelic statues. A church and a greenhouse sit at the base of the seven hundred year old opulence, flanked by pools, fountains, and gardens bursting with greenery.

I'd nearly forgotten places like this still exist.

"Wait till you see the spa," Cade says, reaching for my hand. I whip my head around, jaw hanging, mind racing because I wonder if we'll be escorted by honest-to-God knights when we finally get to the entrance. "Didn't appreciate it much when I was a kid. Now? Christ. Those Swedes mom brings in every time the family visits know exactly what they're doing. Some of it can't be fully human, considering how you'll feel after one of their massages."

I'm smiling for a few seconds before the usual guilt creeps in. *You're not coming here to get pampered,* I remind myself. *It's a job. Not a vacation. And you're not really his.*

I try to shake it before the car lurches to a halt. We're only feet away from the biggest, grandest door I've ever seen outside the old Byzantine churches in Istanbul. No knights, but an entourage of well dressed men and women, who step forward to open the doors for us, retrieving our luggage from the trunk as we follow them inside.

"Almost there," Cade whispers, his grip on my hand tightening.

For once, I don't fight it, or worry how horny it'll make me. It's comforting, and even more soothing to know I'm with someone who feels normal here.

I feel like a child in this place. Sure, I did my homework before we came, read the wiki and glanced through the Turnbladt castle's pictures online. None of it does a lick of justice to being here, though.

Not when I'm standing on these ancient grounds in the flesh, trying to keep up with Cade as we roam a soft purple carpet that looks like it belonged to a king once upon a time.

Not when the awe is making me lose my mind. The life-sized gargoyles, lions, and stallions we pass on our way to the huge glass doors on the other side of the main floor are too much for my young, poor, and American mind to compre-hend with any ease.

Not when the heat in his hands is making my own impos-sible to ignore. Fire washes through my blood the longer I cling to him like a lost little girl, trying to remember my introduction, when the fateful moment comes a second later and I see the Turnbladts waiting on the terrace. A full break-fast bar and steaming tea set surrounds them.

"Cade, Cade, Cade!" Mrs. Turnbladt stands, calling his name louder as she nears, before impacting her son in a bear hug that looks stronger than her short, skinny frame should manage. "We've been waiting for you all morning, son."

"She does mean *all* morning," he says, turning in his mother's grip to face me. "My parents live for the sunrise. Mom, this is –"

"Call me Katrin. It's wonderful to finally meet you, dear." The woman drops her son to wrap me in another bone-crushing embrace. I try to hug back, matching her strength, if only to save myself from being crushed.

"Skye," I whimper, once I'm able to breathe. "It's an honor."

"Nonsense," Katrin snaps, pulling away. I notice she has the same eyes as Cade; furious, bright, and blue. I wonder if she's the source of his manic energy, too. I still can't believe he didn't sleep on the flight. "You're the one who's honoring me. The whole family, to be quite honest. Come, dear, you must be hungry after the trip. There's fruit, bread, honey, butter from the village, and the most exquisite arctic thyme tea you've ever tasted."

I'm beaming, and it isn't forced. My stomach growls ferociously. I stop next to Cade and his father, a genteel man with bifocals and salt and pepper hair. He stops, lifts my hand to his lips, and lays a warm kiss on my skin.

"Pleasure, Skye. I'm Stefan. Thank you for loving our son."

"No thanks necessary," I say, reaching for Cade's hand very obviously. I need this engagement thing to look natural. "We're made for each other."

He gives me a knowing look. His arm goes around my waist, pulls me closer, and – as if I expected anything different – he steals a kiss. Longer than he really needs for an affectionate peck.

I'm barely annoyed. It's this magic place making me intoxicated, probably. There's no recoil, no doubt, none of the usual fear when his tongue touches mine. My fingernails crawl up his neck, claw his skin, wind through his short blond hair until they're needling his scalp.

Cade pulls away first, breaking the kiss, drawing a harsh breath through his sexy lips. "What's gotten into you?" he whispers, so low his parents can't hear. "Kiss me like that again, Skittle, and we're in trouble. Don't know what I want more: another taste, or introducing your ass to my palm for teasing me when we've been here for five minutes. No games."

"None," I agree, wondering what he's getting at. But it's not half as confusing as whatever's happening to me.

You're overcompensating, I decide. *Trying to get the jump on your nerves before they screw you over. What better way than to take this love birds thing a little too far?*

That's got to be it. It's working, too. Stefan gives his son a proud grin.

Then he leads us to the table, where Katrin sits, the sun in her happy eyes and her face resting on her hands. "Let them have their fill. They've got to be starving after the flight."

I nod joyfully, taking the empty spot next to Cade. He tugs a fruit basket close, while a waiter steps forward, serving us three glasses each. Tea, juice, and water.

"Eat, dear," Katrin says to me again, her eyes soft and excited. "Then I want to hear *everything.*"

* * *

"Why history?" she asks, before biting into a biscuit. "It's a very murky subject, but an interesting one. I couldn't bear trying to make sense of things from a thousand years ago. Our ancestry here is plenty for my mind, thanks."

My eyes scan our surroundings before I answer. Plenty? She's living in a freaking museum. More glamor, richness, and age old wonders than anyone deserves. I'm used to the past being cold, distant, clinical, more of a murder-mystery hobbyist's approach than being steeped in the living and breathing bygone.

"Well, I'm sure you've heard the line about how it repeats

itself, right? I don't believe that myself," I say, pausing for another bite of this amazing berry yogurt. If this is ordinary Icelandic fare, I don't think I'll have any problems adjusting to the diet. "I think it's off base, honestly. History's full of lessons, but it never happens the same way twice. It's worth preserving as a guide. It tells us what shape the future could take. If I'm able to help, then well..." I shrug. "It's a decent calling, and a good career, as soon as I've finished my dissertation and found tenure somewhere. I'd really like to be out in the field, rather than cooped up teaching, though."

This is making me more nervous than I should be. It's not the curious looks the Turnbladts are giving me turning my cheeks beet red, but Cade's eyes.

He sees more than a flustered young woman meeting her potential in-laws for the first time.

He hears more than a strained student trying to breakdown her humility for strangers.

He feels more than he's entitled to...his damn hand hasn't left my thigh since the first few minutes after we sat down.

I don't dare bat him away. The same part of me that kissed him doesn't want to, and I know it's insane. There must be something in this fresh mountain air, or the crisp glacial mineral water in the tea, that's putting me in pieces.

"Whatever, love. I think you're just in it for the travel perks." Cade wastes no time getting in a jab. He looks at his parents. "She's been more places in Europe than me. Lots of time in Turkey."

"Ah, a lovely place, Istanbul in the spring," Stefan says, his eyes glazing over with happy memories. "I once spent a week there schmoozing an investor from Dubai. He went with another firm in the end, one of the biggest misses of my career, in fact, but I couldn't care after a week in that place. The art...the music...the food! I'd go to the ends of the earth for lamb that tender again."

"Stefan, please! There's more to life than stuffing your face." Katrin slaps gently at his hand, hiding a raw smile. "And you, boy, lay off our lovely guest. There's a time and place to tease your wife, but it isn't in front of me on our first meeting."

"Yeah, mother. Good point." Cade shoots me a sideways glance, bringing his hand back into his own lap. Why the hell does the skin under my skirt feel so empty without his warmth?

"It's a beautiful place, Stefan," I agree, sipping my tea. It's lukewarm by now, but I honestly prefer it. I'm able to taste even more of the exotic herbs and spices, plus the honey's pleasant sweetness. "Have you seen the Hagia Sophia? Incredible. I thought I'd died and gone to –"

I stop mid-sentence. There's something vibrating against my leg, and it definitely isn't Mr. Relentless returning for a second run at getting my panties off later.

It's the third time in the last hour my phone's been going off. I wonder who it is, what's so urgent it just can't wait. It can't be Vinnie...we gave him Cade's number, too. I think he'd waste no time trying it if something crazy happened.

"Something the matter?" Stefan notices the change in my expression.

All three Turnbladts are staring, their blue eyes narrowed on me, full of questions. I'm not sure how much longer I can keep this up without ripping the needy demon out of my pocket to see who's calling.

There's only one person who ever rang my line stupid until I picked up.

I keep telling myself it isn't him. *It can't be.*

"Forgive me. Breakfast is amazing, but I didn't sleep too well on the flight." I hide an exaggerated yawn behind my palm. Perfect timing.

"Of course, dear! Where would I be without my siesta

after the journey here?" Katrin stands, motioning to the waiter before she looks our way again. "Cade, take the lady to her chamber. I assume you'll be sharing, anyway?"

Crap. I secretly hoped his parents would be more conservative, the kind who pretend their son wouldn't dare consider sharing a bed with a woman until it's official.

Mr. Relentless is all too happy to prove me wrong. His grin says he'd like about a thousand other things, too. "You've got it, mom. Dad, we'll catch up later. We'll see you both for dinner. Wouldn't mind laying down for a few hours myself with my lovely bride."

I want to slap him. But I'm stuck smiling the biggest, fakest Cheshire cat grin of my life.

Oh, and there's that fucking phone *again.*

Cade throws a stern arm around my shoulder and escorts me to the sleek black Tesla that brought us here from the airport. "What's really going on?" he whispers, as soon as we're inside.

"Nothing. Just, my phone keeps ringing, and I want to check on Vinnie." I jerk it from my pocket and hide the screen.

Cade gives me an exasperated look, but then decides it isn't worth it. He settles into the leather seat, eyes to the window, enjoying the rolling countryside. The land around the castle is ridiculously steep. As rough as it is beautiful. I'm just grateful the winding roads are smooth, taking us down the peak, to another point of flat land with a hot spring and several more modern looking cottages.

The number on my screen catches my heart on my ribs. I recognize it. Hell, I only just deleted it days ago, after Adele should've sent him the money.

Uncle Harry. Whatever he wants, it can't be good. I try to hold it in, ignoring Cade's questioning glances, hoping for privacy.

I'm in luck. My fiancé is more tired than he lets on. He barely puts up a fight as soon as we're inside the posh cottage and he's sprawled on the bed, sharing the massive king sized mattress. "Don't get any wild ideas, or I'm taking the chaise I saw in the living room."

"You worry too much, Skittle," he says, stretching his arms over his head, yawning wide. "Remember when I was a perfect gentleman that first night we met? I could've had my way, and then some."

"Oh, I remember. Things were different then. We're a little more...familiar now." Familiar isn't the first word that comes to mind. I don't dare say *intimate*, though.

I lay on the bed and wait, clutching my phone under the heavenly pillow holding my head. Resisting the urge to nap isn't easy, especially when he's watching me through those half-hooded eyes. Smug, sexy, and way too comfortable.

My eyes flit to his trousers, searching for a bulge. There's a pang of disappointment when I don't see anything, and I'm not sure why. I'm just disgusted with myself.

I hear him snoring less than a minute after his head hits the pillow.

The French doors out back are cracked open, letting in a lovely breeze. I sit up, swinging my legs over the bed, and tip-toe over. I pray the hinges won't creak when I push them apart.

I'm in luck. They glide wide without a sound, and so does the screen door I use to slip out a second later.

The dewy grass is cool under my bare feet. I'm careful to put some distance between the house and me. There's too much potential for this conversation to get loud, and angry.

I'm calling Harry back, and doing what I should've done years ago.

It's past time to end this.

* * *

"Took you long enough," he grunts, answering on the third ring. "Thought we had an understanding, screamer, but maybe I was wrong about that so let's try again. When I ring your ass three fucking times, you drop whatever you're doing at that fancy school and –"

"No. I don't answer to you anymore."

He's quiet. I can practically hear him choking on my defiance. "Excuse me? And what, pray tell, led to this sudden epiphany, Skye? A lot of inquiring minds really, really want to know about that Leprechaun gold you magically pulled out of nowhere. One million. Exactly what you owed me. Impressive, screamer, and very, very fucking coincidental."

My blood runs cold. I've heard this curious, vaguely menacing tone before. It's the same he used before he convinced me to steal those artifacts, and I took the bait like an idiot.

"It's none of your business, Harry. Don't make me say it again. We're through. Stay away. I don't want anything else to do with you."

"Aw, kid, is that anyway to treat family? I promised your old man I'd look after you and your brother before he bled out in that back alley on a job. Nasty run-in with the Grizzlies. We were moving a lot of dope on their turf in those days, and he just had to have his piece. Those biker fucks had a very lucrative thing going. Your old man got greedy. Ballsy, too, if he'd lived. Would've been better off for everyone. Then you wouldn't have come screamin' to me for cash like you always do, and I never would've put you up to stealing that Roman shit, and we all would've lived happily ever after."

I sniff, a single angry tear blurring down my cheek. It's been years since I've heard anything about how dad died. Mom never talked much about the details for good reason. I knew he was in a bad business, criminal, in fact. But finding out he threw away his life on a drug run, left us all for nothing, and from this monster's lips...

"Your momma's wracked up quite a fucking debt, too. Remember? Shit, you would've just been a little more than a quarter million in the hole if you just had tuition to worry about and Vinnie's fancy treatments. Bitch really screwed you over, didn't she?"

If he's right about her suicide, I don't say it. The debts, the money she owed...it wasn't her fault.

A bad home equity loan and a foreclosure in my teens. Multiple car loans. Eye surgery a couple years back when we didn't have insurance, and the endless tests, consultations, and experimental treatments to find out what was wrong with Vinnie...

I inherited her burden, and then sold my soul to the devil to get it paid.

"Talk to me, screamer. I'm a busy fucking man," Harry growls.

I don't realize how hard my fingers are clenched in fists until I feel the sting where my nails puncture my skin. Harry coughs, allowing ample time to process his cruel secrets.

"There's no point," I say, forcing every word. "I don't care what happened with mom or dad. I care about the *now*."

"Yeah, I thought so, screamer. Very forward thinking. Too bad life doesn't give a flying piss what you, me, or anybody else thinks. It's drink the fucking blood or bleed for vampires. Your old man had the right idea, even if he was reckless. Take your sword and grab life by the balls. Fly the black flag. Steal every goddamned piece you can get."

"You're no pirate, asshole. And even if you think you are, I'm not following in your footsteps, or my father's. I'm not a part of your world anymore. Neither is Vinnie. It's over."

"Jesus fucking Christ, you keep using that word, over.

Ain't that special? Tell me, was it *over* when you took my dirty deal, said you'd get that shit for me, and then you gave me a cock and bull story about losing it in the damn mail? Was it *over* when I – graciously, I'll remind you – let you shake your cute twenty-one year old ass for those rich slobs without putting out? Was it *over* when I gave you a fucking break just last week, for Vinnie, because I don't want him going to bed with a girl for the first time and flopping around like a leaf? Shit, you're just like your ma. Too proud, too stupid, too goody-good to know what's actually good for you."

I jerk the phone away from my ear, finger poised over the end call button. I can't deal with this torture from an ocean away. This isn't how I wanted it to go down. It's my fault for thinking he'd ever listen, tuck tail, and leave us the hell alone.

"Listen, screamer, I don't give a damn if Adele gives me that check for what you owe with a pretty pink bow on top. Don't even care if you send more to cover the interest I never charged you, which I was stupid not to, thinking you wouldn't turn out to be such an ungrateful little bitch!" He stops shouting and clears his throat. Like it makes any difference. "Start over. A gal like you doesn't show up with a million dollar haul out of nowhere. Tell me where you got it."

Hang up, I tell myself the only logical thing. I hate how much his voice paralyzes me.

"Still not talking? What-the-fuck-ever. I'll get it from Vinnie. He's a good kid. Not at all a hard ass ungrateful little fuck like his sister. Give me a couple days to get in touch, screamer. I don't need you to say shit to find out what's what. I'll track down every penny. I'll ask Vinnie, and he'll talk because he's a good fucking egg. And if there's more where that came from, well, guess who's getting a new dirt bike after I take my cut?"

"Harry, Jesus, just leave us alone! I'm warning you, and it's more than you deserve. I'll go the police, the FBI, Interpol, whoever I need to if you're stupid enough to keep coming when I'm begging you to *stop*. We aren't your slaves. You've got your money. We're done!" I don't know if he ever hears my last frantic words. Somewhere halfway through the screed, my finger stabs at my phone, and doesn't stop until his number is just a blinking mess on the screen.

I collapse on a stone bench next to the quiet pond, staring out across the pristine mountain kingdom. It helps calm my heart. I wish it could help with the root of the problem, too. But miracles are for people who lived fifteen hundred years ago in this ancient mystical land.

What I need to do is no great mystery: warn Vinnie, make sure Harry never finds out I'm in an arranged marriage with a billionaire, and keep Cade from learning my uncle is a west coast mobster.

No big deal.

If there was ever something guaranteed to blow up in my face, it's this. Still, I have to try, even if the odds are crap.

But first, I need to shake off this brutal shock that's drained me since breakfast. Inside the cottage, Cade is dreaming peacefully, his huge, handsome body stretched out across the bed like a lion's.

The longer I stare at him, the more I realize how tired I am.

Surely, saving the world can wait for a nap.

VI: HEARTS ON HIGH (CADE)

I'm on a sauna bench with an angel, and she's down to fuck.

Skittle comes to me wearing nothing but a smile and that cotton candy hair. Thank the sandman because I'm buck naked, too.

I don't know how we got here, and it's not like I care. Something about Iceland makes me lose my mind and forget everything. Except the fact I'm hard as a fucking rock.

"What the hell, Skye?" I whisper, as she climbs on top of me. I don't know what I expected when I saw her voluptuous silhouette coming toward me through the hot springs' steamy haze.

I'm sprawled, arms open, cock throbbing harder than the drumming in my ribs, each beat pounding raw lust through my blood. My arms are in heaven when they reach out, close around her, and yank her pussy close.

"What the hell?" I growl again. I can't figure out where my spitfire is, and why she's been replaced by this pliant little minx who brushes her pussy against my fingers, moaning when I thumb her clit.

Her hips have the answers. Her kiss speaks the truth. Her warm, sweet cunt engulfs me, and breaks the dream like a seething fever.

I jerk up in bed, drawing a jagged breath, sporting the world's worst morning wood. Maybe that's because it's really afternoon, or else because I'm still surrounded by something warm, soft, and sweet as roses.

"Skittle?" She moans in her sleep when I whisper, but doesn't open her eyes.

She's curled up against me, closer than the first night we shared a bed. She's in the same blouse she had on this morning, but her skirt is gone. The pink panties pressed tight against her ass tempts every inch of my cock, rousing me faster than my usual morning cup of espresso.

Oh, fuck. She stirs, rubbing against me, dead to the world and far sexier than any girl in dreamland has any business being.

I can't fuck her like this. I shift her soft body, making my chest her pillow, and I hold her just like that for what seems like forever. In truth, it's probably the next half hour where I'm laid out, sweating through my lust, biting my lip like a damn kid with blue balls after his first date.

My fingers aren't thwarted as easily as my cock. They slide through her hair, skimming the nape of her neck. My thumb circles the tender skin between her shoulders, where she has a raven tattoo I can't quite make out, sticking just over the edge of her shirt. She moans again, her brow furrowed, like her mind can't decide if her dreams are happy or hellish.

Christ, I want her bird in my fire. The black sun I've had inked on my chest, details slowly added over the years, blazes under my skin. It's calling her to fly, come closer, even if our bodies melding puts fucking Icarus to shame.

Her face tilts when she rolls, murmuring softly. We're

face-to-face, mere inches apart. It's a special kind of hell keeping my lips off hers. Especially considering they're the same lips I just had in my dreams, the very same I want to taste over and over and over. And this time I want them alone, solely mine, without any liar theatrics meant for an audience.

One little kiss, asshole. What could it hurt? The devil on my shoulder gets the upper hand, ramming his pitchfork through my conscience. I'm about to give my lips permission to ravish hers when I sense movement.

"Cade? Shit, sorry." Her eyes are open.

I give her a disarming smile and run my fingers through her hair again. The real sin here isn't touching – it's not being able to devour her. "Welcome home, sleepy. We've got a couple hours before dinner."

She sits up, hiding the redness on her cheeks. Doesn't work because we both know she's flushed, remembering she just spent the last couple hours sleeping next to me with next to nothing covering that slice of heaven between her thighs.

"I should clean up," she says, rubbing her cheek. "I'm sorry I didn't stay on my side. Must've rolled over in my sleep, into your space, and –"

"Stop apologizing. You think I'm pissed we're sharing skin, even though I'd love to shred that contract we signed and do a whole lot more?"

She turns, a sharp look in her eyes, but it fades when they hit the bulge between my legs. It's barely concealed under the thin sheet. "Holy...are you sleeping...naked?"

"Only way we do it in the old country. Won't be a suit and tie in sight when we're getting massages tomorrow, in case you wondered." I cock my head, amused by the smitten look on her face. Looks like she can't decide whether she wants to slap me, or come in for a closer look. "Get over yourself, sweetness. There's nothing wrong with a nap and a little admiring. The contract with my lawyer says –"

"No sex!" She stands, retreating, pulling the thin blanket by our feet over her to hide everything from the waist down. I wonder if there's a wet spot on her panties I missed. "We can't keep doing this, Cade. I practically kissed you in my sleep."

"Mm-hmm, practically. Next time, just do it, without the hand wringing. Save the apologies for later. Might help us work this tug-of-war shit out of our systems and admit we're human beings. Don't know about you, Skittle, but I'm done denying what's right in front of me." Game set and match.

Her eyes are angry, but less defiant than usual. "You're insane. There's a hundred reasons why we shouldn't breach the agreement. You know it'll just make things harder, messier than they need to be, complicated like mad. I didn't sign up for –"

"Fuck your reasons," I growl, surprised how feral my voice sounds. "I've got two very good ones of my own we'll be dealing with in exactly an hour and a half. My parents are expecting us to look like we did this morning, which went off pretty well, if I do say so myself. They want us holding hands. They want us smiling. They want my lips on yours. Obviously, I don't get a thrill out of sucking face in front of my folks, or your kid brother, but I overthink it every time when it's the only time it happens. Some practice when it's just you and I would go a long fucking way toward perfect. Natural. Smooth."

She squirms, still unsure, begging me to change her mind.

I sit up, crawling toward the edge of the bed. I'm standing, sheet wrapped around my waist, barely hiding the raging hard-on driving me insane. My hands are on her wrists and they pull, bringing her face to mine.

"Cade..."

"You worry too much. Let go for a second and let your dreams happen in the flesh, for once."

Her moan sizzles in my mouth the instant we connect. *Goddamn.*

Can't believe how much I missed tasting this woman, and it's only been since morning.

Maybe it's a thousand times sweeter in here because it's just her and I for the first time since that screwed up night in Seattle. We're in a different time and place. Just as reluctant, with everything turned upside-down.

It's her turn to see me naked, or near enough.

My arm goes around her waist, pressing her to me, and I take her lips harder. She moans again, louder, pushing her little hand against my chest. It's the kind of conflicted push that speaks with two tongues, *careful* and *more* oozing off her like milk and honey.

I slide my tongue against hers, and it's done talking. Mine isn't hung up on speech anymore. We've done this edgy dialog a hundred times in a silent, scary language designed for hiding our lust.

It's dishonest, infuriating, and so fucking wrong.

There's nothing in my lexicon except the pulse of my heart and the churning heat in my balls when I push my fingers through her hair. They hold her, my willing hostage, while I take my ransom in sucking lips and hungry teeth.

"God!" She whimpers, tearing herself away, a sudden empty coolness on my thigh. "Too much. Too soon. I can't..."

She doubles over against the chair behind her, flushed and panting. I smile when I realize her hand was only inches from my cock. And then I'm frowning like a sourpuss because it never reached ground zero.

"Take your time, beautiful. Go clean up," I say, coming closer, running my hand through her hair one more time. "We don't have to decide the world in one fuck tonight. I'm not into rushing anything when we've got business. Take your shower, get dressed, and look over the menu on the nightstand. Our only job is focusing on the food and keeping my folks company. Promise."

My stomach growls just then for emphasis. Skittles notices, and laughs. Apparently, my raging need to have her under me works up a furious appetite.

I watch her slink away, shooting one last look over her shoulder. It's equally unsure and sexy as hell. Bedroom eyes she won't make peace with.

Sitting on the bed, I check my phone for the latest news from the firm, listening to the steaming double shower heads through the wall. It's hell trying not to think too hard about her soaping that little body, wondering if she lets a few fingers drift between her legs and...

No. I have to stop, before I decide to drop the sheet and wait for her in bed, a command on my lips and a fist around my dick.

I don't know how it'll go down tonight or the rest of this trip.

Don't know if we'll fly home with cousin Jonas swallowing his pride, mom's peace and quiet intact, and the feel of Skye's pussy branded into my brain forever. I don't have a crystal ball.

But while I'm sitting here, swiping through notifications, one thing is crystal fucking clear: I'm making sure my shower comes out ice cold.

* * *

THE EVENING IS A BLUR. I manage to towel off and get dressed without stopping to bust a quick nut before dinner.

Then we head over to my parents' favorite place in Reyk-javik. They've set up a reservation at their usual spot in the private dining room. Having to sit there like a good boy with mom and dad, savoring a five course mix of French and Icelandic cuisine, complete with good scotch, works its usual magic.

I let Skye do most of the talking. For once, I don't think she's forcing every smile. We hear about her digs in the Middle East and a study abroad trip to Samarkand, where she experienced the Silk Road first hand.

There's a sadness in her voice I don't follow when she mentions unearthing some statues. "What's the deal?" I whisper, when my parents get up for a bathroom break. I reach for her hand under the table, and she grips it weakly, but doesn't push me away. "You got a couple new credits for your CV, and helped catalog more unknown, boring Roman stuff, right? Sounds like a win-win to me. Did something bad happen over there?"

"Yeah, it's nothing." Her eyes are slow to meet mine. "Samarkand was great. Honestly. It was another trip to Turkey, last year, when I ran into a weird situation. I know, I shouldn't let it cloud everything else I've done, but sometimes...it's just hard letting go."

She doesn't elaborate. Mom comes back glowing, just in time for dessert, which she always saves room for. She's doubly excited to share the fun with my bride. "The skyr is *to die for*, dear, and so are the macaroons. Truly a shame there's only room for one in this belly tonight. Oh, Stefan, help me make up my mind!"

Dad flashes me a helpless look as she clutches his arm. The real victory tonight isn't mom gorging herself like a happy chipmunk, and maybe it's not even holding Skittle's hand the rest of the evening, until we're heading for our ride.

It's the stress-free smile on dad's face, which hasn't been there for months. It lingers through an extra glass of port. Then mom looks at us and puts the knife through my chest.

"Oh, guys, I almost forgot to tell you! I heard from cousin Jo the other day." I clench on hearing the name. Johanna is my second cousin, and she's also Jonas' mother. "She's thrilled Cade's finally found the one. The whole family, as a matter of fact. Jonas sends his compliments."

Fucking great.

Everyone's eyes are glued to me. It's almost a physical pain to cough up the dreadful words. "Is he coming while we're in town?"

Mom smiles, nods, and the soft Nordic lights around us get a whole lot darker. "Oh, yes! Apparently, he's very eager to spend time with you, Cade. Sounds like he'd very much enjoy a double date. He's finishing a tour in Dublin with his wife, Giselle, but they'll be here later this week, I understand."

I *understand* it's a date with the devil, and everything I'm working for could go up in flames if I don't smoke his ulterior motives first.

"Just name the time and place, mom," I say, draining my wine glass. "We'll be there."

* * *

"YOU WERE GOOD TONIGHT," she says, as soon as we're in the car. Her hand slides into mine, and I grip it hard, even though I'm dead set against her sympathy. "When your mother mentioned your cousin, I thought –"

"It's nothing. Hell, it's exactly what we came here to deal with. I'm glad we don't have to procrastinate anymore." I'm not lying, necessarily, but glad doesn't seem like the right word for the razor blades sliding through my guts.

"How bad is it, anyway? Your mom's heart?"

I sigh, staring out the window, taking in the dark Icelandic night as the city's sparkling lights give way to the moon glow of the villages between us and the castle. "She's not on her last legs, exactly. Her doctor keeps her supplied with steady check-ups and nitro pills after her last heart attack. It's been a year since anything bad happened, but dad and I aren't interested in tempting fate. Heart attack or no, she'd have her ticker busted up in a million pieces if she ever thought there was a risk of losing this place. I'm not letting that happen."

"It's not like we're staring into hell. We'll have a few days to prepare, I think, and plot out the ways this could go."

"I'm here. Whatever you need," she whispers. Her fingers pinch mine so hard I can't ignore her eyes any longer.

I'm not in the right state of mind to read what's really there. I'm pissed off, anxious, and my cock is on fire, but if there was ever a time when I cared about not taking this too far, it's now.

A few hours ago, I would've shaken myself stupid for blowing my chance to finish what we started this afternoon. Before dinner, I had every intention of taking her to bed, ripping off her clothes, and taking her every damn way I started in my dream, and then some.

Now? I can't fuck this up. Not when we're days, maybe hours, away from a reckoning with Jonas.

"I want you well rested," I say, running my fingers up her wrist. They dig into her skin with the fiery confusion stabbing at my veins. I'm torn between the need to fuck her, and also leave her heart thoroughly un-fucked for what's ahead.

Drawing a deep breath, I let my mind wander, mulling the other ways I might be able to make this better. "Let's turn in early tonight. Tomorrow, assuming no surprises, I'll show you my favorite trails. You said you've got the driver taking Vinnie out to the museums tomorrow, right?"

"Oh, yeah. Damn. I forgot about that," she whispers, more to herself than me.

If I didn't have a million other fires going in my mind, I'd wonder what the hell she means. But her soft recovery smile is enough for me on the ride back.

Later, I realize I indulged in more drink than I thought. Skye isn't immune to the rich old world dinner either. We lay down for an hour or two of TV and idle browsing on our phones.

She's the first to drift off. I pull her close when my eyelids are heavy, wrapping my arms tight, ignoring the hungry stirring in my dick.

I can't figure out what this is anymore, or what the fuck's happening, but I decide it doesn't matter.

Tonight, we're here for each other. That's the true, unwritten fine print in that Byzantine contract we signed.

I never bothered spelling it out because I knew we'd both live it, if this was meant to be.

Tomorrow, my cock may have its way.

Tonight, there's something else reigning I can't nail down. I won't dwell on it long enough to make any hard conclusions. I just know it's surprising, intoxicating, and I want to hold onto it like a jealous bastard, even while every shred of reason says trying to makes me certifiably insane.

* * *

CRUNCH GOES ANOTHER BRANCH, snapping loudly under Skittle's boot. She smiles sheepishly. "I never thought these fairy forests would be so rugged."

"Crazier than back home, yeah. Pacific Northwest has nothing on Iceland. Keep it down, Skittle. You're scaring all the animals," I tease, elbowing her softly in the side. She jabs me back, getting in a hit that leaves my lungs breathless. Two hours in, and it's glaringly obvious she's never been a regular on the Washington hiking trails. "Only another mile. Think you can make it that far, or should I carry you?"

"This better be worth it, jackass." She gives me the evil eye and extends a hand. I take it, standing on a rock, helping her over.

"When you see the view, you'll understand. This country doesn't fuck around. Treat it with respect, and it'll pay you back tenfold." I stop, taking a deep breath, loving the fresh air this time of year. "Your turn, Skittle. Fill your lungs with nature. Think it's been my elixir since I was five years old. Grandpa lived to a hundred. I think this air had something to do with it."

"Nope. It was the waterfalls." She points me to a break in the cliff on the other side, where the rolling stream tapers and hits the rocks, giving our hike a calming soundtrack. "Strength and beauty, together. Just like it should be."

Her eyes say she's admiring more than just the scenery. My dick jerks in my pants, remembering its denial last night. Growling, I take her hand, and we walk the last few paces in record time. I scale the rocks harder than I need to, hoping it'll drain some of the demon energy. It's been hounding me like crazy to pull her aside, and take her in the great outdoors with nobody except the trees as witnesses.

But we didn't come all this way to fuck ourselves stupid. Her gasp is almost as satisfying – almost – when we round the last bend, reaching the spot where the mountain levels out, and look over the kingdom that's been in my family for generations.

"Holy...wow. I'm starting to see why you're going through so much trouble for this place." She sinks back against me, hand in mine. I wrap a possessive arm around her waist, giving her lips a second, sharper gasp when my free hand sifts through her hair, takes its blue and pink and gold, and gently pulls. "Oh!"

"Yeah, you love that view, front and fucking back. Welcome to Eden, Skittle. This place, this view is why we're getting married, but it's more than that, too. If you want to know me, here I am."

"Do I?" She turns her face to mine, holding a smile. Tease. "I'm not sure why it matters, Cade. If we settle this business with your cousin and seal the deal...won't this be over in a few months?"

I don't answer. It feels wrong to talk end dates when it feels like we've just gotten started.

Worse, I don't want to think about them. That's what really worries me.

I'm not used to shirking business, especially the big picture, end goal crap.

Except this...this isn't like any client I've ever had to fluff. Making an eight figure investment return seems easier than letting Skye Coyle go. And how fucked is that?

"No answer? Did I say something wrong?" She's so persistent.

I run my hand up her shoulder, slide it up her throat, and slowly cover her mouth. She tenses in my arms. "You talk too much, beautiful. You think even more, when it's high past time to switch off your beautiful brain. No more wrestling. Let's enjoy the now and this billion dollar view."

I'm barely exaggerating. Selling this place would double the considerable Turnbladt family wealth overnight, but it's not even an option while mom is breathing. That's also why Jonas will fight tooth and nail at our meeting this week. It's his free ticket to living the messy rock and roll lifestyle until kingdom come, and I'm the asshole shoving his pass through the shredder.

I hold her while we stare into Icelandic majesty. We're just in time for the sun to peak through the thick ashen clouds. It dances on the streams and lakes, catches itself on the castle's towers, and then skips off the village steeples before it goes racing back into the wild sky.

"I think I'll start counting my lucky stars," she says softly, tilting her face to catch mine. "Before, this was just a job. I didn't think I'd be able to calm down enough to appreciate the trip, even when we stepped onto your plane. Now? It feels like a vacation. Even if this isn't real, Cade, I'm thankful. I never would've seen this place if it weren't for you."

"It's nothing, but the lucky part isn't wrong. You're the first chick I've ever brought up here to share it."

She blinks slowly, and smiles. "Wow. And it isn't even real. I'm honored."

Those words ring hollow. Empty. Regret tinged with gratitude.

My hands grip her a little more tightly, pull her closer, wishing for the first time I hadn't made her sign that stupid fucking contract.

Who's to say what's real and what's pretend? Christ, just asking these questions...who's to say this glacial air and medieval view isn't going to my head, scrambling my brain?

We don't say anything for the better part of the next half hour. The longer we're up here, away from the world, sealed in our embrace, the easier it is to believe this thing is whatever we choose to make it when we head back to earth.

If that means it doesn't end after laying down the law with Jonas, so be it.

If we spend a few more months 'married' than we need to when we're home in Seattle, putting on a show for Vinnie, my friends, just enjoying an artificial romance for the experience, then fine.

If we decide to race down this mountain, bust through the cottage doors, and consummate this fake engagement with the hardest lay of my adult life, then *carpe fucking diem.*

The contract isn't cast in marble. Neither are the ground rules we agreed to.

Up here, I'm inspired – or is it just her warm body snug against mine that's playing muse?

I don't know, but the rest couldn't be clearer: we make the rules.

There are no masters except what's in our hearts, our heads, and thundering in our blood.

* * *

"Shit, sorry. Don't remember this back trail being so over-grown," I say, grunting as I untangle my boot from another mess of fallen birch branches. "You holding up okay?"

"I'm fine. Actually, I'm kind of glad we decided to go through the thick of it. What's awesome scenery worth without paying Mother Nature?"

I chuckle, slowing over a rocky patch before we stumble. "Whatever, Ms. Thoreau, just give me your hand. Never took you for the communing with nature type."

Reluctantly, she jumps into my arms over the rocks and beams a glare at me. "Maybe I never got the chance. This doesn't have to be about us, you know. This place is so magical it just might be the recipe I've been looking for to find myself."

"Yeah, it does that." I smile, holding her longer than I need before we continue onto the overgrown path. "We're hardly the first to mull the deep stuff on this trail. Think it goes back eight hundred years, maybe more. Knights, monks, royalty...they all came here to contemplate. Or maybe just to get the hell away from it all."

"Thieves and bandits, too," she mutters, so low I wonder if I've heard her right. I slow, shooting her a weird look over my shoulder. Her cheeks are red, and I spend the next sixty seconds wondering what she's getting at when it happens.

One minute, she's trotting behind me, bashful and mysterious as ever. The next, she's yelping. Her boot catches a loose rock. It skids out under her heel and throws her down hard.

"Skittle! Damn, you all right?" I'm next to her instantly, hand on her thigh, close to the source of pain causing her to whimper.

I see it before she does. Nasty, raw scrape on the knee. I should've insisted on jeans, but of course, thinking about covering more of those mile high legs when we left was the last thing on my mind.

"Can you stand?" I ask, easing her up, reaching into the small case strapped to my belt for bandages. At least I came prepared. "How's your ankle?"

I'm reaching for the antiseptic and a big Band-Aid when she shakes her head, fighting through the pain. "It's twisted. Not broken. I'll manage if we take it slow."

"Hang on," I lay my hand on her shoulder, digging my fingers in. I'm not letting her up until we've dressed this crap properly. "You're not risking an infection. Bite down. This will sting."

I splash the stuff across her wound and she winces. I see her face tighten, hear the hissing through her teeth, and then the two most conflicted words I've ever heard put together. "Asshole, *thanks!*"

It's not sarcastic. She's serious.

Gripping her hand while I apply the bandage, I put pressure on her knee to help stem the bleeding. "Almost over. Let's rest for a minute, then I'll help you up and we'll take it real slow. No rush to get back tonight. Nothing happening except an evening nightcap with –"

I don't expect dynamite until it's on my lips. Then, sweet fuck, drinking with dad is the very last thing on my mind.

Our kiss comes so hot I'm grateful for the soft, steady mist enveloping us. It's the only thing that cools us down. The trees, the mountains, maybe the spirits who lived here centuries ago, they're all jealous.

No Viking ever had it this good, tasting a wildcat who sucks at my lips so hard, I want to bite her. Sinking my teeth into her bottom lip, pushing a feral growl into her mouth is a good start.

I shove her to the ground. My hands are done healing. They're hellbent on conquest now, crawling up her sides, catching her tit in one palm through her sweater. She moans into my mouth and her hips rock toward mine, calling my cock to full greed.

"Skittle, fuck!" I break the kiss for precious air, twisting my head away, before this Siren swallows me up. "You know what you're asking me to do? Is *this* what you really want?"

Can't believe I'm giving her a way out, but it's only right. Meanwhile, I want to reach down inside myself and strangle my conscience.

"You already know," she purrs, voice so low and husky it makes my dick throb harder. "Take me home."

And I do.

I give Popeye a run for his money and I don't even need a mouthful of spinach. I lift her up, throw her over my shoulder, and take the rest of the trail at breakneck speed. By the time the ground levels off and we're nearing the castle grounds, I'm panting. I stop to shift her lower, and her eyes shine in mine while we take the last few acres to the cottage, sharing one heartbeat.

I'm going to defile this woman in ways I haven't even thought of yet.

And she'll ruin me. This ice princess turned temporary

whore, who never even laid her clients, who swam through the muck without ever getting herself filthy.

It's too much to contemplate with my racing thoughts and savage words. So, I let my body do the talking while I stab at the lock to our cottage and kick down the door. We're inside, and her lips are on my throat. I'm too drunk by the kiss and need to fuck her. Don't realize until later how much I must've looked like a desperate newlywed, carrying his blushing bride over the threshold.

"Cade, please," she whispers. I slow, closing the door to our sanctum and shutting out the world. She's practically tearing at my shirt, the minx.

She isn't supposed to want it rough. I'm not supposed to leave every scrap of clothes on this angel's body in tatters, and pin her under me like a goddamned tiger, but I do, *I do*, and I'll figure out who I owe apologies to later.

It's animal instinct ruling me now. It comes faster, spills out of me, and lights me on fire the more we kiss, the more I taste those lips I've had on my mind all week.

I throw her down on the bed and open her legs. My fingers dance up her thigh, feeling every inch of her, sweeping under her skirt. She moans when I brush my thumb over the striped panties covering her sweetness.

She's fucking soaked. It's my turn to make noise. Growling into our next kiss, I press my lips to hers, famished for her tongue.

I move my hand higher, pressing harder into her. These fingers tease, but they don't let her fuck them.

It's my tongue that's aching to be between her legs.

"Cade!" She mewls my name, eyes wide and rolling, soft grey fires dancing in her pupils. "Wait."

She pushes against my chest. I rear up on my knees, reaching for the buttons, when I notice the sudden uncertainty colliding with lust in her features. "What's wrong, Skittle? Don't tell me you're having second thoughts."

"More like first," she says, sucking softly at her lip. Her eyes close, and she sighs, wracked by a secret stuck on her tongue. "I've never done this before..."

"What, slept with a man in Iceland?" I narrow my eyes, entranced by her legs pinched around me. She can't be doubting a damn thing. Not with the way she strokes her feet up my thighs. "I've had others on this soil, but none who ever mattered. None like you, Skye."

"Yeah? How many *others?*" Her eyes are huge with questions.

I wonder if this is some weird ego thing and consider my next words. "Three, I think. None in the last few years. They were one-night stands. Nothings. Not like my one night bride."

"One night bride?" She echoes the phrase, smiling, reaching up slowly. Her fingernails brush my cheek. They scratch my stubble, and the noise sends current down my spine. "When I said *first,* I meant it. First, and so far, only. That's what I'm trying to tell you. I'm a virgin, Cade. Does it freak you out?"

"Fuck yes, it does." Her eyes pop for a split second before I push her into the mattress and take her lips again. My cock is diamond. "You? Pure? Virgin?"

It doesn't compute.

Holy Hades, at this rate, I might burst an artery before I get my chance to take her balls deep. My heart drums in my chest, thumping bass echoes in my ears, giving the world a spin I've never experienced.

"You'd best not be screwing with me, woman," I say, voice like glowing charcoal. I catch her hair in my fist and pull, seizing her and tilting it to mine, touching my forehead to hers. "Can't *believe* you, Skittle. Can't believe no man's ever had his lips on this skin, this tongue on his cock, this pussy sucking the very life from his balls...fuck!"

The last word comes harsh. It chokes out when I push my hand between her legs, and she grinds into me, raw need returning to her hips. That blackness in her eyes is huge, void, begging to be full of fire, and for me to do the kindling.

"Until you," she whispers. Her fingers graze the nape of my neck, teasing as ever. Can I get any harder? "I can't go on like this, Cade. Whatever I said when we started, no sex, I did it then because I was afraid. I still am."

I pull my hand from under her skirt and lace her fingers. It's the hardest grip ever. "Don't be, Skittle. Whatever happens after tonight, I'll never leave you broken. Never in stitches. If I'd met you under normal circumstances, without your tits hanging out on a grand piano, I'd have wanted you anyway. You're everything I thought I'd always marry, the few times I ever pictured it, without ever thinking for a second you'd be wearing that ring thanks to these fucked up circumstances."

She whimpers, and I wonder if it's the same sound she'll make when I smother her clit. My finger pushes against the diamond under her knuckle. My dick is about to explode in my pants.

"Skittle," I growl her name one more time, forehead pressing harder to hers, ready and willing to burst through my jeans. "I –"

"I want to fuck you, Cade. Please. That's all I truly want."

I seal my lips with another kiss, and this time, there's no stopping. Fire blazes in my tongue and sizzles in my fingertips. They run low, lifting her skirt, then peel off her clothes rapidly.

Her bra clasp pops between my fingers. Those tits I've dreamed about since the first night roll into my palms, nipples peaked, begging to be sucked.

My balls are molten. That heat becomes my soul for the next few furious minutes. My mouth encircles each nipple, sucks until she whimpers, higher and shriller every time my teeth probe tender flesh. My hand presses into her untouched pussy harder. I flick her panties aside, working two fingers up and down her wetness, coating my hands in that honey I'll lick off first chance I get.

I want that fucking O on my mouth, and she's *way* too close already for my liking. Skye's cotton candy hair ripples in my fingers, head rolling frantically on her shoulders, lips parted for the shallow breaths keeping her alive as pleasure takes control.

I haven't even gotten my tongue on her clit yet. Holding her down, I make her wait like a good girl, rumbling my delight when her teeth pinch my lower lip.

I've never wanted my face between a set of legs so bad in my life. Never thought so clearly, so long, or so hard about how she'll scream when my tongue finds her depths.

No more wondering.

I'm breathing mad, ragged breaths, sinking to my knees, stamping rough lips up her thighs. My hand dips into her panties and twists them tight.

One rough tug is what it takes to make her understand. She lifts her little ass, and then they're gone, shimmied down her legs and tossed around her ankles.

I don't even unhook them from her left foot. Can't deny my mouth a second longer, especially when I catch her full scent, and my blood grows needles.

I need this pussy on my tongue.

I need it fucking now.

"Come for me," I whisper, before diving into her core. The way her moan cracks on the first lick, parting her tender lower lips, tells me it won't be long. *Sweetness, come.*

I work it out of her in long, steady laps, each more

furious than the last. The hunger building in my balls takes over. If I wasn't so focused on shaking her apart in the next sixty seconds, I'd stop to tear my jeans off, before my cock rips through the denim.

But there's no pulling me away from her sweet cunt until it tenses. Her legs try to close around my head, fighting the pleasure that's about to tear her in two. My fingers catch her silky thighs, holding them apart, telling her today's not the day she decides when I stop licking.

Hell, not today, or any other I'm lucky enough to be face deep in this pussy.

I wait until she's on the edge to lash her clit. I wait for the glory: knees wobbling, thighs shaking, calves fried in a winding, electric tension bound to flame out in glory when she goes off. Basically, the works.

It's the best fucking O I've ever fucked into anyone.

Her back arching is the first sign of my reward. Her lungs hitch, catching her breath. Hope the last time she inhaled it was plenty because she'll be breathless for the next few minutes.

Her virgin cunt tenses below my tongue, and her clit throbs harder before I know the fireball inside her hits nova.

Sweet, merciful, unholy fuck.

My dick drips venom the whole time she comes on my face. I pull her shaking legs apart harder than before, pinning them to my temples, growling as I taste every last drop her pussy gives.

It's mine now, and then some.

Every twitch, every shake, every jagged curse streaming from her mouth.

Every drawn out moan, every burn in her legs, every turn of her hips as she twists in all directions, and finds more ecstasy delivered by my relentless tongue.

This is goddamned mine.

Every. Fucking. Thing.

My rainbow, my cotton candy, my Skittle. This is the last sweetness I'll ever taste as a sane man.

Because I already know I'm fucked before I even get my first inch in her slick, steaming pink.

After we fuck, I won't be the same man. Won't want to live one more day of the boring ass life before I had this virgin pussy attached to the most infuriating lips I've ever known.

Never, ever again.

She's mine. And I'm so fucking hers.

VII: OFFICIALLY COMPLICATED (SKYE)

*A*ncient Rome was a melting pot of faiths, each with their own vision of heaven.

I've known every one of them in the space of three minutes. Cade's mouth carries me to places I've never studied, much less imagined, and I'm a hot mess by the end of it.

Sex hair, chewed lips, legs that only stop shaking because they're secure in his strong, steady hands. I'm afraid to look directly into his eyes for the first few seconds after returning to earth.

No regrets. No worries. No fears.

Please.

My prayers are answered. Whatever stupid fears I had about my first time, they're gone the second I open my eyes. The same gorgeous, kind man who tore my happy place from the sky and put it in my hands is still there.

His blue eyes are a moonlit ocean. Softer, brighter, vaster than I can understand. They remind me a wicked ache remains between my legs, and offer the only cure.

"Now," I whisper, running my fingers down the buttons on his shirt. They're half-undone from our earlier frenzy.

He's so calm, so collected, I hate it. "Cade," I whine his name, smoothing my feet up his legs, begging him to pull those pants off and fill me.

He hovers over me, held up by fists. His lips come at mine, hungrier than before, surer they'll find their relief inside me. If only he didn't make me wait, didn't make me beg with my hips pressed so sweetly into his, practically dry humping the bulge in his pants.

"Skittle...have you lost your fucking mind?" he growls, palming my cheek, running his thumb over the soft space below my eye. "What's gotten into you?"

"You, not being in me, as a matter of fact. Please, Cade. I need you."

"You *need* to stop tasting so good, love," he says, his tongue flicking over the lips that sent me to paradise just minutes ago. "Stop distracting me. Then maybe I'll let this cock out and fuck you how I always imagined, every damn inch ruining that honeysuckle pussy for anybody else."

"God – please!" I don't recognize my own voice. It's too harsh, too distant, too desperate to impale myself on this man's wilds.

I'm so deep in the zone I don't realize he's moving until he's shirtless. Then my fingers are on him like lightning, clutching at muscles bound in dark inks, pulling myself up on his body, coiling my tongue with his.

Even in his rough, hard body, he's thoroughly Icelandic. The tapestry on his skin is a beautiful chaos. Volcanic fire and shattered glaciers curling up his arms, grounded by the black sun on his chest. Its majesty deepens my trance.

His kiss is an addiction. It's gravity, warmth, rocket fuel. Lust boils over when I hear his belt buckle knocking around. Another blink of my burning eyes and his pants are gone. He smiles, folding his swollen cock against my belly, revealing his fullness.

I gasp. I sputter. I can't believe what he's about to put inside me.

"Any last words, Skittle? As a virgin, I mean." His voice smolders in my ear, deep and dark and dangerously fuckable.

If my pussy gets any wetter...

I close my eyes, pressing my forehead to his. I lick my lips, nodding slightly, fingers sliding down his raging biceps. "Cade, I'm ready."

It's everything he's waited to hear. He kisses me one more time, then dives to the side. I hear him rummaging for something, and realize what it is when he comes back from his suitcase a second later, a foil packet clenched between his fingers.

He holds it to my face, blue eyes drifting fires, growling the next words. "Tear it open, and roll it the fuck on me."

He leans, giving me space. I take the condom's packet in my teeth and pull, fingering its spongy contents. My flush burns hotter on my cheeks. A second later, I'm paralyzed. He grips my hand and smiles, bringing it lower, between his legs, clenching the rubber.

"Pay attention, sweetness. We'll be doing a lot more of this," he whispers, placing the condom over the tip of his cock. His fist closes around mine.

The first time I touch him there, he's pulling my hand down, sheathing himself in the only barrier that's going to be between us when we're in the throes of it.

His cock jerks in my hand. He's bigger than ever when he swells, just sheer muscle sent to rend me in two. It takes both of us squeezing to tame it.

Mercy.

My heart flutters. We lock eyes, and I lose myself in those blues one more time, knowing there's nothing left to hold him back.

He sinks lower again, eclipsing my small body. Cade's

huge, muscular perfection surrounds me. His fingers sink through my hair, fisting locks behind my head, reminding me who has total control.

The time for words is over. I raise my hips, dig my teeth into my bottom lip, and then surrender when he buries me in a newer, harder kiss.

It's the prelude to his hips joining mine a second later.

There's a screaming heat, an exquisite friction, a faint tearing as my virgin silk engulfs his fullness. And he's far from done.

Deeper, deeper, *deeper.* His thrust lifts my body. He's in to the hilt and he holds it in my quivering mess. Every muscle below my waist goes tense and hot, soaked in want, instinct unbearably awakened.

"Cade!" I whimper his name. He rocks back, lifting himself slowly, only to crash forward again, this time faster and harder.

My gasp becomes a moan in his mouth.

It's fire, it's bliss, and yes, it even hurts a little.

But it's the kind of pain that promises goodness. So much fucking good.

It's our essence since we met, our apotheosis. My flesh surrendering in delicate, slick submission, and his raging in full masculine offering.

How could I do anything except fuck him back?

I'm grinding my hips, lifting my ass off the bed, tossing myself against him with a vigor I'm sure surprises us both. He thrusts harder. It's chaotic and sloppy at first, a sexy mess for the girl who's never had it, and never thought she'd be getting it from a Nordic giant who shoved his ring on her finger without really meaning it.

Oh, but does it matter when his hips collide, and I'm so, *so* full of him?

Does it make my tongue against his any weaker, or

lighten the urge to push my nails into his skin, holding on for dear life as he picks up speed? As he seizes my virgin pussy, rough as my hair in his hand, pulling and thrusting, grunting and cursing when he isn't just growling my name, a feral plea for ownership caught between his teeth?

"I'm a fucking goner, Skye. You're tight...wet...hot...perfect. *Perfect.* Stick a damn fork in me, and you, too. We're done. You're so, so, so fucking mine."

And I am.

Our sex is a breathless dance. Flesh and sweat and primal fire. It's smoke in every nerve and raw honey at the tip of my tongue, even when it slides against his, the sweetness spreading down my throat and into my body, where it mingles with inferno.

"Holy, holy hell," I whimper, baring my teeth as his speed quickens.

I won't last much longer. That shouldn't be shameful for a woman, but I'm honestly a little embarrassed how quick I'm ready to come on his thrusting, frantic cock.

Not that Cade minds.

The change in my pulse, my breath, my hips crashing into his only spurs him to wilder heights.

Muscles I didn't know I had tense in my belly, focused around the fireball he fucks bigger every time his length curls against my flesh.

His delicious, intoxicating friction is officially too much. I'm seriously going to –

"Come for me, Skittle – come fucking *hard!*"

He steals the words from my body. We're a shaking tangle of limbs as I hit meltdown, pressing my chin into his shoulder. I bite him when I come because I'll break if I don't.

Orgasm hits me like an uppercut. Everything becomes a blur of black fire, smoking ice, and breath torn from my lungs, transmuted into ecstasy.

My own heartbeat becomes a roar. Somewhere behind it, his voice, still urging me on.

I'm coming my soul out. I don't think I could give it any harder if my life depended on it.

Still, Mr. Relentless wants more. He forces it out of me with harder, longer strokes between my legs, his ass clenching like a bull in rut every time he slams into me.

"Come, Skittle. *Come!*" His sandpaper voice slays what's left of my sanity.

My body hits overdrive and senses go numb. The bed, the room, the Icelandic beauty around us vanishes in a veil of white stars clouding my vision.

It's him, it's me, and this rippling fire that sweeps me up and won't let go until I'm good and ready.

I come for him, all right. I come sweating, pulsing, silently screaming, clutching him with every limb. I come his name raw on my tongue, and come his heat on my throbbing clit. I come in facets of my soul I don't even want to explore, and then come again in every nerve lashed with fire.

Drunk. Depraved. Bound.

Just when I think I'm spent, and the vicious spasms ripping through me are finally through, the roar bursting out of his throat overwhelms everything.

"Wait, Skittle, wait. Don't you fucking stop. I'm coming, too – coming up in you!"

God. The animal edge in his words is enough to forget there's still a condom between us, but hell, I swear I feel the heat.

It's like my body knows when it feels him swell. That beautiful, maddening fullness deep inside me gets so much fuller, and then he's shaking us so hard I think we'll break the bed, growling as our pleasure rends the atmosphere.

Now, my stars, my heat, my sheet-clawing O are his.

They're the same wicked whirlwind possessing me when

his thrusts lift me off the bed, when his fingers tear at my hair, when he groans in my face and rests his forehead on mine, his balls still twitching against my ass, pouring everything quintessentially Cade into me.

It's melting point, and so much more.

"Jesus. I never came like that, Skye. Never in my life," he rumbles, a spark in his eyes wanting to hide the truth in his words as soon as he recovers more of his senses. "What the fuck are you doing to me?"

His question is heavier than the weight of the world.

I don't know. I don't know how. I don't dare to ask why.

He stays rooted in me so long I can't tell where we begin or end. My fingers roam the nape of his neck, gentler than before. I'm still in the place where words are pale shadows, too dim and weak to speak clearer than our trembling, short-circuited flesh.

Even when he pulls out of me after an eternity, parts with one more kiss, and plods away into the bathroom with the tied off condom in his fingers, there's no return.

There's no coming back from wherever we are now, wherever and whatever *here* is.

We're not in Kansas anymore. Not even Reykjavik, or Seattle, or anywhere I've ever known.

When he returns, crashing into bed next to me, pulling me into his arms, I'm still as lost as ever, but I can't stop smiling.

However long we're in this strange, strange land, I'm safe. I'm happy. I'm whole.

I'm just afraid I'll never want to leave.

* * *

"Damn it, just listen to me. Vinnie, I'm not screwing around.

If he calls, if he texts, if he leaves you a voicemail or a note by pigeon...you tell me, okay?"

There's nothing like trying to knock some sense into your little brother to make the ground beneath your feet feel real again. Vinnie sniffs, pushes his glasses up on his nose, refusing to make eye contact.

"Jeez, okay. I really don't see what the big deal is. Uncle Harry's the bad guy now? The man who kept us afloat before you got engaged to Mr. Moneybags? Are you even gonna tell me why?"

I'm scowling. No, I don't want to feed him more than I have to. And not just because I wish he'd just shut up and listen, for once.

He's insulted the man who just rocked my world. "Don't talk about Cade like he's just a giant meal ticket." I'm wagging my finger. "You're having fun here, aren't you?"

He nods. "Well, yeah. Of course. That butler guy's taking me out mountain climbing today. Just little hills, very safe, so don't worry. It's cool and all, but I'd love to know when we're heading home."

"Just a few more days, probably." I'm not interested in admitting I haven't got a clue. "Look, he's going to be your brother-in-law. I'm not asking you to fall all over yourself thanking him for this trip, but show some respect. Understand he's a good man. I wouldn't be marrying him if he weren't."

Except my knight in shining armor is a farce.

It's getting to me, isn't it? I shouldn't sound so defensive, so rustled over Vinnie's dumb comments.

But I do. Here I am, standing with my arms crossed, staring him down and trying to pretend there's not a constant stream of lies dripping off my tongue.

"As for Harry, just trust me. Whatever he did in the past, it doesn't matter. We're not talking to him for a good long while." I don't have the heart to say *forever,* even though that's exactly what I'm planning. I'll figure out how best to break that news when we're home, without Turnbladt family intrigue hanging over my head.

Vinnie still looks unconvinced. He doesn't say anything, but turns back to his phone, screwing around with a Snap from one of his friends.

"Vinnie, look at me." I point two fingers at my eyeballs, and then at him again. "I'm serious. Any contact with Harry, you come to me."

"Whatever. Got it." He sighs, looking over his screen.

I'm secretly hoping someday we'll have a normal relationship, without grating on every nerve. I love the kid, sure, but his fifteen year old attitude and my stress levels don't mix. "Anything else, sis? Should I plan on entertaining myself this evening, too, while you wine and dine with those old farts again?"

"Stefan and Katrin are perfectly nice people, Vinnie. Be nice to my in-laws. I'd really appreciate it if you'd show them some decency."

"I'm not pants-on-head *stupid.* God, Skye," he says finally, throwing his phone on the table next to him. "I'm a big boy. It's not like I'm gonna go talking crap to their faces. I thought we were cool and could keep things just between you and me."

"Well, just between you and me," I pause, wagging my finger, scolding him. I'm officially worse than our mother. "I'd love for you to enjoy your time here without the constant whining. Cade said you're welcome to have his guy bring you anywhere in the city after you're done climbing for that gym credit today. Oh, and I'd like to look over your paper tomorrow, assuming it's in my inbox like you said."

He twists his lips, silent as ever. I've given him all the leeway he's getting with the essay. I'm ready to see proof he's been doing his work, rather than just screwing off the whole time.

I close the door to his room without a goodbye.

Perfect timing. He doesn't see my heart racing when my phone pings, and I read the new text waiting.

CADE: Need you back as soon as you're able. We're doing dinner with Jonas tonight.

CRAP. This just got a whole new kind of serious.

* * *

BRAND new royal blue evening dress that could put a princess to shame? *Check.*

Gold rune pendant for courage? *Check*

Navy blue heels a little taller than I'm used to, secretly picked to drive him wild later? *Check.*

I'm as ready as I'll ever be for the main reason we ever kicked off this fake fiancé thing.

We're early to the same private room where we dined with his parents the other night at Reykjavik's finest French fusion place. I sit quietly while he makes small talk with Stefan, something about the firm's investments in exotic crypto-currencies.

The staff serves our second glasses of wine before I see them. Cade's fingers tense on mine under the table, and there's a twitch in his face like he's ready to murder.

Jonas Turnbladt is just how I imagined. Full goatee, light blond hair too long and too greasy for the polite society I've been immersed in since arriving. He's stuffed into a suit a full size too small. Probably because he hasn't bothered updating his wardrobe since adolescence.

Give him the benefit of the doubt, I tell myself. I really want to, even when he sits across from us wearing an ugly smirk, the skinny and very pregnant French chick at his side looking through us like ghosts.

"There they are! Jonas, Giselle, how are the happy couple?" Stefan booms, grinning ear-to-ear. He's looking at Cade, warning him with his eyes. *Behave.*

"Starving. She has to eat every two hours, and I'm just goddamned ravenous after the drive. Where's the menu?" Jonas' voice is sharp and nasally. I've been around enough to know I'm not confusing jackass with foreign accent.

He looks past Stefan, declining Katrin's airy smile, pulling the menu from his wife's hands. She gives him a dirty look. It's like we don't exist.

Then Cade clears his throat. "I'll let you guys get settled. Then I want to hear all about the honeymoon."

My hand pinches his until he lets go. *Good God. So, we're doing this, starting right off with a challenge.*

Jonas mutters an order for soup to the waiter patiently standing by before he looks our way. "Sure, sure. I'll get on that. A man who's just gotten engaged needs plenty of advice before the big day, after all."

They're locked in a death stare, a not-so-subtle dick waving contest I'm worried even Katrin won't diffuse when she chirps across the table. "Isn't this lovely? They're *so good* together, these two, and it's coming together like lightning. At the rate we're going, I'll barely get to share a few laughs with my daughter-in-law before the grandkids."

Cade's eyes go big on his next sip of scotch. I hear him swallow. I blush, eyes drifting to Giselle's baby bump, who smiles at me knowingly.

"Oh, no, in case there's any misunderstanding, I'm not –"

"Pregnant? Such a shame. Looks like you're made for it." Jonas winks like the pig he is before he reaches for his wine, downing it in one pour. Then he glares at Cade's scotch. "Like water. I want one of those. Say, while we're talking family, I've heard the changes to inheritance laws lately are rather interesting. They're overhauling everything right now."

"Everything?" Katrin echoes the fateful word. Stefan and Cade both look like they're ready to have a stroke.

"I'm clueless when it comes to that legal stuff." I roll my eyes, smiling at Katrin, trying to stop the nuclear warhead Jonas clearly wants to detonate at the table.

"*Ja*, well, so was I before I got my man on it. He's a very good contract lawyer. One of the best in the country, in fact, and he's reviewing what happens with my royalties to make sure the kid is covered when Giselle is due. He's also looking at a few other family properties in the meantime, just to make sure our little nugget is set for life if anything tragic happens. One never knows."

His eyes are on Cade now, who takes a long pull of scotch, holding his gaze. "Smart. I've seen life get rough for plenty of people like my high school buddy. A bully and an underhanded city councilman screwed him over for years. Tragedy, really. It's true what you say – you never, ever know."

The waiters bring our soups, salads, and a scrumptious looking caviar hors d'oeuvre platter, but nobody lifts a fork. The tension is thick, ruining every appetite except Katrin's, who digs into her ancient grains, blissfully ignorant.

"So, when are you due?" I look at Giselle. One last attempt at stopping the knives Jonas and Cade look like they're ready to pull.

She smiles numbly, and then taps Jonas on the shoulder, muttering a few words in French. The jerkoff rock star poser looks at me, smiling. Several gold teeth glitter in his mouth. "She doesn't understand a word of English, I'm afraid. You'll have to speak French, or leave the chit-chat for the folks here who can actually understand each other. So, Cade –"

"Christ, this scotch." He coughs, pushing his chair backward in an explosive jerk. Then he's up, throwing his napkin onto the table.

"Cade?" Stefan is petrified, his son's name a hoarse whisper.

"Sorry, dad. I need to use the restroom. Clear my throat. It's too much, or too strong, perhaps. I'm feeling...off, all of a sudden. Jonas, if you wouldn't mind giving me a hand. I'm worried about my balance." He rocks on his heels, clearly exaggerating.

I stand, leaning into him, eyes searching his as he ignores me.

Don't go. I squeeze his hand, warning him to re-think what he's about to do without using words.

But two seconds later, he's gone. Both of them.

I try to make small talk with a worried Stefan, listening to Katrin's messy French conversation with Giselle in the background. I make it five minutes before I excuse myself, and tip-toe down the hall to find out what the hell he's gotten himself into.

* * *

"MOTHERFUCKER, do you understand what's at stake, or are you just stupid? Her place could house a billion dollar amusement park and resort. Billion, with a B, in your USD funny money. I'm willing to negotiate, if you're smart enough not to stand in my way." Jonas is seething.

I'm listening to them near the restrooms, flattened against the wall, hand against my chest. I can't stop my heart when it's racing a hundred beats per minute, one for every nasty word between them.

"Tough shit, cuz. I'm not interested. A few million extra every year in royalties won't sweeten anything on my end, especially if it makes mother miserable. This is her place. Always has been since she was a little girl. It's her peace of mind. I have a real career, and I know how to handle money. There's nothing for us to work out because it's not about me." Cade pauses, and I'm expecting the next sound to be his cousin's fist plowing into his face.

He leans in closer to Jonas before he continues. "Listen, if you want us wasting a lot of time and money getting lawyers involved, figuring out who's entitled to what when we're both married, be my guest. I dug up the old trust before I flew out here, and it's pretty clear. I think you know that. We're just playing games."

"Oh? And which translation did you read, Cade? Do you have any damn clue how much is lost when you can't understand the language it's written in?" His speech quickens, and then comes to a halt. Then he explodes. "Bastard idiot! You want to fight me on this – and for *what*? A five hundred year old tea house for an old woman who won't be around in ten years to enjoy it? You're stupid and selfish, Cade."

"No. Just sentimental. The castle is seven hundred years old. Get it right. Also, get ready, because I'll take off my jacket and beat your ass blind if you say a fucking thing about mom again."

I'm wincing. I don't want them to hurt each other, but God, I can't even blame him if he throws the first punch.

A rich, plump woman saunters past me, humming to herself. Mercifully oblivious to the furious chaos unfolding just a few feet away. I use the commotion when they swallow their words to peak around the corner, hoping they won't notice.

It's worse than I thought.

Jonas looks like a puffed up alley cat, his dirty blond hair flat against his shoulders, left fist twitching at his side. Cade is a rock. He owns the space in all his Viking glory, scary calm and quiet. He'll knock Jonas out cold if it comes to it, and the consequences? *Shit.*

"You're so defensive. Pathetic. I've heard about your mother's health. Shame, really. Seems if you were really a good son with his mother's health in mind, you'd help rid her of needless burdens. What good is a medieval ruin if it just gives the poor woman a heart attack? Listen to reason: relieve her."

"Careful, asshole, or I'm *relieving* you in about ten seconds. You're not getting the castle."

"Okay," Jonas sneers. "Have it your way, cousin. We'll find out who's right very fucking soon."

He starts walking. I run across the hall, trying to hide behind a birch plant, hoping he won't see me eavesdropping. But before he crosses to the spot where I'm standing, he turns, and pivots so sharply I hear his shoes squeal on the tile.

"Stop being such a monumental dumbass. Don't chase me down and break my nose. I know you're tempted." He isn't wrong. Cade's eyes confirm everything, twin blue fires searching for their excuse to burn him down. "It's over, Cade. We'll end it like men in court."

"You won't end shit," he growls, pacing closer, a glint in his eyes like he still wants to knock his cousin to the floor. "I'm not blind, Jonas. You won't let this go and you won't fight fair. I can't pretend it's through."

"No, but you will tonight. Make it a fight, hit me, and I'll run up to Katrin asking for tissues, bleeding through my fingers. I'll tell her how you smashed my fucking face in because you're such a spoiled brat, you can't let go of what's *rightfully* mine. She'll find out she's losing her place the hard way, and all because her loving son couldn't settle down long enough to make a deal. And as for your lovely fiancée, well...I'm sure she's just after your money. She doesn't need a brute with a criminal assault on his record mucking up her wedding plans, does she? Unless it isn't old fashioned gold digging that's got you two kids together...and there's something else I should know about?" He pauses, waving his hand absently. "No matter. I'll find out very soon."

Oh, God. Surely, he couldn't have seen through our act? He can't possibly know it's a marriage of convenience...right?

Cade's eyes are wider than mine. "What the hell do you mean? Asshole, get back here!" He's yelling down the hall, but his cousin doesn't stop and turn, determined to leave.

I hold my breath as Jonas' heavy footsteps hit the tile again, each echo fainter as he heads for the dining room.

Cade takes off like a lion. I'm barely able to get in front of him before he bowls me over.

"Skittle? What're you –"

"Don't do it," I whisper, pushing my hands against his chest. It's like holding back a semi truck. Desperate heat braises my cheeks. "Cade, you heard him. I *know* it's hard not to go after that little shit after the things he said, but if you...he could ruin everything. Don't be cray. Walk away. Fight another day. It's not too late to fix this."

Listen to me. Please.

"Shit. Whatever. Maybe you're right." He pulls me into his embrace and collapses against the wall, anger still coursing through his huge chest. "No good will come from breaking his jaw tonight, as much as I'd enjoy it, and I'm *not* a violent man."

"No, you're only human. Patience. We'll get him another day, I just know –"

"We? No, Skye, this is *my* problem. Your job is to smile,

look pretty, and give me the nails to hammer his coffin shut legally. I won't have you getting mixed up in anything else, you hear?" His gaze says it all: *you'd fucking better.*

My dark, seething guardian angel. He's ten times more handsome when he's mad, as screwed up as that is.

Maybe it's because he's being honest. A guilty pang shoots through my heart when I remember how I'm keeping him completely in the dark about Harry and my debt.

I'm not a good person. I'm a lying, cowardly tool, if I'm honest, and I don't even know who I'm working for anymore.

Cade leans in for a kiss. After last night, I love those lips more than I ever fathomed, but they're also the world's softest curse.

He wants me to put some serious distance between the family drama? Fine.

I just hope I'm able to give him the same courtesy, and live to see him bury that greasy haired twit.

* * *

"Goodnight, dad. We're probably heading out in the next couple days. It was good to see you tonight...and Jonas, too." Cade says his cousin's name like a curse, barely softening it for his mother's benefit.

We're standing outside the restaurant in the chilly night, waiting for our cars. The asshole and his mysterious wife took off before dessert. I was glad to see their spots abandoned when we made our way to the table.

Stefan embraces his son, planting a kiss on his cheek. I'm just near enough to make out the words. "Tell me everything later. I hope to God there's nothing that shouldn't be coming, son?"

"Nothing. You worry too much, pop."

"Oh, dear, I'm sure it was nothing serious," Katrin says, flashing me her oblivious smile. "He's a very busy man with his music, and the young lady looked well. They're off to Germany this weekend, I believe. I'm sure we'll see them again before –"

"I hope so!" I cut in, giving Mrs. Turnbladt's hands a farewell squeeze. "We didn't talk much, but tonight was a joy. We'll do it again without unexpected business next time. I'd love to sit down someday at peace, and talk, just like we did tonight. Thanks for making me feel like part of the family, Katrin."

Warmth blurs her eyes. "A thousand welcomes, doll. I'm thrilled us ladies had a better time tonight than the boys, it seems."

She glares at Stefan and Cade. The two men turn, uneasy smiles on their faces. Cade's father clears his throat uncomfortably.

"Sorry I wasn't around more, mom. Blame the scotch, like I said. It hit me like a freight train. And Jonas, he was good enough to keep me company, made a lot about the future crystal clear. When my stomach stops churning, I'll be grateful."

"I'm just happy you're laying off the bottle, boy. Next time, you'll have to remember your own tolerance. Your college days are long over."

"Of course, mom. Can't say I miss them. It was good to see you again. There's nothing like spending time with family. All the ones who really count." He pulls her into his embrace, shooting me a sideways glance. There's a resonance in his voice that's surprising, like he's clearing his head after waking up from a long nap.

So, maybe this evening wasn't a complete disaster.

And perhaps there's also life for both of us after his

scheming cousin learns some respect, and I learn how to face him without my own secrets clouding our honesty.

* * *

I CAN'T DECIDE what's louder – the ocean's roar, or the blissful beat in my blood.

We're down near the loading docks in town, bundled in full autumn gear, an outing we promised Vinnie. He's always had a soft spot for ships. We've spent the last hour with him watching Reykjavik shipping come and go, listening to his obsessive comparisons with Seattle freight.

Sometimes, he says he wants to go off and be a Marine or a sailor.

I'm worried I believe him. Noble or not, it scares me to death.

So does watching him walk with his arms out way too close to the water, barely balanced.

"Oh my God. He's going to slip and drown!" I whistle nervously through my teeth, shaking my head.

Cade wraps my wrist in his fingers, pulls my hand up, and gives it the warmest kiss ever. "Kid's having fun. Let him. I remember what it used to be like being cooped up all day with homework. He ought to enjoy himself and unwind before we leave tomorrow. Besides, if anything happens, I'm a damn good swimmer."

I catch myself staring a little too harshly. It only lasts a moment because his eyes, his kiss...can anyone really stay mad at this gorgeous man? Especially after he took us out this morning for the world's most incredible massage. My muscles are still singing, beat to a pulp and loving it.

"It's gone by so fast, our time here. Feels like we just arrived."

He gives a low happy growl, nodding. "Means you're

having fun, Skittle, just like your kid brother. You should do it more often. See how it isn't the end of the world?"

Laughing, I dig my elbow gently into his side. "Ass. We'd be having a much different kind of fun if I hadn't talked you down the other night, after dinner. Jesus, the way you were looking at him..."

"I'm not proud I wanted to beat his ass. Caveman me took over." His smile vanishes. "Guess I owe you, Skye. If I'd lost my better senses and popped Jonas in the nose, there's no telling what might've happened. Still don't know what the sneaky fuck is up to. But at least I didn't have to worry about him crawling up to mom with a broken nose or getting me a shiny new set of handcuffs...that would've really given her a coronary."

He sighs, blurring the line between dark humor and heavy truth. "You should give yourself more credit. You're not a total Viking Caveman, you just look like one."

"And don't you fucking love it, beautiful?" He grins, folding another arm around my back, pulling me in. If my lips don't tell him the truth, my body does in spades.

His lips attack mine and we both know the undeniable.

I'm stuck in that honey sweet fog when I see it out the corner of my eye.

A familiar mousy set of green eyes and jet black hair. A shawl. A baby bump.

"Hey, isn't that..." I whisper, clumsily pulling away from him, pointing over his shoulder. "Giselle?"

The woman turns away before he gets a look, and I get a better one. I rub my eyes, pushing my fingers deep into my sockets, and look toward the small fish market where she was standing only seconds ago.

Assuming it was her, and I'm not hallucinating.

"Don't see anybody, Skye. You sure your eyes aren't playing tricks?" Of course he doesn't notice.

It's like every bad mystery movie I've ever seen. What does that make me? I wonder if I'm becoming the crazy thriller character when I can't make out a shred of her through the meager crowd again.

This doesn't make sense. *Why would she be here?*

Maybe I'm seeing things after all. That's a lot more comforting than thinking Jonas' pregnant wife is trailing us.

I need a better look. Creeping forward into the market, I scan it over, trying to catch a glimpse to verify it's her, or prove I'm flat-out wrong.

"Skittle!" Cade runs after me. I'm too busy eyeing the crowd to listen when he yells. "Watch it, you're about to –"

Oomph! I hit the big guy in the trench coat so hard it leaves me winded, which is really a shame because my body tries gasping from the shock. There's confusion, limbs, stuff on the ground he's desperately trying to collect, ignoring my frantic apologies.

He mumbles something in guttural Icelandic that sounds like an apology, too. It could just as easily be an admonishment, though, and I decide I don't really want to know.

I just peel myself away from him. I also have a new problem when something crunches underfoot.

"Damn!" I reach for the twisted metal and hold it up. One look tells me this set of hair pins will never be the same. Neither will my poor purse, which rolled through the dirty water, reeking of fish.

"You okay, love? Didn't realize how serious you were thinking what you saw..." Cade wraps his arms around my waist, instantly soothing.

I take one last longing look around. No sign of Giselle. No anything except my own stupidity.

I feel like a total freak.

"Nah. Just forget it. I guess I was wrong." Somehow, those words seem more wrong.

"Next time you decide to dart off like a human bullet, say so. I'm a decent runner. Polyphemus over there didn't touch you, did he?" There's a jealous edge in his voice spoiling for a fight as he glares at the giant plodding away from us.

"No. Not intentionally, anyway. I smacked into him pretty hard. Wish I knew enough of this language for a proper apology..."

"What's with the mud, sis? Is this like a new fashion trend?" Vinnie has his biggest shit-eating grin on when I whip around and shoot needles from my eyes. He crouches by my feet, comes up with something black in his hand, and cocks his head as he passes it over. "What, no thank you?"

I'm too busy groaning. It's my checkbook, completely coated in mud.

A minute later, we're all on the ground, pecking with our hands like hungry chickens. There are bits and pieces of my stuff everywhere. Cade wipes my phone with a handkerchief while Vinnie snorts, shoving a few dirty coins in my palm I wanted to save as souvenirs from the trip.

"You should really be more careful next time."

"Same, Vinnie," I snap. He stares, puzzled for a second, before I reach for his ear and pull. I don't stop until he's begging.

Behind me, Cade is on his feet again, laughing. It's happy music to my ears.

If only we were a normal couple. I'd already know he's a keeper since he's able to appreciate what it takes to put my bratty little brother in his place.

VIII: EDEN ON THE EDGE (CADE)

"*J* can't believe I'm doing this. Whatever you've got in store, it better be worth it."

I don't say anything, just smile as I drive our luxury rental higher into the mountains. Honestly, I'm still a little stunned Skittle kept the blindfold on.

She balked when we first left the cottage, and I let her know it was a condition for enjoying our last night in Reykjavik.

"Almost there, beautiful. Keep your panties soaked and un-twisted. Ten more minutes, they'll be gone."

"You hope!" She throws a punch at my shoulder, laughing. Misses me by a longshot. I hear her hand crash into the leather seat.

Not the best timing on these roads up here. She's blind to the crazy twists and turns carved by a psycho construction crew who thought it'd be wise to hide the country's best kept secret behind a gate barely big enough for a car to fit through.

But I've taken this route a hundred times. It's almost second nature.

I stop at the entrance and punch my code into the box. The gate swings open, parting for one more elite member of Iceland's most exclusive spa.

The valet who takes the vehicle when we step off at the curb doesn't even blink at the blindfold she's wearing. I'm sure they've seen crazier things from rich men and their mistresses, and if they haven't, they're paid a princely sum to keep their lips shut anyway.

Vegas has nothing on this place. What happens here, I'm not sure even the NSA knows.

It's the kind of blasphemous, addictive secrecy that makes me throb.

"Come on, Cade, just a little peak!" she whimpers, as soon as I take her hand, giving it a sharp tug.

"No. Be a good girl, though, and you just might get a taste..."

She whimpers after me, wondering what I mean, but my lips are sealed for the next five minutes. I lead her down the stairs slowly to the private spot I've readied. It's a cool night, and the steam surrounds us like a cozy cloak once we're on the pool deck.

Champagne chills in the bucket just like I asked. Two bottles of Dom, which we won't even finish. I've got plenty more enticing ways than booze to keep her occupied tonight.

"Stay there." I walk a few paces over, rip one of the bottles from the bucket, and dig the bottle opener in.

She jumps when the cork flies off with a *pop*. If the resonant fizz doesn't give it away, the two crystal flutes I click together gently do.

Skye's smiling anyway. *Christ, those lips.*

Makes me think twice about whether I want to serve us drinks, or toss them off the edge of the cliff and get busy making that sunshine on her face glow.

"Gently, Skittle. Take it nice and slow," I whisper, bending her glass into her hand, raising it to her lips.

She can't tease me with her eyes, but damn, the way she swallows says it all. My dick jerks in my pants, lips aching to criss-cross her throat, and then work their way down to the nipples guaranteed to be pebbled if I just reach out and –

"Delish," she whispers, tasting her champagne. "So, is this the big send off? Or do I just get to hang out like an extra from *Eyes Wide Shut?*"

I smile, taking a long pull from my drink, trying to dampen the horny edge in my blood. Naturally, it doesn't do shit. "Didn't know you were a Kubrick fan."

"Sure. Art snob kinda goes with history major. If I want to sit in front of the TV for more than an hour, it better be worth it."

"You fret too much, Skittle," I say, grabbing her hand. Slowly, I lead her over to the railing, then stand behind her. Love how she presses into me when my hands wind around her waist, snaking up her shoulders. "You want something worth looking at? Feast your eyes on this."

I undo the blindfold and let it drop. She makes a muffled sound, somewhere between the one she made when we went up the other side of the mountain in the daytime, and the pleasure oozing out of her in bed.

"It's marvelous," she says quietly, eyes taking in the expanse. Stars wink in the distant night like silver and ice. The cool breeze is a summer sigh next to the hot spring at our backs, urging me to stop screwing off every second I'm next to it and rip off our clothes. "You shouldn't have, Cade. It's just going to make home feel more surreal. I'm messed in the head. Can't help looking at this place and feeling like it was here forever, just waiting for us...and after we leave, all this disappears."

There's a sudden sadness in her voice I don't like. I take

her drink, setting it on the small marble platform at the lookover's edge with mine. This is serious. "Damn it, love, don't you get it? If I wanted this fairy tale to end like nothing happened, I wouldn't be pulling you in deeper."

She's silent, a slow, wild blush forming on her cheeks. I turn her around in my arms, press my forehead to hers, pulsing my breath on those lips I'm two-point-five seconds from devouring.

"That sky isn't meant to make you worry, or yearn, or whatever the fuck. It's meant to be a backdrop." Training my eyes on her, I watch the storm in her wide grey pools, and I love it. "This doesn't have to be our stars or our sky. No poetry. None of that Romeo and Juliet bullshit where we hold hands and suck face while nature smiles on. What's here on earth is what really matters, Skye, and so does the moment. That's what's ours. And what the hell would I ever do with more stars when my Skye's right in front of me?"

"Cade..." She leans into me, tits plush against my chest, calling the fire in my balls to drive me mad. "You're a total dork, and I love it."

Fuck, those lips. They get the jump on me, and then I'm on her mouth whole, tongue and teeth claiming what's mine.

I meant everything I said.

Meant it in ways that won't stop fucking with my head even when we're caught in our rapture.

Because when my mouth runs rampant on hers, when my palms catch her ass and can't dream about letting go, when my brain wolfs out with the frantic, animal need to be inside her, I'm afraid to decipher the wicked tempo beating in my ribs.

Fear never scared me off.

And when there's a woman wrapped around me with half her dress pulled down, nipple in my mouth, purring as I fluff it back to perfection with my tongue, fear is an absolute bitch encouraging the lust in my blood.

I need to be inside this sweet chaos I can't forget, and I need it *fucking now.*

My hands peel away our clothes in record time. We're at the pool's edge and I'm on my knees, eyes fixed on the wet spot seeping through her panties. The harder she squirms in my arms, the more I want to taste her.

"Oh, Jesus. Cade..." Lace in hand, I tear her panties down her legs and fling them over one ankle. Her moan is reward enough.

I lay her against the table next to the water and suck her lush little cunt from behind.

She cries out in less than a minute, legs shaking, fists in a ball over her head. Her thighs try to press shut and I rip them apart, bury my face deeper, hellbent on stealing the O from her body.

My tongue is all warrior. It fucks, it strokes, it licks her world apart, and then it thieves.

I push my cock in my fist when she shudders, leans into me, and screams.

Sweet fuck, that's it.

There.

Come, Skittle, come! I want this rainbow turned to lightning.

I suck her clit straight through the grinding, erratic orgasm rending her in two. Every twitch in her muscles turns me on more. Her pussy drips honey on my lips. I give it every scratch of stubble on my chin, make her ride my face like I know she wants to, and fuck, I almost bust a hot mess all over my hand when she arches her back tighter, prolonging her ecstasy.

I can't take a second more of this.

Normally, I like to take things slow. Love to get them so

deep in the zone they have time to savor it, to breathe, to remember their own names.

Not Skye.

I can't remember my own damn initials unless I bury myself in her in the next five seconds. Once her legs stop shaking enough to settle in my grip, I ease her into the pool, diving in the shallow heat with her.

I haven't forgotten the condom in my pocket. Tough and water proof, though a scary part inside me wishes it wasn't. I want to be in her raw, and I want her tight body sucking every seething drop from my balls.

We have to use protection. I remember her words the first night we met, when she thought a quick fuck was where our business would end.

Can't stop thinking about that scared, shaken girl agreeing to do the unthinkable. I wonder where she's gone as I look into her eyes, spread her legs, and smother her in a dozen kisses before I roll the condom on and push between her legs.

The Skye who moans when I fill her to the hilt isn't the shy, sweet, mysterious young thing I met our first time.

I've known her body, and I'm working on her soul.

I'm glad I laid next to her that first night, and didn't consummate the fake marriage she didn't even know about then. In a few more weeks, I'm marrying her, and I know we'll be doing this soon like a proper honeymoon.

So different from what we thought.

So dangerous.

So impossible to stop.

Her eyelids are fluttering. Unless she's a real lightweight, drunk on a splash of champagne and my relentless sex, she can't be coming again...can she?

"Hey, beautiful, look at me!" I pull her slick, steamy hair

behind her neck, loving how that cotton candy melts in my hand.

"No, no. Just fuck me." Her voice is harsher than before. She's climbing all over me, until I have to plant my feet on the stone under us for leverage.

She's grinding. Sucking at my shoulder. Then she bites hard, and I grab her chin, wondering what the fuck's gotten into her.

There's a wet heat in her eyes and it's not the hot spring's reflection. "What's the matter?" I growl, kissing off a tear as it spills down her cheek.

"Nothing." That's not what her eyes are saying. She looks away, leaving me to stew, cock still hard and rooted in her.

Damn it all. I actually *care* why she's going nuts all of a sudden, and not just because I really want to fuck her.

"Tell me," I say, pushing my fingers into her chin. Holding her face, I pull her into another demanding kiss.

"Cade, no. Forget it. Let's just enjoy –"

No. I'm not falling for that fake light in her eyes. Or her little fingernails dancing on the back of my neck. Grabbing her hand, I pull it off, clenching her face tighter, my eyes burning into hers.

"Tell. Me."

She sighs again, looking away. "I don't want to go home. I don't want this to end. It's stupid, and wrong, and we barely know each other, even after we've fucked. But that's how it is. I can't hide it anymore. I was afraid this would happen, when we broke our contract, and decided to –"

"We didn't decide shit, Skittle. Our flesh made the hard decisions for us, so why deny it now?" It's not just my cock talking when I lay my forehead down on hers, arms winding tighter on her hips. I win a soft moan from those fiery lips, shifting her deeper on my cock. "Why worry? Why give the future a second to curdle the now? I'm happy with this, Skye. With you."

Her eyes roll toward me, slow and mellow. There's disbelief I don't like. I want to fuck it right out of her grey-blue gems.

"Because *this* is just making it harder, Cade. Because I thought we'd do this, and keep some distance for both our sakes." She pauses, bites her lip, anger sweeping sadness aside in her eyes because she thinks I still don't get it. "We shouldn't be doing this. We're losing control."

Good. Anger, I can work with, and I understand everything she isn't telling me between the lines.

"Fuck yes, we are. And since when is that a sin?" I rock my hips into hers. Long, hard strokes, thrusting the turmoil out of her face, smoothing it to bliss. "Tell me you don't love it, Skye. Say you're willing to give in just so we can satisfy some prim and proper ego. Don't know about you, but this ego isn't nearly bruised enough for that. Remember the cottage/ You were on me like a cat in heat. I'm still on you because I want this, I want you, I want us. Tonight, I want to revel, beautiful, and whatever the fuck tomorrow brings, it's got nothing on us. *Nothing.*"

That isn't the word that stands out when I take a second to mull what I just said.

It's *us. Us.*

Oh, fuck. Did I go too far?

I bury my questions by thrusting into her harder. Lust grunts through my teeth, hisses with a heat that's fiercer than the steam. If it wasn't for the tan I've kept from a business trip to Arizona a month ago, I'd be blushing like Ms. Totally Pretending She Doesn't Want My Cock. And failing miserably.

Skye moans louder. My cue to quicken my strokes, clenching her ass with one hand. We drift to the wall where I hold her, kiss her, drive into her depths with a passion that's freaking me out more than the bashful heat in my blood.

All the better to make this right.

All the better to let her nails descend my back, and add her mark to my mess of tattoos.

All the better for me to brand her, inside and out.

I piston my hips into hers. Her pulse matches mine. Our hearts, our bodies, our heads are one, gloriously one, and we race toward our release, continuing a dialogue too warped for any words.

She's the first to give it up. Skye comes like a rocket, hips quaking, whimpering because I've fixed the fever inside her. I hope like hell I've cured the feels bug, too.

I'll never get sick of hearing those noises she makes. They reach through me, pepper my cock with the urge to bring her off harder.

Fuck, yes!

Every thought in my head melts in sweet friction, churning water and the grind of my pubic bone on her clit, stealing the air from her lungs. My hand rips through the water, smacks her little ass when she comes, and her pussy grips my dick so hard I see stars.

"Can't. Fucking. Hold it!"

I don't try. There's just enough time to put my mouth on hers one more time, and suck every whimper out when my cock swells, burns, and shoots fire up my spine.

Good goddamn.

There's no doubt or fear or future where we're going. For a wonderful, star-crossed second, we're in the moment ruled by the flesh, where everything is two, and also one.

Two thudding hearts.

Two pumping balls.

Two breathless, shaking, clutching bodies.

Sweet dualist fuckery, and one steady breath.

* * *

A SEVEN O'CLOCK flight isn't exactly the Red Eye. But when I've spent the whole night fucking the woman who's already passed out next to me, her sweet face resting on my shoulder as the jet drifts on at twenty thousand feet, and my eyes are very red, I think it qualifies.

She took my advice, or maybe I just screwed good sense back into her. Our tongues stopped lashing each other with words, turning to fleshly pursuits between several more glasses of Dom.

When she took me in her mouth...Christ.

It was new, it was fresh, it was better than any champagne blowjob I ever had, even though I coaxed her through every step of giving head for the first time.

We didn't return to the castle until well after one in the morning. Of course we were famished. Fortunately, the cottage's kitchen is always stocked with fancy cheese, bread, and my guilty boyhood pleasure, a whole case of Matarkex biscuits.

We ate laughing, telling jokes, staying as far off the heavy stuff as we could.

No, even with Iceland a couple hundred miles away, I'm no closer to sorting out the crap running through my head while we were there. Neither is she.

But am I happy? Yes.

Fuck yes.

Can't remember the last time I went overseas and came home feeling truly refreshed. Feeling alive, even.

Every trip before was more of the same: family visits, mountain hiking, drinking my ass off into my early twenties, and when that got boring, poaching local pussy I'd never see again, much less bring to bed for seconds.

This trip was different. What should've been a high stress

do or die talk with Jonas vanished in the sticky haze of her kiss and the first real smile I pulled out of her on that mountain.

I'm smiling, sipping my morning coffee, reluctantly sliding a pillow under her head when she stirs. She needs it if she doesn't want to wake up with a stiff neck, but damn I miss her heat.

I miss it already. It takes me back to the bliss we've enjoyed for the better part of a week. Everything I don't want to let go of, even though the serious business at home won't wait to leap up and bite me in the ass like a rabid poodle.

Reclining my seat all the way back, arm around her, I close my eyes. I'm hoping to catch a few winks while I've got the caffeine in my system. Nothing like a coffee nap to slash my sleep time and amp up the energy.

Or just make me want to rip her skirt off first thing after we touch down on Seattle's sacred soil again.

I'm almost out when I hear a crash near the back of the plane. I sit up, heart racing, bracing for an apocalyptic announcement from the flight crew. It never comes.

It's not something mechanical failing. It's in the cabin.

I get up and walk to the plane's rear, step into my room, wondering what the kid's gotten himself into. Skye thought he'd sleep the whole way home, sprawled out on my bed, but he's very much awake when I knock. He practically rips the sliding door off its rollers.

"You okay in there, Vinnie? Heard the noise and wondered." I stop when I see his face. That teenage rage and angst is too familiar.

How many times did I see it in the mirror when dad grounded me for fucking off at Maynard? Or when I got into a fistfight with Spence over that chick we both wanted to take to homecoming, whatever the hell her name was? Only reason we both walked away with our teeth intact is because Cal broke it up that day.

"Sorry. Didn't mean to throw it so hard..." He's busted and ashamed.

I don't have to ask. He just steps aside, lets me through, and I see his phone in the corner with a crack in the case.

Walking over, I pick it up. It's taken quite a beating. "They ought to pay you for quality control. You've clearly found the weakness in the design," I say, trying to lighten the mood.

Kid isn't having it. He slumps down, fist on his chin, a fifteen year old *Thinker* with more emotion than Rodin ever captured in bronze.

"Want to tell me what's wrong, or just keep sulking?"

He looks up, surprised. Until now, I've been the distant, genteel rich douchebag his older sister is marrying. A benefactor who paid for an awesome trip with lots of frills, including this private jet he's on now, without ever getting real.

"Nothing," he says, turning away.

Inwardly, I smile. Looks like he's got one thing in common with his older sis: they're both stubborn fucking mules.

"Bullshit." One word, and he does a double take. I stand there, arms folded, head cocked. "Talk to me, young man. I'm old enough to know nothing is almost always a load. You wouldn't have almost dented the gold trim on my wall if you were upset over an undercooked burrito."

I nod toward the uneaten breakfast on the table next to the bed. He sighs, taking his sweet time gathering his words, scratching his head like he doesn't know how to begin. I walk over and plop down next to him, never taking my eyes away.

"It's this guy. He's just an old friend of the family. Always good to me, but kind of an asshole, sometimes. Skye doesn't like him much..."

"No? Why's that?" My ears are ringing. Might be more than teen spirit storm and angst here after all.

"They had a falling out recently. A few times in the past, too, I guess. Never really understood over what because he tried to help her...both of us, really. Anyway, she's doing the usual big sister thing. Says he's a bad influence, more or less. Wants me to stay away from him. But the thing is, he's like family. He's not a monster. He's just making sure we're okay, even if he's not the most upstanding guy." Vinnie's eyes go the floor. "I've known him too long to just ghost like she wants. It isn't fair. I told him Skye isn't treating him right, and he got kind of crazy. Real hot under the collar, I mean. He yelled at me a little, but then he apologized. It's frustrating, is all."

What the hell is really going on here? I'm trying not to let skepticism bleed through to my face.

Vinnie pauses, rubbing his temples. "Christ, nobody can just level with each other! If she'd be more open about her beef with him, talk it through, then maybe I'd get it. Everything is such a big damn secret. Skye never tells me anything!"

"Easy, Vinnie. She holds her cards tight, yeah, but she's got her reasons."

Does she? I wouldn't bet a spare dime on it, knowing how well she hides the parts of her she doesn't want me seeing. But if she's going to these lengths to keep Vinnie away, treating this mystery man like a danger...was that debt I paid to Adele owed to someone else?

"You don't get it." The kid whips his head around, anger flashing behind his lenses. "He was always there. Only constant in our lives. He was close to mom, before she offed herself."

Holy fuck. He's hurt, but way too casual when he says it.

Maybe he's blocked it out to numb the pain, the way brains do when they can't hold more poison.

"Say no more. You've had it rough, and I'm sorry." I slap him on the shoulder and give it a brotherly squeeze. "You want my two cents? Sounds like this guy is taking advantage of you, whoever he is. Look how upset he's got you, and for what?"

I'm not just playing devil's advocate. I want to know more.

"Yeah, whatever. Maybe." Vinnie twists away, rubbing his face. At least he doesn't look so pissed off anymore. "He's no angel, like I said. He got Skye to do some things in the past she wasn't proud of. I did stuff, too. And I told him too much today like an idiot, when he got up my butt about her. I never should've picked up the dumb phone..."

Whatever *stuff* means. Drugs? Petty crime?

How old is this guy? Is he tied in with the same assholes Skye owed mega-money?

No grad student I know wracks up a cool million on Starbucks and tuition. Nate told me her place was lower on the great digs meter, too.

I'm baffled. The background check I ran on them both before signing off on the wedding didn't turn up anything. No convictions, no criminal record. Nothing worse than a single parking ticket for Skittle.

If I had serious reason to worry, we never would've gotten this far. But I can't just pretend she wasn't in some level of hell I thought I'd ended when I wiped her debt out, and saved her from more musical peep shows.

If she's still in danger, hell, if Vinnie is...I need her to come clean.

Can't have her legally hitched, and maybe for a lot longer than we first agreed, if she's sitting on secrets that could go nuclear.

I smile, hiding the questions lashing my brain. "You did the right thing. You're entitled to blow off a little steam. Let's just save it for when we're back on the ground, okay? Then you can knock yourself out in my gym. The Ass Kicker loves a good beating. If that's not good enough, I'll put Fields on standby to take you somewhere better."

"Thanks," he whispers, reaching for his phone on the bed. He winces when he feels the broken protector screen.

I'm halfway out the door when I stop, turn, and look back at the kid whose soul is so trampled I think there's footprints on his shadow. "Don't worry about the case. I'll take care of that, too. You rest. We've got a few more hours before we're home."

I walk back to the cabin lounge and take my seat. Skittle hasn't moved, curled up with her blanket, sleeping like a kitten. I settle in, shifting her pillow to my shoulder, gingerly stroking her brow every time she moans in her sleep.

"What's happening in those dreams, beautiful?" I whisper. I hope they aren't nightmares.

Because if we've got a future, and I haven't just bought the world's most expensive mail order bride, then I can't have her pretty head full of darkness.

It's my job to bring this woman paradise.

IX: PHONE TAG (SKYE)

*I*t's weeks since we came back from Eden, and I'm wondering when it ends. Things are so much better than I ever expected at home.

There's time to settle in, catch our breath before the big day. I spend the evenings with Cade and the wedding planner he's hired when I'm not at the university.

We go over décor, guests, food, and venue. Everything that would take a normal couple months to set up. Not surprising his billionaire pockets are a shortcut through the usual hang-ups.

It's a good thing, too. He hasn't heard anything else from Jonas since we left, but I know he's out there, looking for the perfect opportunity to call us on our wedding bluff and snatch Katrin Turnbladt's beautiful little tea house away.

She called me into it the morning before we left for one more chat. Probably the only thing that made me feel human after our late night together in the hot springs, before we had to head for the airport.

I sat marveling at the handcrafted glass, sipping the finest cup of herbal tea folded in a splash of honey. Katrin rattled in her soft sing-song voice, charitable as ever. I smiled at her family stories and the anecdotes about little Cade. It wasn't even forced.

When we touched down on the runway and I woke up, so much more peaceful than the first trip there, I waited for the shock.

There has to be a moment when he looks me in the eye, when the going gets rough, and everything boils over...right? When I ask myself just one last time *what the holy hell am I doing,* marrying a billionaire who hand rolls sushi for my spoiled little brother, and actually makes it taste good when we sit down for dinner?

Iceland should've been the end of everything that's too good to be true. It should've kept our overdrive lusts, too, but they haven't let up either since the day we came home.

Every time we share the bed, I'm having the best sex of my life. The only sex, of course, but if it gets any better than this, I don't want to know.

Not if it doesn't involve Cade Relentless Turnbladt.

Just thinking he's the only man I ever want to bed *should* tell me how screwed I am.

Trying not to *should* be the screaming warning my heart has gone crazy.

Pretending it's okay, and wondering if heaven lasts forever, most definitely *should* be a sign the end of Skye Coyle is nigh.

Yeah. It's really a shame his smirking, gorgeous, kiss teasing face comes with so many *shoulds* attached. I'm having a harder time seeing them every hour we're together.

Every new kiss turns shoulds into could, and maybes into will.

It's a scathing sort of poetry that's bound to put me on my knees.

Kneeling for this man involves tears, that much is certain.

There are too many hidden spikes perched under my life, ready to catch me in agony. I just wish I knew whether there's joy or sorrow after the inevitable pain.

* * *

MY DISSERTATION IS COMING ALONG. Hell, at the rate I'm stress-writing, I think I'll have a draft for my professor with a full bibliography before wedding week. I've never been more enthralled by *The Plague of Justinian and Late Roman Labor.*

And it's nothing compared to what's waiting that evening.

Fields picks me up from campus and drives us downtown. He waits patiently while I walk into the expensive bridal shop. I put on a brave face, pretending I'm totally ready for this, but I'm three seconds from breaking down by the time the pleasant woman is taking my measurements.

I'm able to wipe a few secret tears away when she leaves, telling me to wait near the changing room while she retrieves my best options. I sit on the bench, trying to hide the sour regret that keeps foaming at the back of my mind.

Five minutes later, I've stuffed myself into a model ivory outfit complete with flowery flourishes around the neckline, and it happens. My reflection in the long mirror gets the evil eye when the tears come, hoping they won't ruin my mascara.

"Selfish bitch. Why do I still wish you were here?" I'm not talking to myself.

There's a ghost in my head. I haven't been able to shake it all morning.

Mom.

Obviously, she wouldn't approve of anything about this screwed up wedding. Like the fact it isn't real, technically, even if it's starting to feel like it is so much it's maddening.

But every girl should have her mother around to help try

on dresses. I wish mine hadn't thrown herself off a Seattle bridge, drowning herself in the Puget Sound.

If I'd made more friends in my history program, it wouldn't be so bad. The peer group never meshed with me since the suicide, though. The rest is my fault.

Guilt is a heavy burden. I shut down anyone getting too close to a girl who's willing to steal just to keep her little brother healthy, and who took too much money from a depraved, soulless asshole who just happens to be family.

Is my parents' curse in the DNA we share? Sometimes, I wonder.

Desperation is no excuse for what Harry made me do. However much the guilt tears me up in the present, I would've sold him those artifacts if I'd had a chance, without a second thought. I'd have become a thief for a cause, and right or wrong, I wouldn't have looked back.

Fear is no excuse either. That's what ruled mom, and ultimately ruined her. I feel plenty of it, too. It's there behind every soft smile and flirtatious night in Cade's arms, trying to let go, and fool myself into thinking I'm not just being used for this wedding, this body, this madness he's adopted to save Katrin a heart attack.

"Who the fuck are you – really?" I whisper again, trying to blot the tears on my hand so they don't stain the fine fabric.

I don't know why I bother. Easy answers never come. Just more savage questions patented for stinging the heart.

Do these torn up eyes on top of a fancy dress staring back at me belong to a criminal?

How about a coward? Mom was so afraid, so defeated, she killed herself. That's why she isn't here today, living my lie, rather than the ones I'm sure she told us to get by.

"Everything all right, miss?" The owner knocks softly, and

I grunt back through the door, staring at four more dresses hanging neatly on their hooks I have left to try.

They're easier than the first. I'm able to get through it and even like how sexy I look in the last without a full on descent into ugly crying.

"We have a winner," I say, stepping out, wearing the cream colored thing with the low neckline. It's not exactly my style, but I think we have something to work with. Breathable shoulders are a girl's best friend.

It just needs more color. Leave that to me.

"A lovely choice. Simple and elegant, I'm sure you'll agree." Concern pricks at the woman's eyes. She notices the mess around my eyes. I'm already in too deep to look like a normal Seattle princess seeking her dream wedding, so why not drop the final bomb? "This particular item also has a number of add-ons we can do. Our seamstress, Shelly, is known around the world for her –"

"Yeah, sure, about that. Can we do some pink and blue up and down the sides? Maybe like...a unicorn stripey pattern up the back?"

"Unicorn?" Her eyes are marbles.

"Tell you what, I'll get this off, change back into my clothes, and send a sketch over to help explain it better. You've got a business card?"

She quietly reaches into her pocket and holds out the slim, glossy scrap with her name and info. There's a tremor in her fingers.

I palm it and smile sweetly. "Thanks. There's not a problem, is there? When you said add-ons, I figured –"

"Whatever it takes to make your big day wonderful! Mr. and Mrs. Turnbladt deserve the finest. No questions here!" Flustered, she walks away, trying to pacify me like the rich, high strung wife I'm sure she thinks I'm about to be.

Joke's on her.

Maybe everyone.

I won't let mom's absence, past mistakes, or a million questions ruin this. I'll enjoy my damn wedding day because it's the only one I might ever get. It's worth remembering, regardless of how long this charade lasts.

For Cade, I'll walk down the aisle, but I'll do it *my way*. That's one thing I've never had.

* * *

"WHERE'S MY SUGAR, Skittle? Come closer. Might be the last time before I'm back, and we have to suit up as bride and groom." He's standing just outside the door, dressed in a sinfully sexy flannel shirt and jeans, an extra inch of five o'clock scruff on his face. I'm a little disappointed I won't be heading to Alaska with him for his friend's birthday.

I wrap my arms around his neck and kiss him deeply. We kiss so long – no, so *longing* – Fields looks away with a smile, waiting next to the car with the suitcase he's loading.

"Shit, don't do that," he growls, hand sliding down my back. "It's hard enough to leave."

"Good. Because it would be a shame to forget me while you're off communing with grizzly bears, or whatever."

"Careful, love. Just because I'll wife you so fucking hard in the next week doesn't mean you're exempt from a spanking."

"You went too easy last night," I whisper, wondering if I should be careful what I wish for. My ass is still singed and I'm already wet, even though he was in me less than twelve hours ago. "When you get back, and we do the honeymoon...harder."

Poor Fields. I really feel for him as Cade lifts me off the ground, throws me against the wall, and sucks my bottom lip into his mouth until I feel his teeth.

The butler is clearly underpaid for everything he's seen in this house since we returned.

And I think – *I hope* – it's going to get a whole lot wilder in the months to come.

* * *

CADE FINALLY BREAKS AWAY and leaves with one last smoldering look through the window. I feel like a dumb kid who's just been blown a kiss by her high school sweetheart.

Then I turn, step back inside, and jump halfway out of my skin. "Vincent, you scared me! How long were you lurking there?"

He's in the hall, leaning on a fancy stone end table I really wish he wouldn't touch. "Long enough to see you suck face with Mr. Moneybags. Spankings, sis? Gross. I don't even want to imagine you and all that Fifty Shades crap."

"I'll give *you* Fifty Shades where the sun doesn't shine if you stand there talking crap about your future brother-in-law." My heart shouldn't be drumming this fast over typical Vinnie antics. Maybe I'm secretly disappointed. "I thought you two were warming up. Stupid me."

"Aw, come on, he's an okay guy." Vinnie pauses, and I keep my back turned, waiting for him to come closer. "Sis, I didn't mean it. Really. This is still a little weird to me, I guess I'm just – sis?"

I spin around and dig my hand into his stomach. The tickle-monster isn't done until he's on the floor, rolling, begging for sweet mercy.

"Okay, okay, okay!" He still isn't winded. That's unfortunate.

It's at least another ten seconds before he's able to fight me off and I give up. "How's it feel? Think I've had my payback, or should I go for more?"

He's shaking his head furiously, sitting up with a scowl on his face, flicking his glasses back over his nose. "Christ. And you're supposed to be the mature one..."

"And you're not supposed to scare me out of my wits and dump on Cade when I'm thinking about getting you out of the house, kiddo." I extend a hand from my hips, helping him up.

"You're such a hardass, Skye. Why's it gotta be like that when we – wait, what? Get out where?"

"Show me your math quiz first. If you've got yourself a B or better, you can hang out with me around campus while I go in to get some work done."

"B-plus!" he says with a huge grin. "Can we go by that awesome music shop on the corner again, right outside your building? They've got incense."

"We'll see." I'm left smiling in a thunder of footsteps, watching him fly up the stairs to get his laptop from his room.

Cade won't be home for close to a week. If I have to be alone with my brother for the first time since our world flipped over, maybe there's a chance I can make him less of a dick.

* * *

I'M HUMMING, hunched over a thick corpus of Latin translations, records from the Eastern Roman empire. It's the icing on this beast of a book I've been working on forever.

What better way to end the year than a married woman with a doctorate? It's not all roses from here, of course. There's still oral exams, a few last credits, and a final seal of approval from the faculty before I've got my degree in hand. Then there's the one way ticket to uncertain employment in this expensive city. I'm safe from that as long as I'm with

Cade, but I'm not comfortable using him as an endless security blanket.

I'm also not letting these worries detract from the accomplishment. I've done something marvelous here, and it's been an eternity since I knew that feeling.

Keep your head down, I tell myself. *Just a little while longer.*

And the end is coming so close I can feel it in the TA office, marking a few last quotes to cite with sticky notes. I'm so deep in my groove I barely hear my phone buzz. But as soon as I lift it up, the demon number on the screen ices my blood.

"Harry." The bastard's name is a curse and a question on my lips.

I'll never understand why he won't just leave us alone, especially when I've sacrificed so much to hold up my end of his hellish bargain.

I can't keep living in fear. I do a quick look around and then get up from the desk, ducking into the small study room around the corner I know is never occupied.

I'm just in time for his second call. He plows straight through voice mail, hangs up, and dials me again like he always does.

"What?" I wish this phone had a cord so I could yank it out of the wall.

"Still pissed at your uncle? Figured as much, screamer, so I'll keep this brief. Vinnie had a nice chat with me a few weeks back." Asshole pauses, letting it sink in.

My fingers form a fist. I can't decide who deserves more rage. My clueless brother, for not doing the very serious, very simple fucking thing I asked him to – come to me ASAP if Harry calls. Or the monster himself on the line, taunting me with his silence.

"What do you want? Just spit it out, Harry." My voice trembles.

I hate it.

I'm sputtering. Cracking. Breaking down exactly like I don't want to.

"How fucking gracious, Skye, showing me some respect. Finally. I've missed it more than you'll ever know. Let's see...what is it I called you for? Oh, yeah. Turns out some investments I made with the cool million you dropped on my ledger didn't pay off like I hoped. Now, I'm looking for a loan, and I think you can help me out. Hilarious how the world works sometimes, ain't it? I loan you cash, and then I come asking, hat-in-hand? Screamer, you still there?"

I don't know where I am, honestly. My head feels like it's going to explode.

"I can't loan you money. I paid back everything...everything I had."

"That's a real shame, Skye. Real *big* shame that you have to lie to me, and you're so fucking bad at it, too."

There's nothing to say. It doesn't faze him for more than a few seconds because he rolls right over me.

"I'm *not* lying. I don't have money, and if I did, I damn sure wouldn't give it to you."

"Aw, hell, that's where you're wrong, screamer. See how you mix two truths and a lie? You just love to keep me guessing, don't you? Chasing my own fucking tail like a stupid back alley mutt?"

What the hell does he really want? It can't be a loan. He's loaded from a life of crime. I'm trying to breathe, waiting for this to pass, or at least find the courage to hang up, and never answer another unknown call after I block his main number.

"Truth is, I don't want your fuckin' money. I want a nice fat cut from new guy joining our family; Mr. Moneybags, as Vinnie calls him. Your new hubby's loaded, isn't he? I know you thought you'd play dumb and I'd just eat it, leaving me holding onto my clueless dick, yeah?"

The world drops out. Now, I get what this is about, and I couldn't be more numb.

But I know what I need to do.

First, I'm going to hunt down my stupid little brother and strangle him with my bare hands. Then I'll find some way to throw mud in this asshole's eyes, right after I figure out how much he knows.

"You're not getting anything, so stop trying," I snap. Maybe this isn't completely hopeless. "Shut up and listen for a second, Harry. Whatever game you think we're playing, I'm out. I told you once, and I'll say it again, until I'm beyond blue in the face: leave. Don't contact me. Don't call Vinnie. Stay away from Cade. Don't threaten us. This is your last and final warning. I *will* go to the police, and I'll tell them everything I know."

For the first time in my life, I'm sad it isn't much. My uncle is always on the go, up and down the west coast, leaving his network of amoral underlings like Adele to do his dirty work in the pimping department. Whatever else he has a hand in, I know even less. Dad was into dealing drugs, which means his brother is too, but I have no specifics.

All I know is I'm teasing fire, and there's a horrific chance someone is bound to get burned. I'm blind to how deep, how dangerous my uncle's network really goes.

"Brave words. I'm a little choked up, screamer." Even the exaggerated sniffing sounds he makes pours fire in my blood. "Thing is, you're fucked. Come on, we both know it. I just wanted to have a little fun before I told you how fucking fucked you really are, whore. Vinnie and I talked about more than how beautifully loaded your new fiancé is...see, the kid has a hell of a conscience. He *cares* about you, about family, about shitting up your life without even knowing it. Remember those artifacts? The thousand year old multimillion dollar jewelry we thought was gone? Turns out – and you won't believe this – it was right under our fucking noses all along. It didn't get lost in the mail or swiped by customs or whatever the fuck excuses you told me."

Oh, God. I don't even want to know.

"Don't. Please!" I'm covering my mouth, courage leaking out of me in a whimper.

He's laughing. Deep down, I'm screaming.

"You know where they went? Those rings, those Caesar busts, those expensive ass rocks from Persia? Right to Manny's Pawn shop in Bremerton, an easy damn ferry ride away. I sent my men over there. Lucky the owner didn't have a clue what he'd bought, and he pissed it away for a couple thousand tops. Your dumbass brother, God love him, pawned the shit for a few video games. Did it right under our noses. I'd be pissed, if he didn't just hand me the perfect excuse to make your life absolutely fucking miserable if you don't do exactly what I say."

Can't think. Can't breathe. Can't bear to learn this demon's demands.

Harry notices. "Go ahead, screamer. Ask. I want you to."

"What...what is it you want?"

"Looking for a nice juicy piece of Mr. Moneybags. If the man can cough up a million plus for a bitch like you, there's plenty more where that came from. A whole lot fucking more. I done my homework on Mr. Turnbladt, sweets. That sick sonofabitch is loaded to the gills. I want to shave a few off him. Here's what's gonna happen..."

"No. No. No!" Each time I say it, my throat goes raw, anguish oozing out. "You can't do this. I won't let you."

"Yeah, yeah, yeah, screamer. You will," he growls. "Thing is, I'm doing you and the rich chucklefuck you're marrying a big favor. Don't think he'd fancy my boys hanging around everywhere he goes. Slipping through his big bay windows, denting his car, giving him one fuck a bodyguard bill that won't even do a lick of good when we decide we're done playing cat and mouse. It's easier for everybody if he just shuts his mouth like a nice little boy and pays me up front. Shit, I'll do you another favor, and treat this like a real transaction. Maybe that'll help with that stick-up-the-ass ego you've always had. I'll sell you this dusty Roman shit for five million. I'll hand it off wrapped up with a pink little bow, and you can throw it off the nearest ferry or whatever the fuck, so you can pretend you were never a common fucking thief, nobody else ever gets to have this kinda fun with you again. Fair?"

You know it isn't, monster. I want to say it, scream it in his face, but it won't help.

I know what he wants.

Has bartering with a hungry lion ever saved anyone backed into its cage? There's just as much chance reasoning, pleading, asking this asshole for a mercy that's never been in his makeup.

"Yeah, shit, I didn't think so," he says after I don't answer. "Tell you what, I'll send an invoice through Adele. Price non-negotiable."

Non-negotiable. It's that phrase, more than any other, that cuts through the last shred of sanity in my brain. I sink to my knees, phone pressed against my ear like a scalding iron, wishing I didn't have to listen to another vicious second of this.

"It's a hard fucking bargain, so I'll leave you to your tears. You're a smart girl, Skye. Always were. I know you'll come around. You're the brainy sorta coward, and they're the kind who survive. Not like your mother. She thought she was smart, but she got real damn dumb in the end. So, little missy, you do whatever you need to convince your new squeeze it's well worth his money to pay me every red cent.

Lie, threaten, drug him, and pull the money out yourself. I don't give a fuck. I just want to get paid."

My phone chirps. The screen is flashing. It's finally over.

No, it's barely begun.

Before I dig into this mess, there's one thing that's at the top of the list. Harry knows far too much, but I still don't know what, and that's where I need to start.

I'm finding Vinnie. He has to know what's at stake, how much he's hurt us. And after I finish pumping him for information, I don't know if I'll ever be able to look him in the eye again.

* * *

HE'S SITTING on a bench at the edge of the university, blissfully ignorant of my disaster. It's the usual he's stuffing into his mouth: a mocha and a jumbo cinnamon apple muffin. I think I try a million times to reason with myself, to promise I won't be too harsh, but damn it...he's signed our *death warrant.*

"You're early, sis. What's happening? Are we getting dinner tonight before we – " His smile fades when he sees me blocking his evening light, my long shadow cast over him. "Hey, what's the matter?"

"You. You talked to Uncle Harry, Vincent, and you didn't tell me."

His eyes drop. "He's family. He called when we were coming home, on the flight, weeks ago. I couldn't ignore him. He kept on dialing. What else could I do? He didn't – "

"Shut up for a second. Just tell me what he said. No excuses, please. What the hell did he ask you, Vinnie?"

"Just the usual. Sort of. He wanted to know how we're doing, how school's going for me, if I'm up on my meds and if you're taking care of me." Lies. And not even innocent lies.

My brother's eyes are sad behind his glasses, grey and heavy as the new wave of Pacific rain brewing in the distance. "Okay. So, please don't kill me, sis, but maybe it was a little more serious than I said."

He doesn't realize he's handling dynamite until my hand explodes toward his. No more games. I yank the mocha out of his hand and whip it at the sidewalk, then grab his shirt, and yank him up, until we're face to face.

"This is serious, *so* serious, Vinnie, you don't even know. Stop bullshitting!" Fear flickers in his eyes. "I need you to tell me everything, no matter how bad."

I catch my own reflection in his glasses, tiny and seething. My heart sinks.

What are you doing? Pain deepens the longer I look at him. He's just a kid.

As stupid, disobedient, and reckless as he's been, he's still my little brother. I'll always love him.

I can't let Harry turn me into this. I let go, trying not to cry, and slowly turn away, rubbing at my eyes.

Vinnie reaches out, trying to comfort me, but I push him away. "Just...no. Give me a minute."

It's much less. My heart beats through stomach-knotting nausea. But I manage to turn without losing my lunch all over the pavement, and look him calmly in the eye.

"You're an idiot, and so am I. Come here." We hug. I squeeze him, so hard I think it hurts us both, but mostly me.

I'd almost forgotten who's really to blame in this screwed up situation. It isn't Vinnie, it's the asshole putting him up to this, pulling the innocent mistakes out of him, threatening our way of life, old and new.

"Vinnie, whatever he did, I forgive you. This anger, it isn't me. I'm trying like hell to let go. But I just...I need to know. You can tell me what happened, all right? I'm worried for us."

The tears in his eyes gut what's left of me. Jesus, no, I promise I won't cry a second time.

Vinnie looks through his fogged up glasses, nodding, and slowly spills the black guilt he's been holding in. "You remember the stuff you sent back from Turkey? Well...the box came. It was never lost. Signed for it with FedEx myself. I opened it and saw...stuff worth a lot of money. Money that should've been for both of us, I know. I stole it, sis, and I'm sorry. Pawned it for an X-box and a couple games. James and Mike were there, too. They told me I was getting ripped off. I should've listened to them. But I went and did it anyway and...and I'm so fucking sorry, again."

He grabs me and doesn't let go. I haven't seen him like this since mom's funeral. He's a child again, lost and working through the crap hand he's been dealt in life, the same hand I've worked my tail off to reshuffle.

"Vinnie, stop. Harry told me everything. You really screwed up bad, but it's not the end of the world."

If only he knew how close we came. But honestly, he never will, and that's how I want it.

I'm not telling him about the work I did with Adele, the desperate penny pinching, the full-on thieving I planned with those artifacts and Harry, though he's probably worked that part out.

I can't keep letting our uncle's evil consume us.

Not Vinnie.

Not Cade.

Not me.

My arms grip him tighter, holding on. I rock him until his sadness and shame melts away, and he's able to look at me again through raw, red eyes without trembling. "I'm sorry," he whimpers again. I think it's the tenth time.

"Enough apologies. I'm the idiot who stole the stuff for him," I say, trying to take away as much guilt as I can.

"And I'm the dummy who told him everything, sis. He got to me. Made it seem like he cares...and I guess he doesn't. I don't know. Sometimes, I wonder if he really does, deep down."

"No. Vinnie, he's a monster. A conniving one. I know you don't see it quite like I do – I don't want you to – but you have to believe me. Please. Whatever happens next, just promise me you won't talk to him again."

"I won't, sis. This time, I mean it. If he's got you this upset, this worried, he's no good. Just wish I'd gotten it through my head sooner." We sit down on the bench, watching a few cars go by with students laughing through the open windows. Then he turns, a new look in his eyes that's worse than the brazing sadness. "Will we be okay, Skye? Should I worry?"

We should fear for our very lives. But there's no good telling him that.

Panic won't help, and if Vinnie freaks out and does his own thing again, this only gets worse.

"We'll be fine, Vinnie, but I need one more promise." I reach for his hand, holding onto my words until our eyes are locked. "Listen to me, please. Everything I say over the next few weeks. No crazy questions, no doubts, no disrespect. Whatever I'm telling you to do, it's for your good. It's for mine, and for Cade's. You hear?"

He hesitates. "Yeah. I promise, sis. Loud and clear."

"This will all be over soon. One way or another, I'll deal with it, Vinnie. That's my promise."

It's another hour before we make our way home. I stay up late, long after Vinnie retires to his room, checking the locks on the doors and windows when the sparse night staff aren't watching.

It's not like this place is defenseless. There's always someone around, and a world class security system with cameras and built-in tamper alarms. But I don't think Cade's place has ever faced a threat like this.

Harry probably won't dispatch his goons until I've seen the hellish invoice, but it doesn't matter. I'm not taking chances.

* * *

CADE'S TRIP to Alaska rips a hole through my life. It's not just Harry's ultimatum creating the chasm in his absence.

There's a weird number sending texts. I don't understand a word of them.

It's like someone ran text through an online translator, and spat out choppy English.

I read the words that keep coming over and over again, always some variation of the same thing.

Obsess...spychip...poker...Jonas.

The last word is perfectly clear, though I wish it weren't. Like we don't have enough problems.

I reply every time, always a little angrier, asking who the hell it is and what they want.

There's no response. I also can't do anything while Cade is out in the wilds, where his cell isn't working. He doesn't respond to the sugary texts and emails I send trying to get his attention.

Paranoia is a hell of a drug. It's deep in my veins and the hits keep coming, making me afraid to leave the house for the next week.

One night, Vinnie stays out late with his friends, not answering his phone. I ball him out when he drags himself home at two a.m. He's more understanding than I expect, apologetic, even.

I'm the train wreck.

A message shows up roughly a day before Cade is due

home. I see the blank envelope with Adele's handwriting in the mail basket by his office, where the housekeepers leave my things.

I wonder if my heart will explode before I'm able to slide the opener through the seal.

Harry wasn't kidding when he said invoice. It looks like a bill from any old place, a hospital or ratty auto-shop, only the line named SERVICE isn't more specific.

The seven digits next to it put me on the brink of passing out.

Five million dollars. *He's fucking serious.*

My vision goes red. Lungs heaving, throat pulsing, hands clammy like a fever, I fall against the wall, trying not to pass out.

Yep, it's as big a disaster as I expected. It's also *here.*

"I'm sorry," I whisper to Cade, as much as to myself. "So, so, so, so, so fucking sorry..."

There's an imaginary hole opening under me. I'm falling, just a little at a time, onto my knees.

I don't know how long I'm on the floor, knees pulled up to my chest, eyes glazed over.

You know those shock moments when a late night phone call comes in, and tells you someone dear has passed away unexpectedly? The world shifts on its axis, the poison seeps in, and life will never, ever be the same, even if the full atomic loss hasn't yet exploded.

I lived it the night I found out mom threw herself off the bridge, when I rushed to the morgue to identify her body.

That feeling is with me again tonight. It's like a heavy sickness I can't shake no matter how long I'm crumpled in the corner, probably until near dawn. It takes a security guard making his rounds through the library on morning watch to break my stupor.

"Miss? You all right? Hey!" his flashlight hits my eyes like a second sun, hand over his face.

He's reaching for his phone, probably to get a paramedic, when I'm finally able to move. "I'm okay. Sorry. I must've fallen asleep."

I get up and turn without another word, leaving him to stare after me. The man doesn't follow.

He knows better.

There's an escape. One, and no other. And it's sure to be as hopeless, as final, and as soul killing as mom destroying herself.

This is the end. It can't be anything less if I want to make sure Cade and Vinnie have a new beginning.

X: LET IT BURN (CADE)

"*Y*ou're a genius," I tell Cal, smacking him on the shoulder. He's just told me his plans for the firm's next big marketing push. "Fuck me, we're going to be rich. Richer, I mean. I can see us clawing back what we spent on the security upgrades in a month. Then it's pure profit."

It's smart. Deceptively simple. It would've sounded good even if it weren't accompanied by the most savory elk sausages in the world hissing their aroma into the night, speared on our sticks over the fire.

"You're welcome. We spent a fortune making things right after those damn hacks. I'm just glad it's smooth sailing from here." He looks at me, bright blue eyes glowing, pushing the dark hair up over his forehead. He's been growing it out since the wedding, giving him that sort of wizened look men get when they settle into family life. "You're a huge asshole, by the way."

"Me?" I thumb my chest, puzzled as hell.

"Yeah, bro. You think we want to talk business all night instead of this girl you're screwing?" Spence pushes his sausage deeper into the fire, completely charring it. I'll never understand how he savors the black, bitter end like it's an ice cream sandwich on a California day, but to each their own. "More than screwing, I should say. Why the fuck didn't you say it was serious?"

Because up until Iceland, it wasn't. I don't have the heart to admit I played the same dumb game Cal did with Maddie, before they got real.

Wait. Played? My brain is stuck on past-tense, too. Another reminder I'm more serious than I care to admit about marrying this girl next week. That's scary.

"I wasn't sure how to break the news, guys. Hell, I'm still trying."

"Dude, you're over-thinking," Cal says, plinking his canteen on the rock in front of us, and filling it half full of scotch. "Come on, Cade. Admit it. You've fallen head over heels if you're this torn up talking about her."

"Your mom's heels," I growl, smiling like a fool. Spence chortles over my shoulder. Whenever we're away from the office, we regress back to the seventeen year old shitheads we used to be at Maynard. "You want to know the truth? Fine. I'm getting married in about a week."

"That's –" Cal chokes on his scotch, spitting a mouthful on the ground.

"Holy shit!" Spence's jaw drops. "You glorious bastard, now I'm *really* pissed. Making me the odd man out on all our future outings while you two prattle on about your wives and kids? Fuck you, Turnbladt."

I'm laughing. Cal tackles me first, but Spence isn't far behind. He crashes on top of us both.

It's ridiculous. I just dropped the biggest news of my life, and here we are rolling on Alaskan soil like a trio of five year olds drunk on pixie sticks.

These guys are complete pricks sometimes, and even harder to work with, but goddamn, do I love them.

The feeling must be mutual. They don't ease up until I kick them off, wearing a face full of rich dirt. We're fleshy targets for whatever bears are waiting out there in the night, stomachs growling each time they sniff our camp. Good thing the ruckus we're making would frighten away Lucifer.

"Guys, come on, let me breathe," I say, coming up for air.

Cal whacks me across the face again, playfully, and nods at Spence. They pin my wrists to the ground. "No. Not unless you tell us we get a chance to meet the unlucky lady before the rehearsal dinner. Maddie also needs another girl she can squawk about chick-shit with. She's got baby fever and it's only getting worse after her work ends in China, and she's back here full time..."

"My heart's bleeding for you, bro," Spence says. "Knocking up your wife. What torture."

"Like you'd know anything about pussy that actually counts." Cal glares. "Let's not get distracted. We're having words with Cade, and I'm far from done."

"Nah, I think you are, Calvin." Spence lets go and dive bombs Cal in the chest.

I'm up on my feet, sensing an escape, still laughing my ass off. It's their turn to tear into each other like teenagers again.

Five minutes later, we're licking our very adult wounds, sitting on the logs, breaking into the stuff for s'mores. Soon, the night smells sticky sweet, roasting marshmallows speared on sticks releasing their perfume. I reach into the bag behind me and pull out the small box wrapped in gold, then fling it onto Cal's lap.

"Here you go, birthday boy. It's not the keys to a new toy, so don't get too excited."

Spence and I unpack our chocolate and graham crackers

while he digs through wrapping paper. I bound it extra tight, and it's the kind that doesn't tear easy, asshole friend that I am.

Cal eyeballs both of us with a sideways glare. He's used to it by now. The gifts we give are either heartwreckers or stupid gags. There's no point in anything else when we're three rich guys in our prime, each of us able to afford whatever material fun our hearts desire.

"What the hell is this?" he growls, opening the box, pulling out the broken piece of wood inside. "Is it...no fucking way!"

"Way. That's a piece of the fishing lure we lost years ago, that time we took your old man's boat out with your brother, John. We were all like fifteen. I've been holding onto it for years."

"What the hell? John was pissed. Told me we'd lost it when Spence caught that thing on the buoy, and ripped the line." His older brother was our chaperone. That was before the deadly day in Afghanistan that cost him his life, another tragedy turning my buddy's life upside-down.

"He was totally busting your balls," Spence says, smiling in the corner. "You're so gullible, Randolph. We laughed about it later with him, when he told us your parents grounded you over it. Cost you the date with what's her face – the slutty girl Cade wound up boning."

"You mean the one I almost broke your nose over?" We're all cringing for different reasons.

Cal because he pretended to be the older, wiser one who stopped us from fighting over the same pussy he wanted to get his young dick wet in. Spence because he missed out. Me, because I actually had her. Just thinking about that skank today makes me realize how stupid, blind, and lost I was once upon a time.

None of my conquests were Skye.

They wore their designer lipstick like all the rich girls who went to Maynard. They were trial runs for the women who came later; faceless, greedy bitches I took to bed and never called twice. I fucked through a small harem with the same excitement as hitting the gym after awhile because I could, and because my body needed sex to function.

But I never felt the spark I did with her, Ms. Grey Eyed Cotton Candy. My smiling, sexy rainbow spitfire waiting back home.

How was I ever so stupid? Then I look at the two men who knew me in those days, and I remember, because they were the same.

"Yeah, well, you lost your v-card to her and freaked over having the clap a week later," Spence says, driving in the screws. "Can't say I missed much."

"Fuck you, it was a bladder infection. Bad timing." I'm completely serious.

The last thing a clueless boy needs is his innards lighting up a couple days after he's had his first time – and being dumb enough to think he could still get rusty after wrapping it up. "Anyway, this one's from both of us, Cal. Might not have remembered I still had it if this asshole hadn't brought it up. This seemed like the perfect occasion." I nod Spence's way.

"Man tears, assholes. Thanks a lot." Cal only exaggerates a little. He stands, walks over, and forces us to sit close with one arm slung over each of us. "I'm serious. If John is anywhere, he's looking down from those northern lights, laughing at what we've become. Married men, muckity-mucks richer than our parents, idiots or geniuses who are about to start families...he never got the chance. But some-where, I know he's happy."

I'm the first to grab the scotch off the flat boulder next to us, but Spence was reaching, too. We each take a swig and do our own little toast to Cal's fallen brother.

He was older, never as close as the three of us, but I think of him a lot. Doesn't tear me up like Cal, his own flesh and blood. Still hits me between the ribs a different way.

John Randolph's death is a reminder – the messiest kind.

Life is brutal. Unfair. Twisted.

It'll gnaw you up and spit you out if you give it half a chance, if you don't come ready for every day alive. Now, thanks to Skittle, I know it'll do it anyway without something worth holding onto, worth finding and loving so hard it lights your blood on fire.

I've found it in her.

Cal's not the only one a little choked up, taking his turn at the bottle, thumbing the old lure in his hand. On his other side, Spence stares off into the wild starry night. Green and gold and blue break through the shifting sky above us. It's *aurora borealis* in all her majesty.

I don't know what's up with him. Maybe I've got a better idea what's running through Cal's brain, but I'll never experience it like he does.

I just know me. I know myself too well. I know what's coming the second I step off my jet in Seattle again, and head home to the paradise I've found in her arms.

I can't fuck around.

This girl who's got my diamond and a big sappy piece of my heart deserves the stone cold truth. She deserves better than a fake ass wedding and a bunch of legalese asking her to fake it.

She needs real, and I need a wife.

More than a one night bride I hired to fix family trouble.

God willing, when I get down on one knee and pop the question like a man who's always been smitten from day fucking one, she'll say *yes*.

* * *

WE'VE BARELY TEXTED since I got on the plane. I asked her if everything was all right, and she told me not to worry. *A few things to talk about when you get back,* she said.

No details. No explanation. Nothing.

Sure, it makes me worry a little, but I'm on the plane, anxious and fully committed to doing what I planned.

Nate is parked on the curb like clockwork, a smile on his face and a spring in his step. "Welcome home, sir," he says, opening the door.

I slide in and tell him to take me to Skye. No, I don't care if she's home, at the school, or dog watching in the fucking park.

We need to talk now. I need to get this out of my system. Just like I need to pull that ring off her, without shoving it back on her finger unless she's decided it belongs there.

No more denial. I want to wife Skye Coyle for real.

Nate knows the score. He ferries me across Seattle and parks on one of the bustling campus streets. I head for her building, a hopeful beat in my heart and a spring in my step.

Remember what you practiced on the plane, asshole. This is it. No do-overs.

I'm grateful there's nobody else around in the archeology department when I find her behind the glass door. She's got her back to me, gloves on, brushing off a palm-sized bust underneath a bright white lamp.

She gasps when I come up behind her, brace my arms around her waist, pulling her into me. Lips on her ear, I start the words I'm hellbent on getting perfect.

"I'm here. Couldn't wait for you to get home, Skittle." She twists in my grasp, laying a reflexive hand on my arm. "Not yet. Don't turn around. Stay right there. Just give me your hand. There's something important I need."

I can't figure out why she's so tense. There's no fight in her, but there's an electric resistance. I grab her palm, lay it across mine, and reach for the ring with my free hand. It comes off easy. For a second, I stand there like an idiot, relishing her heat, asking for its courage before the most important thirty seconds of my life.

I don't expect the crying before I'm even on my knee, whispering the words. "Turn around, beautiful."

Skye's breath catches in her lungs, harsh and sweet. I practically feel the current running through her.

I definitely don't expect the eyes. Rather than the happy smiling sheen I expect over her soft greys, they're ghostly, sad, poisoned. If I were a lesser man, it'd stop me in my tracks.

Doesn't make any sense. If she knows what's coming, then why the hell does she look so upset?

Doesn't she want this as bad as I do? *Christ.*

There's only one way to find out.

"We started as a lie," I say, reaching for her hand, grasping it like gold in mine. "Then crazy happened. These months we've had together, Skittle, they've been the best time of my life. I'd be a fool to walk away, pretend it didn't happen, try to find it anywhere else, or with anybody, but the only woman I'll ever need is standing right in front of me."

Shit, shit. Her lips are trembling now. She's either about to explode, showering joy, or lay into me like the world's biggest jackass for doing this.

Grandpa had a saying, an old Icelandic one: *Faint heart never won fair lady.*

Mine is beating now. Pounding every manly, take-no-prisoners molecule of me numb, turning my blood to venom, and I'm still *not* backing down.

"There it is. The reason I'm here today, on my knees, asking you for...shit, is any of this making sense? Maybe it isn't clear." I take a deep breath, close my eyes, and squeeze until I feel her pulse. "I love you, woman. Loved you some kind of crazy even before the day we hiked up that mountain, overlooking the castle we're supposed to save, and I knew it was about more. You deserve better than a fake engagement and a rushed wedding. *We* deserve better, Skye. Do me the greatest honor of my life: marry me."

Her tremors are worse. The storm in her eyes breaks, and the tears come, harsher than any happy ones ever should be. I'm so fucking stunned I can't say anything, squeezing her hand off, waiting for her to open those beautiful lips, and give me a sentence.

More than words, I mean, sentence in every sense of the word. *Sweet, maddening judgment.*

"Cade, I want to...I want to so bad...you don't even know." Her voice goes ragged. My eyes are double moons, big and pleading, waiting for the rest.

Fuck, please. Please, no buts.

She's sobbing, choking on a grief I don't understand, like she's watching someone she loves bleed out in front of her. I grab her other hand, pressing the ring into her palm, catching her before she falls. We stand like that, me halfway up, face-to-face and mortally wounded.

I have to pull it out of her. "What's wrong, Skittle? Tell me the truth. What's keeping you from saying yes?"

"I can't do this, Cade. We can't. It's a terrible idea." It comes out fast, a quick moving dagger lancing my heart. "I'm sorry. If this were different, if it wasn't so complicated, then *of course* I'd say – no. No. Don't make me do this. Please, Cade. I'm so, so fucking sorry."

Tears spill down her face, melting on the beat up lab floor beneath us. Once I'm sure she's able to stand, I raise myself up, and take her with me, jerking her into my arms. She's fighting and whimpering and I don't care.

Nothing about this makes any fucking sense.

"This isn't you. What's the real reason? Is it the man Vinnie mentioned? The asshole friend who had you in debt? Is that what's stopping you from being happy?"

Whoever he is, I want him dead. There's a raw, vicious hatred in my blood, the kind that snakes through my guts in such a violent rush it makes me sick. I catch myself on her wild, frantic eyes. They tell the truth, even if her sweet tongue can't.

"Cade –"

"No, Skittle. No. I need answers, not excuses. I ripped my heart out and practically threw it at you. You want this, I can see it in your eyes, and *nothing* should come between us. What's stealing my yes? What's between us? What's your problem? Because if it's him, if he's got something hanging over you, it's my fucking problem, too. I don't care what it takes to make it go away. Talk to me!"

"Cade..." She sniffs harder, blotting at her eyes with her fingertips, looking away. "Cade, please..."

The blackness drowning her pupils says it all. *Don't make this harder.*

I won't listen. I don't know what *this* is, and I sure as hell won't let it ruin the future we're supposed to have, the one begging to come out in her strained, confused gaze.

"You don't have to be afraid as long as I'm here. For you, for your brother, for us, I'll do whatever it takes, Skittle. If you want me to get down on my knees again right now and write it in blood, I fucking will, and –"

"Cade!" Her shrillness is the only reason I stop. Then I take a long, hard look at the desperate frustration burning away in her, the pain written on every pinched line of her face. "Just shut up for a second. Listen. We can't do this. There are a million reasons why, but what it really comes down to is simple. What's happening is all on me, and no, I'm not interested in talking details. So, please. *Please.* Stop making me your problem. I don't need you, and neither does Vinnie. We'll handle it like we always have. I'll pay back the money and move on. I don't want your damn job or your money, Cade. It's over. I'm sorry."

Whatever I expected, it wasn't this.

This shit is apocalyptic.

She's so cold, despite the tears. It's like she's been working up to this for a long time. My battered ego snaps. Skye just rattled off everything she's trying to shut out, but the biggest part of all is missing.

"And what about love, Skittle? You want to stand here and tell me you don't need that, too?"

I give her an entire minute. She doesn't answer. I wait in the silence, expecting her to crack, to tell me everything that's corroding her heart so we can fix it, work this out together, just like we're meant to.

But I'm left holding ice when she turns around, without so much as a second look, and stares into that fancy long lab mirror behind her, avoiding my eyes.

I'm willing to take plenty of punishment, but I'm not a stupid man, or a patient one.

Today, all the demands, hopes, and prayers in the world won't put a dent in the glacial fucking wall she's built, and turned into concrete.

"Just go," she whispers, voice as low and weak as rustling leaves. "Leave me. You'll hear from me soon to discuss my stuff in your place, and Vinnie...just leave him to me. We'll be out of your life soon."

No more. I can't take it. The thought of talking those details right now when she's ripped herself away from me, when I thought I'd caress that cotton candy hair and spend the rest of my life taming those lips...fuck.

I turn, storming down the hall. I don't stop when I nearly

crash into the bottle-eyed professor coming down the hall, or when my ears absorb the smothered sobs coming from the lab room. I don't even look back when I hear the crash on the ground, and Skittle swearing, slapping the ground with her palm as she reaches to salvage whatever treasure our private hell just destroyed.

I can't believe she doesn't get it.

Her ignorance defeats me.

Her denial shreds my soul.

Her lies – I mean whatever the fuck she had to tell herself to seal truth deep inside her – is cold blooded murder.

Why is the heaviest load of all. It's crushing me from the inside out when I get to the car and slam the door shut, without saying a word to Nate.

And grappling with it longer won't help because it doesn't do anything to change the new bitch of a reality we've just stepped into, sick to its very core.

If something else doused our paradise in kerosene, then Skye just threw the match. That's what I can't get over.

I'm the helpless bastard watching Eden burn.

We could have faced anything together.

Secrets were the only flaw in our armor, and she just chose them over me.

My fingernails dig into the leather armrest, leaving permanent marks, and I flick the switch for the intercom, ordering Nate to drive us to my favorite watering hole. "Let it burn," I say to myself softly, spoiling for a bar fight and a hot joint. Two damning, childish things I haven't had since high school, when I used to sneak into the dark places meant for Seattle's roughnecks, and do the typical stuff that comes natural for edgy kids.

My edge today is so harsh it could cut the world in half.

There's no fixing this, and no escape from the humiliation, the agony, the hell to come.

I might as well get a jump start fucking up my head, before making any rash decisions. It's guaranteed to be a simmering chaos over the next week, while I try to figure out how I live without Skye Coyle, or how to drag her back to me kicking and screaming.

"*Y*ou're asking for a lot of firepower, little mama. You sure you know how to handle one of these?" The tall man in the leather cut twirls the handgun around his finger, before he slams it into his palm, fingers clutching the handle. "Relax, honey. It's not loaded. Obviously."

"I've got your money, just like I promised inside." I nod toward the bar. It's a living irony, the same dive where I begged Harry for a reprieve from my payments just months ago, only blocks from the ratty little apartment we used to call home.

It was the only place where I knew I'd have a chance to find my salvation. The man inside wearing the Grizzlies MC cut didn't disappoint. STRYKER, his name badge says, and he looks at me through hooded dark eyes, wondering if I'm trying to stiff him.

Sighing, I reach into my purse, scrounging for the wad of money I withdrew from the ATM. "Take it. Count it. You'll see it's all there, and then some. I don't care about making change. I need this gun today. *Please.*"

He stares at me a second longer, and then his rough lips curl into a smile. "Throw it in the saddlebag. You've made it worth my while, especially with Prez cracking down on us dealing guns like we used to. Good thing I'm a long way from Redding. Follow me out back."

He climbs off his bike, leaving me to drop his money. I tuck my jacket tighter, cold and nervous, heading behind the dirty dive into an enclosed part I've never seen before. When he pushes the cold gun into my hand, I freeze, already hating how my nerves aren't cut out for this crap.

Too bad. Need to learn fast if you want to survive, I tell myself, staring at the weapon while he comes up behind me, and unlatches the gate in front of me. It creaks open, revealing what looks like a mess of bullet riddled targets. It's a makeshift range, totally in violation of all kinds of city codes.

"I don't understand. I thought we were done here?" I whisper.

Stryker digs into his pocket, draws out the blocky lump inside, and pushes the small cardboard box into my hand. It's surprisingly heavy. "I'm giving you an extra box free. Wanna see you take a few practice hits, darlin'. If you're as bad a gunslinger as I think, you'll want to buy a few more off me."

He's an asshole, but also a good salesman. I step into the little booth, pushing the earmuffs over my head. They're freezing cold, a stark contrast to the hot, seething blood my heart pours in my temples.

Relax. You've done this before.

It's been four years since I fired a gun. I did it then because mom insisted. She made me learn in case anyone ever broke into our crappy place while she was out, and I was alone with Vinnie. She told me I had to know how to use the firearm stashed next to her bed.

I thought it was cool at the time. It always is when life is a manageable hell and all the threats are abstract.

Lifting the weapon in front of me, I bite my lip, line my shot as best I can, and fire.

It goes off like a rocket.

It's a miracle my shoulder isn't broken. He wasn't kidding about the recoil, the firepower, the *good as dead* bite in this beastly little toy.

I almost forget to check how I did, but even through the earmuffs, I hear him whistle. "My, my fucking *my*, Sniper Girl. Let's see that shit again!"

I nearly hit the middle, dead center. But not quite. I pull the trigger several more times, adjusting better to the kick after each shot, emptying the gun until it clicks in my hand.

The biker's heavy hand falls on my shoulder. I whirl around, anger in my eyes.

His touch is too much like Cade's. But the man I gutted and loved would never look so amused with such a dirty, dark smile.

This is a game to him. For me, it's way too real, risking the ultimate sacrifice to save us from that asshole.

"Forget the fees, princess. Your ammo's on the house. Haven't seen a chick shoot like that in forever. You single?"

"Married," I say in a hurry, holding out my ring finger. What's one more lie on top of infinity?

I'm still wearing it. Even though it rips a new piece of my heart out every day since I told him we were over, I can't stop, I can't take it off, and he hasn't asked to have it back.

Cade hasn't said anything.

"I need to get going," I say. "If you've got those bullets –"

"Yeah, yeah, Sniper Queen," he growls, leading me back to the alley where he's parked his bike. "Shame about the ring. Chicks who know a thing or two about kicking ass are hard to come by in these parts, and back home, too."

* * *

IT'S EVENING. I'm back in the hotel room burning through the last of my money, clutching the phone, thinking through everything I need to do.

I cleaned out my account this morning, stuffing several hundred dollars in an envelope addressed to Vinnie, sent to Cade's house. Not that they need it.

Despite the huge bitch I've been, I know he won't toss my little brother into the cold.

But every bit helps, especially if I don't survive what's coming. And if I do...

No. I don't let myself think about the future, or the insane consequences.

I'm looking at a disaster no matter what. If Harry doesn't off me the second he realizes I'm not really there to do business, it's not like everything I've done to protect us goes away.

I can't just go running to Cade after destroying his heart.

If only he'd known the damage on my end was worse. It's hard to breathe every time I let myself remember his stern blue eyes, big and pleading, staring up at me while he gripped my hand and made that killing confession.

Love? Jesus Christ.

That's a word I wasn't sure I'd ever be ready for outside the sisterly affection left for Vinnie.

Not after the last couple years, living the unthinkable, and then agreeing to the best deal I ever made on a whim with a man I totally wasn't supposed to feel anything for.

Too bad sex changes that.

Too bad it wasn't even the sex that started it.

Too bad I've lived with butterflies since the first night we met, when he brought me to his bed, and began risking his life every screwed up second he decided to mesh his existence into mine. And without even knowing it.

It's not that I wasn't ready for love, or the heavier marriage we were supposed to treat like a cold hearted joke. On the contrary, I was.

I still am.

It's a fucking atrocity that the man I have to kill won't let me have it.

I couldn't let Cade put himself in danger for me. Couldn't even let him realize how real, how deep, how awful the danger we're in really is.

I have to save him myself, alone, and the first step is waiting for me just a quick call away.

Forget waiting for the tears to pass. They run down my cheeks anyway when I dial the number, waiting for the sharp, impatient voice on the other end of the line.

"Hello, Adele? It's Skye. I'll keep this brief. You need to get me in touch with Harry. I've got a payment I think he'll be very pleased with, and I'd love to hand it over in person..."

* * *

WHEN I WAKE up the next day, I wonder if I'm living the last day of my life.

Worst part is, there's no manual for how a person should approach the bitter end. I contemplate visiting my favorite coffee shop, a walk through the Seattle Art Museum, where I used to go for a cheap distraction, but none of it seems right.

There's only two places where I really belong, where I can get out the words I've sat on, before they blow everything.

I haven't seen the bridge for months. Last time I took the ferry to Bremerton, I was angry, and I cursed her out. The bums several paces away must've thought I was one of them.

Just another junkie with a lot of venom aimed at the world, too messed in the head to articulate it any healthy way.

Today, I don't have the energy left to care what anybody thinks.

I'm leaning on the pillar, looking across the Sound, back out to sea. It's a rainy, hazy day. The ships are dark silhouettes moving near the ports, occasionally blasting their horns whenever they pass near the terminals.

"I still think you're a huge, selfish ass for leaving us. But would it be any different if you hadn't, mom? Knowing what he did to you, to us, it wouldn't have changed anything. Just would've made me more determined."

I lower my head, staring into the drifting waters. Something moves below the surface, probably a large fish. Is this the spot where she ended it?

Not that it matters. Wherever she is, she can't hear my fretting, and she certainly doesn't care.

"This is stupid," I whisper to myself. Then I turn and start heading back to the terminal, hoping I'm able to get there to catch the next ride back.

Whatever I wanted to find here, it isn't peace. Hanging around the spot where she died just makes me more anxious. If I'm approaching the end of the road, then I'm better off spending it with someone alive who still matters.

I told myself I wouldn't, but I need to see Vinnie.

* * *

My LITTLE BROTHER meets me at the same chowder place where we had our huge argument before. It seems like ancient history now.

I'm enjoying the soup today more than usual. I dug in before he showed up, hoping it'd help settle my stomach, maybe bring some composure before I tell him what a fine young man he's becoming. I've got one chance to get out all the things a dying sister should say.

"You're such a drama queen, Skye." He plops into his seat with a narrow glance, anger shining through his spectacles. "I don't know what the problem is, but he's real torn up over it. Found him in the gym last night with a bottle of rum. Poor guy looked like crap."

"Vinnie, I didn't bring you here to talk about Cade." My spoon stabs at what's left in my bowl, and I wonder if this is just another bad idea.

"No? Then why the disappearing act? I figured this meet up was your way of getting through to him. Finding out what he's like since you left, so you can kiss and make up. Or maybe you wanted to apologize for feeding me such a weak story, but hey..."

I'm cringing. Inside and out.

I knew Vinnie wouldn't buy the conference excuse for long. It's not like I expected Cade to play along, really, but I wish he hadn't made it obvious I'm still in town, ruining him from afar, when I'm trying like hell to save lives.

"I just wanted to see you again. Look, things are complicated right now, and it's got nothing to do with –"

"Spare me," he growls, ignoring the hand I've extended across the table. "You know, I thought Cade was just a rich guy and you were gold digging. I was okay with that until just recently. But he really loves you, Skye. He wouldn't be moping around the house, putting on a brave face for me, if he didn't. I asked him point-blank what was going on, and he finally admitted you two have issues. He swore up and down he'd get them figured out."

"Well, it's not your problem. Let's just enjoy our time together, okay?"

Please. He can't see it, but he doesn't have a clue, the damage he's doing. I don't need to spend the last few hours before the big showdown reminded how badly I've hurt him. Or is this the karma I'm owed for taking matters into my own hands?

I don't know. Second guesses might be fatal at this point.

"Sure, sure. I'll eat the soup and smile like a good kid." Vinnie does exactly that, an exaggerated grin plastered on his face, tapping his fingers on the table while he waits for his order. "Never talk about anything that matters, right? Shit, you're just like mom, right before she –"

He freezes before the words are out.

Bullet, meet my chest.

"That was a low blow. Sorry, sis, I didn't mean –"

I'm having the strangest sense of déjà vu. Before he's done apologizing, I sweep my hands through the air, shaking my head. "Let it go. You're right."

He looks up, surprise twinkling behind his frames. "Wait...what?"

"You're right about me. I've done nothing except crap all over the people who don't deserve it lately. You, Cade, Professor Olivers." I wince on the last name more than I should. With everything else happening, I haven't had time to feel bad about skipping out on my TA duties until now. "I'm not a good person, Vinnie. I try, but I make huge mistakes. Don't be like me when you're older."

He shakes his head, ignoring the delicious smell piping off the steaming bowl a waiter slides in front of him. "Skye, what *are* you saying?"

"Nothing important. Like always. Because you nailed it, and that's not my style when things get crazy, or rough. They're kind of both right now. Someday, you'll understand. Until then, because I don't say it often enough, I just need you to know this, Vinnie, okay? I love you." I slide my hand back across the table. This time, he lets me take his, and I'm thankful because the next part really hurts. "And yeah, I love

Cade, too. Love him so much it hurts like hell, and I always will...even if there's no chance this ever works."

He smiles softly. "Took you long enough to admit it."

I'm puzzled. At first, I think he's just being a brat, but then I see the warmth in his face, the encouragement. His hold on my hand tightens.

No, it doesn't change anything, but damn it, it matters.

"Always wondered about you two because I never heard the L-word much. Glad you're coming around, sis. Next time cut the impossible crap. You guys *will* work this out. You're too good together not to. You've found your one and only, dumb as it sounds."

Now, I'm the one smiling like a fool.

He's a sweet kid. I'm grateful Cade has his back, whatever happens. He'll keep my brother safe, at least until they figure out what to do.

I'd owe him my life for that, if I didn't have to risk it facing down a demon.

"You're right, Vinnie. I don't know about the future, but I know what's true. We were made for each other. Always and only inevitable."

We eat the rest of our soup in peace. Before he goes, I reach into my purse, and hand him an envelope. The note I wrote Cade this morning is sealed inside. I'm careful to tap the edge with my thumb, where I've written Vinnie's only instructions in huge bold letters.

DO NOT OPEN. CADE ONLY.

We share an anxious look. "That's for Cade's eyes only, understood?"

Vinnie gives a look like he gets it for once. I hope to God he does.

I hug him for the last time before he hops on his bike. I'm frowning because it looks like a shiny new set of wheels, probably a gift from Cade. There's a million things I could say about the man I've abandoned giving my little brother a new toy, but this isn't the time.

For once in my miserable life, I hold the criticisms in.

Vinnie rides away, looking back exactly once. Fresh tears sting my eyes, but I'm too determined to let them fall. The time for mourning ended hours ago.

Now, it's time for vengeance. For duty. For everything I always promised I'd die doing – protecting the people I love – even if it takes my very last breath.

I say a quiet prayer for protection, good luck, and whatever else a girl who's never shot another human being in anger needs. It seems so hollow after the last secret wish, just minutes ago.

I prayed my dinner with Vinnie was the last time I'll ever have to lie to someone I love.

XII: BROKEN CIRCLE (CADE)

Hours earlier

I'M DONE with the bottle and beating my knuckles raw on the punching bag in my gym after a couple days. This isn't helping me do anything except blow off steam, and it damned sure won't win her back.

Not that I'm about to come crawling.

I don't know what I'm dealing with.

I talk with the kid when he comes around, feeling him out for info. He doesn't know where she's gone, or why, or what she's truly thinking. I believe him.

I've never let my personal life bleed into my career. I spend the next couple days at the office, plowing through work. With the hacking situation behind us, I've got Cal's marketing campaign in review, going through final approval.

Forecasting the new millions bound to enrich this firm and ourselves has never been so fucking boring.

I'm guzzling coffee, trying not to fall asleep, or else let the potent brew put the chip back on my shoulder when my line to the front desk rings. I'm not expecting any heavy calls, but I'll welcome any distraction from burnout.

"Sir? There's a man from Iceland calling. Says it's urgent."

My fist freezes on my desk, coiled like a rattlesnake. *Jonas.* When it rains, apparently it fucking pours.

"Put him through, Rachel," I tell the secretary. I hear his nasally breath the second the line picks up. "I don't have much time, cousin. Make it fast."

"Wonderful. You'll shut up and listen then, Cade, because I only need a minute. Just wanted to give you a courtesy call to let you know the shit show's over. You're not marrying her. You're pretending, trying to pull the wool over everybody's eyes, and I've got proof. My lawyer has it together real neat, too."

Fuck. There's no end in sight to my problems multiplying. I try not to let rage take full control of my mouth. Whatever he thinks he knows, I need to get it out of him. No easy task when my heart is busy kickboxing my ribs.

"Let's talk about this. Whatever you think you've got, it's wrong. Take a deep breath before you make a huge ass of yourself. Does our family really need this? Us bickering over that goddamned place? Think about it, Jonas. Think hard, before you get yourself into a sticky situation your lawyer won't be able to pull you out of." I'm totally bluffing, using my most diplomatic voice.

"Ah, there's the asshole I was waiting to hear from. Thanks for reminding me why I'll *relish* taking Turnbladt away from you, Cade. Your side was always uptight. Better than us. More money, more entitled, more impatient when the entire world didn't fall down and kiss your barely Icelandic-American asses. You shut up and listen, Yankee Doodle, because I'm not saying this twice. You're not getting what's mine. Ever. The courts have plenty to nullify your inheritance rights. Sorry your fake marriage scheme didn't work."

"You're delusional, Jonas. Stop and listen to what you're saying. Jesus Christ, you think I don't love her? You think I'm not ready to haul Skye over my shoulder any day just to marry her, proudly, and disprove whatever the fuck it is you *think* you've found? You make me goddamned sick!" My fist bangs my chest.

So much for calm, collected, diplomatic. Just talking about Skye fills my veins with vinegar.

I'm losing it on these lies, these wishes. Everything I'm dead serious about doing, and everything I can't because she's nowhere to be found, and the heart I thought I had locked down is wilder and more unpredictable than ever.

"Good. We're both gagging then. Expect to hear from my lawyer tomorrow. I suppose this is goodbye, cousin. I'd say it was a pleasure...but it never was. Dealing with your lying, pompous, prideful ass has been a special hell. Don't bother trying to cut any last minute deals. I'm not negotiating with you or your idiot parents. Oh, and before we go, you'll appreciate the fact I called your mother first. I knew she'd take the news better than you."

"You...what?" My heart stops. Then the world.

It's my worst nightmare realized.

Fuck! Hellfire rushes out of me, and my stomach gurgles, digesting a shock so intense it sends me racing for my seat, before I fall down cold.

"You heard me the first time. Goodbye, Cade. Let your riches be a lovely consolation. Maybe someday, when the amusement park is built, I'll send you a day pass."

The line clicks dead. Static buzzes in my hot ear, glued to the phone, before I rip it away and slam it into its dock.

My face is in my hands. There's no time to call legal, who probably has a better idea than I do how the asshole got the information he's so sure of, or they certainly will shortly.

I need to check on mother. I race down the hall, slapping the elevator button impatiently at the end of it, ignoring Spence when he walks past, and does a double take before I'm rushing down.

Dad isn't answering my frantic calls. Not on the way into the garage, where I've got my car parked after driving myself this morning, or after I'm inside, barking voice commands at the digital assistant to connect his number over and over again.

I wish to holy hell Skittle were here. She'd soothe me before I light my life on fire, before I give into the urge to purchase a one way ticket to Europe to skin that weasel alive.

If anything happened to mom, he's dead. Several times over.

I fight the rush hour traffic to my parents' place, wheel gripped in icy silence, praying I don't see an ambulance once I roll through their wrought iron gates.

* * *

THE ROADS ARE complete bullshit today. I've always been good at navigating the evening rush, being Seattle born and raised, but not today.

It takes forever to make my way across town. I'm halfway to their place in the first rung high end suburbs before the calls start coming in, none from anyone I want to talk to right now.

First Cal, then Spence, both leaving worried messages on my voicemail, asking what the fuck is up.

I'll fill them in later. But I can't ignore my lawyer so easy.

"Yeah?" I growl into my Bluetooth. "What have you heard?"

"Ah, you already know. Well, I suppose that makes this easier..."

Carter's voice is soft, tentative, afraid. And he should be. The one thing that pisses me off more with bad news are the people holding it in.

"Just spit it the fuck out," I tell him. My patience has run out. I wonder if my mind is already in the same gutter where I left my heart after Skittle tore it out. "What does he have? Tell me!"

Sure, I don't have the foul, shoot-the-messenger temper other guys in this industry are known for, but anybody who serves me understands I have zero tolerance for sugar-coating fuckery.

"Big dump came in today from Iceland. Your cousin's lawyer, of course. There's a lot redacted in the files he sent over...but it's damning, I'm sorry to say. I don't know how to say this, Cade, but I think we're hosed. He has an audio recording of you and Ms. Coyle, both admitting your relationship is less than authentic."

"Shit!" My fist hits the wheel. I get a grip again before I narrowly miss a reckless truck flying past. A small part of me is disappointed it doesn't smash through my door, and end my misery now. "How'd he get his paws on that? I don't understand, Carter. Makes no fucking sense."

"We're working that out, and we'll get to the bottom of it soon, I'm sure. I hate to tell you, there's more."

I resist the urge to bang my head against the dashboard. I wait for him to carve another piece of hell and plop it down on my plate.

"He got a copy of the pre-nup somehow," Carter says, almost in a whisper. "He had access to our systems, or an email tied into them. We've been compromised."

Ice. Needles. Chills worse than any I ever felt on a Reykjavik winter courses up my spine, hits my brain, and douses the raging fire in my soul.

I'm not livid anymore. I'm gobsmacked. I'm beaten, and I don't even know how.

"I'll have to go to IT with this." He's still talking. "We need forensics to find out where this breach came from. I'm sure they'll love me after the last situation, just a couple weeks ago, but there's no choice. We have to figure out –"

"It's the same hack. The sneaky, greasy haired puke was behind them all the whole time, and I was too fucking blind to see it. He's been fucking with us before Skye ever came into the picture." I'm grinding each word through my teeth.

It's physically painful.

Just a couple months ago, when the biggest thing on my mind was how to get Skittle in my bed, Cal and Spence sat with me in a meeting with the tech wonks. We considered it a small miracle whatever asshole broke into our system wasn't making any big moves with the client data.

They downloaded so much, threatened to leak it to the media, but then never followed through with dumping those files on the deep web for sale to every other vicious shark and fraudster.

Now, we know why.

Jonas was always a few steps ahead. He never trusted me. He broke into our database, combing through it, searching for anything juicy he could use on me or the firm by proxy.

Before Skittle, there was nothing. He must have worked like a dog to find anything new, and probably struck gold just recently, after I sent him packing at dinner, tail tucked between his legs.

That still doesn't explain the audio, though. Were we bugged?

If only I had time to fly to Iceland to find out, and then strangle his conniving ass...

"I...don't know about that, sir. But we'll figure it out, I promise. I'll have an update by morning."

"Work off my theory. Don't care how much you don't want to believe it. Call me when you've got something concrete." I'm done.

It's a long, rainy drive to my parents' place. Tension boils my gut for another half hour. I hope to every god in heaven I won't find my mother suffering or dead.

That goes double for my AWOL fiancée, too. There's no time to track her down like I want, not with so many wolves ripping my day apart. But damn if I won't be on her, first chance I get, and it won't be Mr. Nice Guy next time.

There's a fierce sadness, a longing when I think of her. And it's got nothing on how bad she's pissed me off.

How fucking dare you, Skittle.

How dare you shut me out.

How dare you walk away.

How dare you cling to your poison secrets.

Are you pretending they're stronger than our love, or are you so delusional you believe it?

I don't know. I don't care. I don't know what life is if I can't have her back, after I've turned her world right-side up, but first I've got to make sure mine doesn't chew me up.

* * *

"DAD? DAD, OPEN THE DOOR!" I'm soaked, standing on their porch, slamming my fist on the stained glass so hard I'm worried it'll break.

This seems weirdly familiar. Then I remember why.

Flashback to sixteen.

I came home limping after the fistfight with Spence. My best friend bit me – yes, fucking *bit* me – and the blood seeping out of my arm made me look like a bigger mess than I was.

I slapped the door just like this. Worried as hell how hard dad would come down on me when he saw my torn skin, and then how I'd explain chasing the little slut who caused this.

I hadn't learned no pussy is worth violence between brothers yet.

Someone else was on my side that day, despite the sin I laid on Spence.

Mom opened the door. She gasped, pulled me in, and marched me up to the bathroom. She didn't ask for details beyond a mandatory *is this the end of it?* I didn't give her any. She dressed my scratches and bruises with a tender touch and a warning in her eyes. I slunk off to my room later, sleeping off the humiliation, an understanding between us never hashed out in words.

That's the funny thing about mothers. You never appreciate how kind the good ones are until they're gone, or so close to the end it makes a heart run cold.

Mine's barely beating when I finally see a silhouette behind the glass. Dad rips the door open. I know his look right away. He's older, wiser, more feeble than the bulldog he used to be, but damn if he doesn't have the same tone of voice he did before I knew right and wrong from my own ass.

"I don't even want to hear it, Cade." He holds his hand out, pushing it into my chest.

"You heard my calls, and you didn't answer? What the hell? Where is she?" I hate having to push back, but he's left me no choice. Dad stumbles against the big closet in our mudroom, reluctantly making way for me. "Is mom okay? Is she alive? Christ, just answer me!"

His eyes go harder, the pinprick light left in them dwindling. "No, son. Neither of us are, if you want to know the harsh truth. You *lied* to us. Played us for goddamn fools."

He isn't telling me anything. I guess that's why his savage accusation only feels like an arrow, and not Excalibur's sword plunging through my chest. "Skye? The marriage? Come on. It's not like I had any choice. Don't you realize I only did this to look after –"

I stop mid-sentence, ears ringing, wondering why the world just exploded red. Then my nose aches like I rammed it into a wall, a split second before the hot blood seeps into my mouth.

"Holy shit," I mumble, staring at the red splash on my fingers for confirmation, before I look him in the eye seeing stars. "Did you just...punch me?"

"I did, son. Damn it, I did, and I'm sorry. Doesn't mean you didn't deserve it." Rage hisses out his nostrils. Then he throws an arm around my neck, reaching into his pocket for the handkerchief he always keeps handy. "I don't know what came over me. I know you're worried about her. You hurt us, but you didn't deserve –"

"Stefan! What's the meaning of this?" My very feisty, very alive mother appears in the hall, blocking us.

I've never been more thrilled to see her pissed and disappointed. It lasts for roughly a second before I realize she has every reason to be, and I'm the asshole responsible.

"Mom! Listen, I –"

"No, Cade. I've heard plenty today. I don't have the heart for more excuses. We'll talk." She pauses in front of me, staring at the hand on my face. It's impossible to hold onto her anger the longer she sees me hurt. I'm almost sorry she can't because I really hate seeing her heartsick rather than pissed. "But first, I want you to clean yourself up, and think very carefully what you have to say before we sit down. I know everything. Your father filled me in after Jonas called.

I'm never going to see my tea house again, but that's not the worst of it."

Oh, Christ. It's worse than I thought. I don't know how she's standing.

"That's not why I'm hurting. Stefan, please." She clucks her tongue, shooting my father a dirty look when he sends me a far dirtier one. "I don't care about losing Turnbladt. That's nothing compared to my only son deciding he'd rather weave an extravagant lie – and over such happy news! – rather than treat me like an adult. I'm not so fragile I'll break like bad China over a few disappointments, you know."

I'm torched. And I deserve every last burn, inside and out, hanging my head like a scorned animal. "Mom, wait. It isn't like that. I –"

"Go clean up, son." Dad growls next to her. "We'll sit down and talk about this like she said. Sorry again about getting physical. Haven't done that in years, and I wish I hadn't. If you need anything, holler."

I drag my miserable ass upstairs, taking the bathroom not far from my old room. Taking my sweet time, I stare at the rusty liquid spiraling down the drain. If only it were this easy to purify everything else.

My eyes go to the reflection in the mirror. Dad got in a good one, busting my lip slightly on top of the crunched nose.

Honestly, I'm fucking glad. The pain makes this more real, forces me to think harder than I've been able to over the past week since she left.

Lies are what got me here. But damn it, they also got me Skittle.

Our white lie marriage fix was far from noble. I'm done pretending it ever was.

Still, there's no denying it became a whole lot more. What began as a bid to protect my mother like she never needed just jammed itself like a key through my heart, twisting and opening truths I never saw.

Confessions haven't helped much lately. There's only one I wish I could change.

Telling Skittle the truth about us, blowing my proposal...those were mistakes. And then I made the biggest one, letting her walk away without telling me how the fuck to fix it.

No more.

If dad wants to throw another punch, or mom chews me out, I'm ready. I'm giving them the bitter truth. Everything. Then I'm washing my hands of this mess and going after the only thing I might still salvage.

Not that I've given up on Turnbladt, or getting even with Jonas. Maybe the laws are clear about his inheritance, per royal bullshit that was laid down long before I was born. I'll still make sure he enjoys his theme park royalties from a padded fucking cell for his hack attack on my company.

Too bad I can't do anything if I don't finish drying my hands, and step back into reality ready to bite so many bullets, I'll lose some teeth.

First thing's first. I'm back at the table, face-to-face with my very hurt parents.

"Okay. Mom, dad, I screwed up and there's no two ways about it. Also know the reasons don't really count anymore. I need you to hear me out." I feel guilty as hell for sipping the warm tea mom lays out like second nature. Anger never stopped her from loving her family like always.

"Screwed up? Cade, this isn't one of your high school pranks we left behind years ago. You lied to us. Went behind my back and found yourself a wife when I told you not to. Gave me a lot of false hope, and yeah, treated your mother like a fool." That last part is such an afterthought I think he's more scorned than her.

Irony has no mercy. Never thought dad would be the one I'd have to worry about, but here we are.

"True, everything you just said. If I could do it again, it'd be different. I'd have let you sort it out with the lawyers, like you wanted. Maybe we could've sat down and broken the news gently."

"Oh, you men. I'm *not* that fragile." Mom clinks her cup on its saucer sharply. "All this nonsense would've been avoided if you'd just been honest, Cade. Don't you see?"

"I do now. That's the part I'll regret for a good, long while, and mom...I'm sorry." I reach for her hands, grasping them in mine, so small and frail. When I look at her, knowing her health, it's easy to remember why I did this stupid shit. Easier to forget she's made of tougher stuff, and maybe she always had more of it in her than me. "There's also one part I wouldn't change. No excuses, no regrets, no apologies. It's Skye."

"That girl you hired?" Dad turns his face up, looking down at me.

"Stefan!" Mom slaps at his arm, then looks my way and nods. *Continue.*

"I'm sorry we couldn't come clean right away. Even sorrier I strung you both along. There's something you don't understand about what happened between her and I."

Something? No. So much more. They'll never comprehend the majestic chaos I had with that woman when she was in my arms, and the evil void that's there when she isn't. "We started on a lie. I hired her, just like you said, dad, hoping I'd have a cheap ticket to screw over Jonas and save the old place. Then we spent more time together. We had our dinners and hiked up mountains. We started kissing, more than we did for appearances just for you two. It was for us. Before I knew what was happening, we were real."

What the fuck is happening to my face? This heat, this

agony. Somebody pinch me. Tell me I'm not blushing like a damn kid in front of my folks.

"Cade?" Mom's voice is softer, too many questions hanging on her lips. She slides her chair over, the better to lay her soft hand on my back, and coax the poison out of me.

"It's true, mom. Before we ran into some trouble last week, I ran to her, got down on one knee, asked her to marry me. I meant it, too. I want to make Skye my wife. I want her in this family, wearing my ring, rocking your grandkids in front of the tree over Christmas...I *have* to do it, mom. And whatever the hell just happened between us, there's no way I'm letting her slip away."

"Son..." Dad isn't so pissed anymore. He just looks dumb-founded. "Katrin, you were right from the get-go. This whole thing is stupid."

I'm blinking, trying to understand. "Are you...smiling?"

What the hell? It's like I've slipped into an alternate universe where I'm still the good son, and I haven't just bombed their hearts into the stone age.

"I knew there was more to it," she says, nodding. "Just wanted to hear it from the horse's mouth."

"Will somebody explain what's happening?"

"You pissed me off, son. Then I found out you had a good reason, and now I *really* regret the fist in your face. Why are you still waiting around here?"

I shake my head, taking another long pull of tea.

He sighs, mirroring my motion. "Katrin?"

My parents share a look. Then it's mom's turn to shake her head, wipe a few tears from her eyes, and squeeze my hand like it's taking everything she's got. "Go find her, Cade. Whatever it takes. Life is too short to spend another minute upset about an old tea house thousands of miles away. Love is no relic. It's alive, it's magnetic, and boy, listen good – all is right between us if you've learned to cherish it."

She's right.

Hell, she's never been more right in my entire life.

I stand. Hug and kiss them both like I haven't for years before I go. Dad pounds me on the back one last time.

The bullshit with Jonas and these roller coaster emotions are vapor by the time I'm through the door.

I shift my car into gear, slowly winding down the driveway, scrolling through my contacts. I punch dial and wait for Fields to pick up.

"Master Turnbladt?" His voice is eager to serve as ever. Today, I'll take it.

"I need you to get my boys on conference call. Now."

* * *

THE KID HAS tears in his eyes at home. I find Vinnie sitting on the landing next to my reception room, knees tucked under his chin, fiddling with something in his hand. It's an envelope, Skittle's girly writing, a big DO NOT OPEN scrawled on the front.

Of course, he hasn't obeyed a single word. It's been torn and read.

"Vinnie?"

He jumps up as soon as I'm less than a foot away. Hiding his face, he pushes the crumpled paper in my hand, sniffing back hot rage. "Just take it. This really sucks. I'm sorry."

"Wait!" Predictably, the kid doesn't listen, running off. I let him go, remembering how shameful a teenager's tears can be. Plus my heart is beating through my ribs when I unfurl the note in my hand and scan the three terse lines she's scrawled in jelly pink.

TAKE CARE OF HIM, *Cade. Please. One last favor.*

Don't come looking for me.
I always loved you.

I DON'T KNOW how long I'm standing there like a fucking statue. I never hear anyone come in, just spin around, ready to bust a lip when a heavy hand falls on my shoulder.

"Bro? What's in your hand?" Spence's wolf blue eyes demand answers.

I wish I had them.

Cal wastes no time waiting for words. He rips it from my hand. He reads the words before I have time for a dirty look. "Start talking. We need answers if you want our help with this...whatever the fuck this is."

"She's gone." It's painfully obvious coming out of my mouth, but no less brutal. "Don't know where. She's got an uncle, this asshole criminal –"

"Oh, Christ. Not another one." Cal is already face palming, letting out a heavy sigh. It doesn't take much for him to remember the unique hell he crawled out of not so long ago. "I can't take the fall this time, but I'm here, Cade."

"Me too," Spence growls, rolling up his sleeves. "Let's talk dirt."

* * *

IT TAKES HOURS. It's late, we're making very little progress, and there's nothing in our stomachs except adrenaline and a shot or two of scotch.

We man the lines like in the old days at RET, when our fathers put us to work cold calling rich future clients, before the SEC clamped down. We're working through the company Rolodex, hitting every damn contact we have in government and tech to find someone who owes us a favor big enough to bend the law.

It's Spence who jumps out of his seat so hard his chair rolls, impacting the wall with a loud *twack!* "Eureka, bros. My man says he's got her cell. He can track it within the hour. Those big gains dad's special funds sent his way and his old NSA connections go a long fucking way."

I share a look with Cal. He reaches over, slaps my shoulder, and the hardest part comes: wait.

Just wait.

I sit there with my fists balled under the table for the next half hour, watching my laptop, waiting for my phone to vibrate with a message from her. I'm a fool for holding out, thinking she'll realize she's in over her head, and come home on her own. But hope springs eternal. I'm also terrified what I'll do if anything happens to her.

My fingers drift idly over the keys. Between calls, I've been mining data, pulling up old police records in the system our company uses for client security and background checks.

I read about Ophelia Coyle's suicide, something I should have done weeks ago. She was just another anonymous stiff dragged out of the sea cold and lifeless. Took them over a day to identify her, and then receive her writeup in the local news.

Just another mystery death nobody cared about. Not enough to investigate beyond the usual procedural paperwork, anyway.

Amateur detectives knocked it around online later that year. There were two suspects connected with her suicide, a random bum and a man named Harry Coyle. Skye's uncle. Doesn't take long to find his gritty background, his three stints in prison in two different states, and realize this is the 'family friend' Vinnie talked about.

The trail runs cold the deeper I dig. No hobbyists ever

found anything damning, and Harry dropped off the face of the earth after he changed his residence to Portland, supposedly to live a quiet life repairing motorcycles.

The Ophelia case is nothing but more questions, and they all make my bile churn.

Ten minutes in, when I've stepped outside my office where we're holed up, pacing toward the water cooler, I see a skinny figure slink behind me. I do a slow turn, the bitter anger I've held in forever breaking out. "Where is she, Vinnie? Did you see anything?"

His eyes go huge behind his black frames after I close in. I feel like an asshole right away and back up, giving him space, draining my water cup. "Sorry. We're working on finding Skye right now. Been under a lot of stress."

"It's okay. We had lunch earlier today. She brought me down to our old soup place, said she had some things to talk over, and when I got there...she couldn't shut up about you. She loves you, Cade."

If his words aren't enough, the sorrow in his eyes twists the arrow in my heart like a screw. I lean against the wall, waiting for more, knowing full well this is the last time for weakness. "What else? What did you two talk about? Think, Vinnie."

He's wracking his brain. His young eyes jerk from side to side, desperately searching. He stands up straight a second later, scratching his cheek. "I brought up our mom like an idiot. She didn't get mad, just said I was right, which really, *really* weird. I'm scared for her. Got an awful feeling she's doing something crazy."

"She could be." There's no use lying to the boy. I walk up, lay both hands on his shoulders, and squeeze like we're staring down the end of the world. "But you don't have to worry. I've got this, Vinnie. I'll bring her home, safe and sound, because I love her like mad. I'll die before I lose my chance to make Skye the happiest woman on this planet."

His eyes are glazed over behind those glasses when he looks up and smiles. Hell, I think mine are, too. My heart strums more venom to my head.

I hope like hell this is a moment my little brother-in-law will remember forever because we beat this.

Not because we lost her.

"You believe me?" I whisper, stooping low so I can look him dead in the eye.

"Yeah," he says, his soft smile fading. "Yeah, Cade, I do. You're a good guy."

"Run along and stop worrying. I'll have her home in no time. Tell Fields where you'd like to have dinner tonight. It's on me."

I watch him go. His footsteps are still padding upstairs when Spence crashes into my back, grinning. "We've got her. Traced the phone to a place in –"

"Let me guess – Bremerton?"

His mouth hangs open mid-sentence. "Shit, Cade. How'd you know?"

Again, Ophelia's suicide. I read the police records. I can practically see an older woman with Skittle's good looks and none of the rainbow dye staring into the choppy, cold waters, willing herself to die.

I remember Vinnie's words, how shaken he was when he told me what they talked about. It's obvious where she'll meet her bastard uncle, if that's what she's gone to do.

"We done talking, or what?" Cal says, catching up to us, chugging a coffee. "I'm ready."

"First, I need to talk to Woollsey. He's got a line to that woman I met at the party, Adele."

"Adele Allure?" Spence wiggles his eyebrows. "Damn, my man, we *need* to hear this story."

"Spencer!" Cal slaps a domineering hand on his shoulder, a warning in his eyes. Then he turns to me. "Seriously, though, what the hell were you doing running around with the richest madam in Seattle? Thought it was a little odd months ago, when I heard you had a chit-chat with Woollsey in private."

"The how's not important right now," I growl, swallowing my pride.

Later, they'll hear my confession. I'll tell them how I set off to find a fake bride, crashing my ego into the ground before the love bug got its teeth in for real. Right now, we need to bring her home.

"Just get that player asshole on the line," I say, nudging Spence hard with my elbow. "He listens when you call. Guess you've got new money and old owing you big favors. Even flippant fucks who have to soak their dicks in champagne pussy twice a week."

He smiles, pulling out his phone. "Because Mr. Popularity is feeling so generous today, I'll hook you up. And I won't even bother asking you to check that bossy tone."

I'm ready to bark back, but Cal grabs me around the shoulder, and leads me through the door onto my patio. The blistering cold blowing in across the Puget Sound helps calm me down.

Thank God for these boys. Without their calm, their support, and even their smart-assed quips, I can't fathom where I'd be.

Cal reaches into his coat pocket. My eyes follow his hand as he draws out a long cigar. "One of my old man's last Cubans. Found a couple boxes before he shuffled off his mortal coil. Been saving them for the times that matter."

He gives it a light and offers me the first hit. I haven't smoked anything in years, not since we were kids, and neither has he.

What the hell? It's customary to have a final smoke before facing death, isn't it?

I suck the rich, dense smoke between my lips. The inner burn sharpens my senses. It billows out of my mouth, wafting toward the heavens like one last smoke signal prayer before we walk into who the fuck knows.

"Woollsey," Spence says, joining us a minute later, pressing his hot phone into my hand. "Don't be too long. Asshole's drunk again. We'll be lucky if he gives you the right digits."

I keep it brief. Just ask for Adele and punch her number into my contacts, then dial. The woman changes her number every month to stay under the radar.

She picks up on the second ring. I tell her I know there's a deal going down, and Skittle must've left without the money her uncle wanted.

It's a massive risk. I don't know what's really involved. But it's worth a guess it's money, the same rocket fuel that makes the world spin. Double for the criminal underworld.

Very good guess, it turns out.

She gives me a time and place. It's close to the last ping from Skye's phone, a vacant warehouse by the docks, not far from the bridge where her mother drowned.

I hang up. We enjoy our smoke in silence, each of us passing it back and forth.

"Haven't done this shit since prison," Cal says, staring at the glow on the shrinking tip, shaking his head.

It doesn't seem fair for him. He's already been through personal hell. Small miracle he came out the other side okay, no thanks to Spence and I having his back.

"Times change, bro, but one thing stays the same: we always come out in one piece. Fuck the storm coming. I'm celebrating early. We kept you from losing your stake in the company and your life. We'll do it for Cade, too, and be home early for drinks."

I look at him sideways, wishing I had his devil confidence.

My gut is eating itself alive. It's pain, the kind that's only trouble.

Except this trouble makes me marvel. And that marvel is the glow in my heart, the crazy wildfire Skittle lit, the blaze I can't control unless she's home.

I need her in my arms, in my bed, sharing in my name.

She's become my life. Heart, soul, and every other flowery, fucked up thing a man like me swore he'd never say, before a twisted angel caught my heart and threw me down to earth.

Cal passes me the Cuban for one last puff. I drink it in, until the heat is almost at my fingertips, alive in this fire.

We talk details one last time. Cal and Spence say they'll do their part when the time comes. I give them a second to make the right calls, setting up the fail safe should prevent us from leaving in body bags, if it's really the standoff we're expecting.

"Let's go," I say, flicking the cigar stub on the pavement, dashing it with my shoe.

My best friends follow to my car after we make one last stop downstairs, behind the hidden bookcase, where I keep my spare cash and precious metals for emergencies. Whatever crazy scenario I imagined when my old man insisted on having a vault in the home, I never thought it'd be this.

It takes us half an hour to stuff the cash into a gym bag and then get on the ferry for Bremerton. We stare into the cold sloshing waters without a word, pulsing dragon smoke out of our mouths into the night, making peace with the next few hours.

I have my friends.

I have my mission.

I have my incessant drum of a heart beating a vicious voice in my blood, its rhythm louder every pulse, a plea and a promise and an echo in every corner of my skin.

Bring her home.

I will. I tell myself the same thing over and over, until I start to believe it, infected with Spence's wicked confidence.

It lasts an hour. Just enough time to drive to the warehouse and meet the devil face to fucking face.

Then I'm surrounded by death in every direction, and I wonder how insane I had to be to think fate would ever let us off without blood.

XIII: SHOW ME (SKYE)

An Hour Earlier

I'M FROZEN in the back of my ride, eyes glued to my phone, hand stuffed into my small black backpack. I can't stop fingering the cold, deadly metal tucked inside.

This gun holds twelve chances to kill him. I'm treating every bullet like one chance with two possibilities: walk away, or else leave this world just like mom did.

I should be scared. Hell, I almost want to be, because maybe then this will all seem real.

But I've been numb ever since I left the chowder place. Ice runs through my veins, so frigid it's strangely comforting. I take deep, slow breaths, focusing my one-track mind on what needs to happen.

There's another voicemail on my phone during the drive in. *Cade.*

My finger swipes over the delete button, but God, I can't

do it. The tears will be too much if I don't let myself hear his voice one more time.

I press play, holding it to my ear. "Skittle, come home. Wherever the hell you are, call me. Let's fix this. Keep you safe. Forget the fighting, the secrets, whatever went down between us. I love you, Skye, and I mean forever."

It's the last word that gets me. The bitter lump in my throat is a rock, and its edges are sharp.

I don't deserve his love, I've treated him like shit, and he's offering me heaven.

Forever. An eternity so deep and distant it cuts into my eyes when the tears come.

No, it hurts. I finally hit the delete button and sigh, stuffing my phone back into my bag.

It can't come out again.

If I even so much as see his name, or hear another word, there *will* be second guessing. And of all the things that could be fatal tonight, doubt is the worst.

The Uber driver drops me off across Bremerton after a short ride. I don't even thank him on my way out, pushing the door shut behind me, ready to walk the last few paces to the rundown warehouse.

There's no rewinding this. No re-do and no escape. It's on.

If I ever walk out of here again, I'll have a man's blood on my hands.

Assuming this goes according to plan, of course.

My greatest worry is Harry not showing at all, and what I'll do if he doesn't. There are no guarantees.

He could have lied to me, decided to send Adele or his numerous pack of goons, leaving me in a pinch I have no plan for. I don't have five million dollars tucked into my bag.

I'm hoping his overbearing ego, his desire to grind my heart to dust one more time, will be enough to bring his demon face to me one more time. But the time for hopes and fantasies is over.

As soon as I see the chasm in the rusty, chain link fence and the two black sedans parked near the rear, I *know* what's waiting. I'm three paces onto the property before a car pulls up, the window comes down, and one of the three grim faced men inside says two damning words. "Get in."

I listen. The man in the back slides across his seat, making space.

It's a thirty second drive across the old complex. The only surprise is that we're not going to the warehouse, but rather, the small beat up office across the broken pavement. Probably an old manager's office from the time when the docks were still working.

The car parks and the men exit. They wait for me. When I stand, they're on every side, leading me in through the back door. There's a dim lamp, a scratched up table, and on the other side of the room, Satan incarnate.

Harry sits in front of three more goons wearing a faded black jacket. Same mackerel eyes and pitchfork shaped beard I remember.

"Been forever, screamer. I'd say it's nice to see you again, but we both know it's fuckin' not. Have a seat." He kicks under the table, sending the chair flying out next to me. "Let's get this over with. Show me the fucking money."

Straight for the throat. I tell myself I'm not rattled.

As much as he should, this asshole doesn't scare me tonight.

He just makes me nauseous. How could we share the same blood, the same grey eyes, and be so different?

There's a black bag in front of him.

No, make that two big black bags, one bloated with what I'm guessing are the artifacts. The other is much lighter, waiting for the money I'm supposed to hand over.

"Well? What's the goddamn holdup?" His eyes never leave mine as he pulls a cigarette from his breast pocket, giving it a light. He takes a long drag and laughs as the smoke falls out of his mouth. "Still the same bashful, slow cunt of a niece, I see. Nothing like my brother. Makes me wonder who really knocked your bitch ma up sometimes."

"Give me a second. I'll find it." I hope these are the only words I have to say before I blow a hole through his brain.

"No. On the table now," the big man behind my uncle growls. "Sammy, Soft Lips, do the count. Make sure every damn dollar she promised is there."

I start a long slow breath. So quiet they can't hear it, filling my lungs a little at a time, timing the mechanical movement I've made myself practice a hundred times over the last few days.

Fingers tight.

Trigger ready.

Clear shot.

Then hell itself opens. My phone is ringing. The dull electric default ringtone echoes through the room, louder than if I'd pulled the trigger.

Men move like a whirlwind, ripping me up by one arm. I shove the gun aside with my other hand, and pluck the phone out, trembling at the elbow.

Harry looks my way, narrowing his eyes. "Soft Lips, answer that shit. This better not be some surveillance shit."

The goon rips my phone away. The room is dead silent and I fall back in my seat, hand snaking for the gun. I'm expecting the apocalypse – Cade's voice.

But that would make far too much sense.

It's a woman. She speaks hurriedly in a thick accent and barely makes any sense. "Skye, Skye? Listen...Jonas crazy. Hot. Mad! I try to get through you forever. He is not right. Husband...my husband is asking for help punish you...all for his fucking castle. He paid my brother. He's working...he hit you in Reykjavik. You spill. He put it in your bag before leave. You never see. Listen, do not say anything with your purse! Do not –"

A man's voice interrupts with explosive, nasally rage. "Giselle? Qu'est-ce que tu fais?!"

The call goes dead. Harry and his goons stare, not knowing what to make of it.

Soft Lips drops my phone on the table and gives his boss a look. "Want us to do a strip search? Check her for wires?"

Several men shift anxiously, eyeballing me up and down, a hot flicker already in their eyes. I think my heart re-starts several times. There isn't even time to think about what Giselle said. Our last day in Iceland was a million years ago, another disaster completely hidden until now.

"Hold it, idiots. That's my niece you're talking about. How about a little goddamn respect? Bitch or not, you won't see her naked that easy." Harry raises his arms, blocking his men, an uneven smile creeping across his lips. He stares through my soul. "Look, clearly something stinks. Can't say I like the sound of that goofy ass call one bit. But it wasn't the police. Some bullshit about a castle? Fuck, that's stupid, and it's none of our business! I don't care if you don't, screamer."

Thank God. I'm silent, teeth digging into my bottom lip. *Don't give him anything.*

If only that ever shut him up.

Harry steps closer, his smile wilting. "Gotta say, I *really* don't like how you're looking at me right now, Skye. This the thanks I get? Excuse me, princess, I could've made a mountain out of this shit and I let it go like a sterling goddamn angel. You're welcome! If you can't cough up some respect, how 'bout some fuckin' fear?"

I swallow hard, quietly cursing myself for stalling. If it wasn't for that stupid interruption...

This demon shouldn't get another chance to speak. I press my fingers tighter to the gun, deep inside my bag where it's out of their view, but I hesitate. Again.

"You've got some stones, you know. Coming out here all alone with so much money your driver could probably smell it seeping through your little books." Harry pauses, far from finished, nodding at my backpack. "Funny how you up and decide to pay without so much as a fight. I mean, shit, how *did* Mr. Moneybags take doling out millions in cold hard cash? He just *gave* it to you? Holy shit, girl. Your pussy's either made of gold, or he's so fucking rich I should've asked for double the invoice."

I don't say a word. I just stare, trying not to let his disgusting dig at Cade wreck my calm.

There's no time, no room for error, and definitely no second chances if I screw this up.

Mistake number one: too slow.

I feel a pressure on my neck a second later. It's one of the goon's hands. His grimy fingers tighten on my skin, making it very clear it wouldn't take much effort to snap my spine.

"Answer your uncle," the man snarls. As if this stranger is supposed to give me the respect I've never had.

I can't even fake it. I just look at Harry, venom pulsing through my teeth, oh-so-ready to end him if I can just find my cool again without these ridiculous distractions.

"What's to tell? Really? Let me just give you the money and –"

"Shut up." Harry stares down his cigarette at me, taking another vicious drag, his eyes narrowed behind the glowing tip. "Tell you what, I don't need to hear your shit. Maybe I'm more interested in telling you a little story before you drop the money, we shake hands, and go our separate ways. This time for good...or until I'm a little short again."

He grins, revealing several gold teeth. I don't know

whether I should pretend I'm outraged, or just try to get through whatever sick game he's playing so I get another opening to do what I came here for.

Just a few seconds of silence, please. That's all I ask.

If I'm not listening to his wretched voice, I'll find my focus, and then he'll never bother me again. Nothing ever will.

"Just tell me," I say, an exaggerated sigh falling out.

He takes his sweet time, stubbing out his half-burned cigarette, before he stands. Harry paces the table, a slow moving shark closing in, his men clearing a space around him. *Great. I never practiced on a moving target.*

"Funny thing, really. I've been thinking a lot about the past on my way out here, screamer. Can't get over how much you're like her. How both you and the dead bitch my dickless brother shacked up with cost me big." He stops. My grip on the magnum tightens. At least he's close. "I put your ma to work for me before she decided to take a nice nasty dip in the ocean. Had her muling up till the day she died, you know?"

It's not a question I can ignore. Harry slams his hand on the table, his eyes searching mine, forcing me to sputter an answer. "No. I had no clue..."

"Yeah. She must have really fuckin' loved you, Skye. Had her doing double shift outside that shitty job she worked, and I was paying her far better, too. Then she wanted out. I got pissed. Told her I'd pull you out of school and put *you* in the family smuggling trade if she was so damn set on stupid. She talked real sweet on the phone the last time to me. Almost like my promises got through her pretty head. I thought we were cool. Fuck, I even upped her little kickback, promised her a cool thousand more for every wad of my shit she drove up from Portland."

I can't help closing my eyes. I remember those weird trips

the last few years she was alive. They'd been getting more frequent. She always left with little explanation, telling me to watch Vinnie, which I grumbled over. I thought she had a boyfriend and just didn't want to tell us.

"How'd she repay me? *How?*" It's more sour the second time Harry repeats it. "I'll tell you, screamer: she fucking drowned herself and took over a pound of good coke in the goddamn fucking drink!"

His hand slaps the table again. It's the first time he really rattles me tonight. I can't control my jump reflex.

I want to shoot him. But I'm shaking when he pulls away. So is he. For a second, he looks pathetic, almost human.

Then the dark-eyed monster returns. "I offered her the world once upon a time, you know. If your ma had just shut up and married me like I asked, none of this would've happened. Christ, I would've taken you and Vinnie under my wing. Just like my own. Bitch left me sick after her suicide. That's why I went so easy on you, screamer. I thought I'd do right to win back the karma I fucked up pushing her too hard."

I can't look at him anymore. Every evil word drives a little deeper in my heart. I never wanted this bastardized confession, this certainty my uncle is not only evil, but so screwed up he thinks wrong is right.

He was dangerous before. I came here to kill him, to protect Cade and Vinnie, but now I have a new reason: shame.

Mom's suicide wasn't a selfish escape. I believed it, no thanks to this asshole, and I was wrong.

Atrociously wrong.

"What's the matter, screamer? Truth is the ultimate bitch, ain't she?" He digs in his pocket for another cigarette. I take a deep breath, brushing the trigger with my finger, getting ready. He looks up, new anger in his eyes. "Hey, fuck you, too. I get maybe the cat's got your tongue after I dropped this much shit in your lap, but that look you're giving me again? Don't make me wipe it off your face, little girl. You're too damn much like her for your own good."

I don't say anything. The glint in his pupils brightens fury red. I start counting with his footsteps, waiting for the precise second he's in my face.

One.

Two.

Now!

My gun is out and pointed at him. The next split second happens in slow motion. The entire world goes silent. I'm temporarily deaf before everything explodes in a stunning crash.

Except, it's not a bullet barking from my gun.

It's someone banging at the door. Then I'm surrounded by his goons, their guns shoved in my face, just as they start yelling.

Nobody does it louder than Harry. "Holy fuck, screamer! Holy Moses. Can't say I've seen a bigger pair on any man I've killed or hired than the set you've been hiding up those long legs, but *damn.* One chance to put the gun down, bitch, or my boys will break your arm. And will somebody get that goddamn door?!"

I don't know what to do. He's behind them, and there's already a man's hand over my barrel. I could fire again anyway, try to empty every bullet hoping one will find its mark in Harry's sick brain.

Too bad the odds of that happening are nil. The nano second I shoot, I'll take two shots in the chest and another in the back, courtesy of the grim faced men behind me who are a thousand times better with their weapons than I'll ever be.

It's over.

The worst part is, I don't even have time to process how

completely screwed I am. Not for another ten seconds, when I see the door open in my peripheral vision.

A ruthless smile pulls at my uncle's lips.

Cade. He gives me a fierce, but helpless look before the man with a gun to his back shoves him inside.

"Shit, Harry. What'd I miss? I go find you this sneaky little shit prowling around, and miss a good old standoff in here?" The goon looks around the room amused.

My uncle ignores him. I watch him step up to Cade while the men press him into a corner. A man pulls the magnum limply from my hand. My thudding heartbeat washes over my senses, turning everything blind and dumb and red.

"Nice of you to drop by, Mr. Moneybags. Good timing, seeing how your woman planned to paint the walls with my brain, fuckface," Harry says. "Start talking. I'll give you ten seconds."

I'm on the verge of blacking out. It's the look from the love of my life that keeps me awake.

Those blue eyes are twin storms. They're Cade to their core, the beautiful fool I was *never* supposed to see again, giving me a glance that's way too real.

"I've got your money," Cade growls at my uncle, never taking his eyes off me. He lets go of the large bag in his hand. It hits the floor like a brick. "Payment for Skye and the arti-facts. Debts in full. Take it, and let us go."

"Sounds like a sweet deal," Harry says. Not even close to the words I'm expecting. He smiles, steps closer to Cade, his head tilted like he's found something fascinating. "For you, I mean, Ebenezer Fuckwit. Soft Lips, take this crap and see what he's brought us." Harry kicks the bag across the floor. "Should give us a nice idea how much more I need before I think twice about blowing out his maggot brains in front of my lovely niece."

"No!" For the first time since being disarmed, I'm struggling. I can't fight instinct. "Leave him alone, Harry, you can't!"

"Can, and *will.*" Harry turns, slowly pacing his way toward me. The goons have thrown me back in my seat, and this time, they don't take their hands off me.

Goddamn, do I hate how I missed my chance. "Harry, please, just listen to him. He's trying to make a deal. Let's forget this. I made a big mistake, and I'm sorry. I –"

"You, little missy, are so fucking done." In one quick jerk, he pushes his dirty fingers through my hair and pulls. It hurts. "That's right. Shut the fuck up, and let me finish talking. You make another peep, he loses the tongue I'm sure you love to suck when you two love birds are all alone. And if you still don't listen, he loses something else."

My eyes flick to Cade. My teeth sink into my own tongue so hard I taste blood.

It isn't fair. I have to listen to this psycho, which isn't easy when there's sorrow pouring out, every glance desperate to tell him how fucking sorry I am.

Cade doesn't move. Just stands there like a blond, blue eyed sentinel. A Viking captain prepared to drown with this ship, if there ever was one, and all because I'd been stupid enough to think I could go off and do this alone.

Cade, I'm sorry. So sorry. You don't even know.

The room is eerily silent for the next few minutes. There's a scuffling noise near the door, right before it swings open again, and I see another goon marching two more men inside. A big man with blue eyes and dark hair has a busted lip.

Cal. Spencer. I've never met them, but it has to be his friends.

No one else would share Cade's good looks or his crazy defiance. Not to mention the regal air around them that sticks, even when we're at hell's throat.

Jesus, where does it end? Without anyone getting killed?

The three men don't make eye contact. Several thugs peel off Cade's side, walking their new prisoners to the opposite corner. They shove them against the wall with their backs to us, guns drawn.

It'll take a miracle for us to walk away alive. And when I'm face-to-face with my demon uncle, it's hard to believe those exist.

At last, the goon called Soft Lips looks up, letting out a sly whistle between his teeth. "Six million even. Plenty more than Ms. Twitchy owed."

Harry taps his foot loudly on the floor, stroking his chin. "All right, we'll talk. Congratulations, Ebenezer. You can thank the ghosts of past, present, and fuckin' future your balls don't have to meet my switchblade just yet."

Cade gives him a dirty look. He's not impressed. My heart dive bombs my stomach and roars up again. If only I'd had his courage less than an hour ago.

"I wonder how much this brat is really worth to you?" Harry nods my way. "She's been a royal pain in the ass, trying to kill me and all. If you hadn't shown up like a good boy with a big wad of cash, this whole thing would be a huge waste of my precious time, considering she brought jack shit. Not counting the bullet with my name on it. Let's not kid ourselves, Ebenezer. You're rich as fuckballs, and I'm *still* in the mood for vengeance. Six mil? I dunno. Think you're gonna have to do better to sweeten the deal if you want to walk out of here whole, with her, too. Fair compensation for my pain and suffering."

"Name your price. Let's start at eight."

"Shit, you're stupid. Eight mil? What did I say again about my precious time?" Harry slams his fist into Cade's stomach.

Oh, God. Jesus.

I didn't know it was possible to be this mad, disgusted, and terrified simultaneously.

A short, sharp scream slips out before I remember to bite my bottom lip, afraid for what he'll do next if I don't.

Harry gives me an evil look, before he turns back to Cade, who's slumped on his knees. My beautiful man clutches his stomach, but shows no fear. Only brute rage. "We'll let that little squeal go on the house. But she does it again, and well, you just might meet my blade after all. Tell you what, Ebenezer..."

Harry pauses, marches to the table, and digs through the bag with the artifacts. His hand reappears with a bust of Diocletian clutched in his palm. He turns the Roman Emperor's face to his, a dull look in his eyes, before he walks over to Cade and holds it high in the air.

"Make the next offer *good,* or we'll find out how much abuse this old piece of shit can take before it cracks apart on a human skull."

"Ten million," Cade growls again.

It's my turn to suffer. I can't breathe, can't think, can't control the rabid fear rattling my bones.

What are you doing? I want to scream. *This isn't a game, Cade. He'll kill you!*

It's so quiet I swear I hear the wind howling off the ocean. Exactly like the stillness before an executioner makes his move, and I'm expecting to watch Cade's beautiful face beaten in any bloody second.

Then Harry loses it. The bust slips out of his hand and hits the floor. He's laughing. A raw, low, evil booming sound, echoing through the room. Spence grunts his confusion across the room.

"You're *killing* me, Ebenezer. Christ almighty. Didn't think a boring, rich fuck like you had such a sick sense of humor. I love it!" Harry slaps his shoulder, pinching his fingers together across Cade's muscular shoulder. "Now let's get serious. Already told you how I feel about my time, so how about we call it twenty mil and walk away like men? I'll even let you shake my hand."

Cade gives him the death stare. Unflinching. Unmoving. A tiger ready to explode any second.

Don't. Please, Cade, just give him what he wants. He's a sadist, but its our only chance.

Desperation suffocates me. My lips fall open, make a tiny sound, and one of the goons smiles, crushing his hand to my mouth. "Careful," he whispers. "Next cry will cost you."

"Handshake is a mighty big honor, Ebenezer." Harry is still talking. It's amazing how this violent lunatic never learned when to shut up. "I'm letting you off light. Unless you think, maybe, I should pick up Caesar off the floor and find out how many whacks it takes to ransom my way to billionaire?"

Another long pause. Another piece of my soul dies.

Harry's brow furrows. He reaches for the Diocletian bust, grips it, and lifts it high over Cade's head. "Come the fuck on. Do we got ourselves a deal, or what? I don't have all day."

"Cade!" I whimper his name, forcing it through the goon's fingers. It comes out mush, and Jesus, I wish he would look at me.

Just tell him there's a deal. I'm begging, holding in my thoughts. *Please.*

Cade shifts on his knees, staring up, angrier than ever. He'd be a nightmare to anyone except my hardened thug mafia uncle. Harry sniffs, a prelude to the long, low sigh he releases. "Okay, asshole. Have it your way..."

He's lifting the statue higher, ready to ram it into my love's forehead, when a new voice joins the fray. "Cade, are we done with this asshole now, or what?"

"Almost." It's all Mr. Relentless says before his knees

swing. He leaps up so hard, so fast, everyone hears the sound of his fist crashing across Harry's jaw.

My uncle howls, half-curse and half-agony. Hell breaks lose several times over.

I still haven't managed to replenish the air in my lungs by the time I take it in.

Harry and Cade have traded places. Now, my uncle is on the floor, a neatly polished shoe on his chest, Cade leaning on him. Every gun in the room is drawn, fixed on him, half a dozen ways to die in a tidy circle.

He doesn't even flinch. "I'm only leaving your evil ass alive so we find out how many other people you've killed, hurt, or made missing persons. Besides, I'm too fucking good to stain my soul killing a worm."

He's crazy.

Cade's polished shoe digs deeper into my uncle's ribs. Harry unleashes another strained growl, still struggling, one hand on his jaw. It must be broken, judging by how drunk and slurred his next command sounds. "Shoot him, shoot him! The fuck you idiots waiting for? Kill this asshole!"

I close my eyes, heartbeat reaching a crescendo, Cal and Spence chuckling in the corner for reasons I'll never understand. *This is it.*

I think I'm already dead during the next sixty seconds. When I open my eyes, I'm still in this worldly hell, but the walls are moving. They're shaking, a voice as loud as God's ringing through them.

"Federal agents! Lay down your weapons! Put down the guns! You're under arrest."

The goons have time for one panicked look before the door gets blown off its hinges. I'm screaming when the big burly men in wetsuits rush in, military rifles drawn. It's sudden, fierce, and frightening enough to disarm every man in the room. Nobody has time to fire a shot in the commotion.

"Nice work," Cade says numbly, once he makes his way over to me, laying a warm hand on my icy shoulder. He looks at the stranger next to us. "A second later, though, and I'm not sure we'd have made it."

"It's harder running up on land in this crap than it looks" the man with the gold badge on his wetsuit says. "Gotta hand it to you boys. If it weren't for your little plan, we'd have missed our chance to try out our new toys, and nab these sonsofbitches."

The men are grinning. So are Cal and Spence. They stand next to us while the police, FBI, guardian angels in frogsuits – or whatever they are – haul the evil out.

At last, he looks at me. "Next time you go off and do something like this on your own, Skittle, I'd love a heads up. You're lucky. I'm so fucking glad you're alive and mine. There's no point wasting breath on a lecture."

"Cade..."

I don't even try to hold it in. I'm on him in a frenzy, with a life I wasn't sure I still had.

This man.

This manic, fearless, selfless man who just won the key to my heart forever.

What do I say? There are no words. Only warmth, flesh, and spirit.

We kiss. We embrace. We clutch at each other's clothes.

We're two famished beasts in need of love. We spend the better part of the next hour with our mouths glued to each other and our limbs tangled, even when more men come in to shoo us away from the crime scene, ushering us out into the moonlit ruin around the warehouse.

I never thought it could be so bright, so beautiful, and so full on a Fall Seattle night.

I was wrong.

If there's anything Cade Turnbladt has proven a thousand times over, it's how damn good he is at bending the world to his knee.

I'm going to marry an artist, an explorer, and possibly a crazy person all in one. And I swear, forehead pressed to his, I couldn't be happier.

XIV: NO MORE DREAMING (CADE)

Three Months Later

"How's our hero holding up?" Spence slaps my shoulder raw for the fourth time today. It's only nine o'clock, and he's already given me so much crap I'm afraid it'll stain my fancy tux.

"I told you to stop calling me that, dick."

"Why's that again? We're several thousand miles from home, all is right with the universe, and you've even got a damn *castle.*" He laughs, marching across the room to Cal, who shares my annoyance. "You've got yourself a wedding that'd make most princes jealous. And it's a fucking miracle, too."

"Spare me," I say, rolling my eyes, fixing my tie in the mirror. "We were all on this rocket ride together."

"Yeah, and it's still uncanny as hell sometimes." Cal looks over, a smile on his face. I think he's secretly marveling at how we almost died just a few short months ago. "You still think your asshole cousin won't crash the party today? I've seen what people do once they've whet their appetite for revenge."

"Nah!" I practically spit it out like the sour taste it is. "Jonas is far too busy chasing his kid around. He came an inch from divorce after finding out his wife flipped on him. Asshole could use her conscience. I think – *I hope* – he's finally manning up. There's a chance he'll stop being such a gigantic prick and do something more important with his life than making ragtag screech metal."

"Gotta love a man who screams himself hoarse for a living." Spence drops into the chair next to us, a glass in his hand. He's too fast, and already a little hammered. Liquid escapes and splashes his trousers before he pulls back, swearing under his breath. "Fuck."

I frown. "That better be water."

"Whatever, bro. This fine Swedish vodka is so common here it might as well be. I'm celebrating early."

Laughing, Cal yanks the glass out of his hand, shaking a finger. "You're *always* celebrating, Spencer. Have some respect. A man gets hitched once in his damn life, and you're up for the honor after Cade."

Spence's eyes grow big before he looks away, grumbling more insults too muddled to hear. "You wish. I'll be the last bachelor standing at the firm, thank hell. Somebody needs to do the detective work every so often when we're getting our asses breached left and right."

"Please, my team did *plenty.* You helped. We all did." I look across to my two best friends, smoothing things over, throwing an arm around them both. "If it weren't for you boys, not only would I have lost my girl, mom's castle, and maybe my life...I'd have lost my fucking edge. I've got you to thank for keeping me straight, and making that asshole roll over like a dog."

"Which one?" Cal raises an eyebrow.

He isn't wrong.

It's been a whirlwind ninety days since we stared death in the eye.

I spent the following week in Seattle after saving Skittle's life, without any distractions. Had to be there for her night and day when we filed the formal police report, gave our statements to the FBI, and then sat through her professor's judgment.

Doc Olivers could've been a huge asshole once he found out what she did. But he forgave her, and so did the dean, happy to have their musty Byzantine stuff back. Oh, and going against the blushing bride of a hometown hero all over the Seattle press didn't hurt. As much as I hate that fucking word – hero – I tolerate it because it's helped us save our skin.

"Yeah, not sure what's worse." Spence pauses, shaking his head. "Having a couple guns to my head, or dealing with the headache after I took the weekend organizing that shit from IT. We're lucky Cousin Thor was so damn sloppy."

"I know." I nod, using a phrase I've leaned on a lot lately.

It's nothing less than miraculous. Everything.

It would've been harder forcing a confession from my rat cousin if Giselle hadn't turned on him. She called Skittle again a day after the showdown with Harry and his mafia men. They talked in broken English over speaker phone. She filled in the missing gaps, told us how she couldn't live with what her hubby planned to do, turning that beautiful castle into a clown show.

"Count your blessings, my man. It's over. *Finally.*" Cal shares my relief.

He's right. I haven't stopped counting them since the second I tasted her sweet lips on that frigid pier next to the dirty warehouse where it all went down. I've never let up since.

It's such a blur now. Isn't it always when a man beats the odds in everything?

I still can't believe it sometimes.

Bringing Skye home and letting her feet touch the floor just long enough to give her kid brother some love.

Waking up the next morning with her eager little lips all over my skin, twining that cotton candy hair around my fingers in three seconds flat, before I re-claimed what's always been mine. Can't wait to do it ten more times tonight.

Her bastard uncle's rapid fire, goosebump stoking trial. We sat on the bench through it and he gave us the evil eye. We wanted justice, but fate had other plans. The trial lasted two days before it was cut short by the mafia hit in prison.

Nobody knows how the fuck they got a man with a knife in solitary, but when a criminal syndicate wants to keep a bird from singing too many secrets, evil magic happens.

No tears were shed the day we heard Harry Coyle died. Only on the evening I had Nate drive us out to Bremerton for the last time.

I stood there with my arms around her waist while she handed the kid a rose to lay in the water. Vinnie cried a little, held his sister's hand, and then turned away to walk off his sorrow, saying goodbye to their mom a second time.

Life comes full circle in the cool, steady echoes left by the waves. I may never understand how the life lost there led to us finding each other in Iceland, and then sealing the deal in front of the Sound, but it did.

I was less nervous the second time I dropped to my knees, took her ring, and worked to hear the words I'd been starving for since our disaster in her lab. *Marry me, Skye. This time for real. This time forever. No more playing.*

Skittle had more tears this time, I think, but they were

253

happy. Every last one of them. I was already up on my feet, lips to her cheeks, kissing them away before she grabbed my hand and spoke the unforgettable.

You're too good to me. I should be the one begging for a second chance. Cade, of course I will!

We might've set a new record for the world's longest, hottest kisses if Vinnie hadn't started clapping, the biggest grin I'd ever seen on his young face.

"Hey, you okay?" Cal brings me back to the present.

Don't know how long I stood there, smiling like a fool. "Yeah. Guys, come on. Show's up soon. Let's make this count like it should with two best men ready to help me tear the world a brand new hole."

* * *

I MUST'VE stood on the castle grounds a thousand times as a boy playing king.

Gone are the dragons and the treasure I liked to imagine. All the beasts are slain, and the last treasure I'll ever need is making her way across the moat in a gold carriage pulled by two white horses. Her ride stops when she's at the gates, and the servants escort her through the door, down the long carpet leading to our altar.

Fuck, Skittle looks divine. Her hair is pinned up, colorful as ever, a rainbow peeking out through her veil, a traditional flower crown neatly tossed in cotton candy tinctured blonde. A couple mouths drop when they see her – stogy old associates from the firm. They can't believe a sane young woman would ever go out on her wedding day dressed brighter than a peacock.

I can't believe they're caught up in protocol. I'm about to marry the most beautiful woman on the face of the earth, and I'm mad thankful her dress matches her hair.

I told her to go to town before this was real, and she listened. Even my distant ancestors who once lived in this place couldn't outdo her in their splendor. No royal ever wore a rainbow.

She's not just the love of my life anymore. She's no ordinary bride.

She's glory itself, the beginning and the end of me.

Jungle green, sun fire red, orchid violet, rustic yellow. I try to take them in one at a time, and then together. I try and fail about a dozen times, but damn if I stop once.

Skye is a kaleidoscope, shifting like the starry sky every time she shimmers toward me. Between the colors, gold and ivory sequins give her a shine like an angel.

None of it outdoes her smile.

It'd be blinding, overwhelming, if I hadn't already sworn my eyes to her.

Every look that's hers from this day forward is love. Nothing less.

My gaze is a mirror to my own damn heart, throbbing like a piston in my chest. Can't decide whether I want to admire her just this way forever, or strip that rainbow off at the first opportunity to devour the sweetness underneath.

This woman. Thief of my heart, my senses, my forever, straight through my own bones.

It's fucking madness. The most awesome, unforgettable, beautiful kind.

I manage to shake the flowery crap out of my head by the time she's next to me. The live chorus mom insisted on falls silent, and so does the organ, leaving the silence to swell.

Grasping her hands, they've never been warmer. The priest starts the ceremony, his words like whispers on these ancient grounds, timeless as the promise I'm about to make.

I don't take it lightly. Fuck, I don't think I could.

I've bumped shoulders with death for her once. I'd do it a

million more times if it keeps her smiling, her eyes fuller than ever, dressed in the happy glow she's wearing that's bound to persist long after the peacock dress is gone.

Just as long as she has my love. And after today, it's hers forever.

The wood burning behind us tickles our noses. Downy birch blisters, cracks, and sends its aroma across the crowds, grey smoke curling toward heaven.

She wrinkles her nose slightly, leaning in to escape the smell, teasing me every inch closer those lips get to mine. Wish like hell we could just skip to the bride kissing part.

The priest reads his blessing in Icelandic – one more tradition my loving mother insisted on – and then moves to English.

I squeeze her fingers tighter, lacing them in mine. It's an impatient grip, and also one that says I wish it would never end.

Is paradox a part of getting hitched?

It seems like seconds before the fateful words wash over us. I listen to the priest for my cue, but first it's her turn.

"Do you, Skye Coyle, take this man?"

Isn't that the billion dollar question?

To have, to hold, to love, to cherish, in sickness and in health.

Until death do you part.

And not even then, I think to myself, quietly following along in my head. I'll follow her into the next life guaranteed.

There's a moment to look across the crowd before I hear her answer.

"I do," she whispers, the love bigger than ever in her smiling eyes.

My parents are huddled in the first row. Mom beaming, of course. Dad looks on like I always hoped he would, assuming I ever got my crap together to do something this monumental. Besides becoming a wedded man, this is also the day I become the good son. This time, for real.

"And do you, Cade Turnbladt, take this woman to be your lawfully wedded wife?"

In sickness. In health. In faith. For richer, for poorer, and all the rest.

I'm up. Time to unleash the words I've practiced in the mirror for weeks, the words I'm holding in like a fool. "Forever. I do, woman, and I'll never stop. You've got my heart and half my soul. You've got it when we're handsome and young, graceful and old, even when we're fighting. You've got me forever, Skye, and I've got you. You're mine. Always were, before I ever asked you to be my wife, the very first time I kissed away your tears." That part is our secret, just enough to drop in public without anyone noticing. Apparently, it works, because there's plenty more to kiss away rolling down her cheeks before I'm finished. First, my fingers stroke hers, tightening with every word. "The one night bride thing is long over, beautiful. Forever just began. I do, I do, *I do.*"

Time slows around the priest as he reaches up, wipes his brow with his sleeve, and smiles. I told him I'd be adding my own brief vows, but I never said what. His voice is trembling a little and his eyes are no drier than anybody else's in these walls when he opens his mouth to say the words I've waited an eternity for.

"Glorious. You may now – "

Oh, hell, do I ever kiss my bride.

I kiss her through the laughter, the cheers, the standing ovation springing up around us. Through my parents bawling, and Vinnie drowning out the chaos, clapping his hands together like a hungry seal. Through Cal and Maddie smiling on, his knowing hand curled around her waist, spread along her belly. And yeah, even through Spence raising his fucking vodka glass, toasting us before the reception has even begun.

* * *

NEXT TIME I get to lay my lips on hers good and deep, we're in each other's arms. It's perfection itself, except for the fact we're still wearing our clothes.

That's how it goes though when we're having our first dance as man and wife.

"I can't believe we're here. Doing this. You and me." Skye whispers the same awe-struck words for the third time this evening.

"Believe, Skittle, or do you need another reminder?" I pause mid-sway, pulling her closer, laying my lips on hers. Pure addicting honey. "Real enough for you?"

She smiles, brushing her hips against mine, the music swelling around us. There are too many eyes on us to thrust back like I want to. Damn if it stops the growl in my throat, which thunders into hers, when I press my hand along her neck and kiss her yet again.

There's a demon energy running through me tonight. Really impressive after the feast, champagne, wedding cake, and even a few handfuls of the signature sugary treat – Skittles. What else?

"I never thought we'd make it sometimes, Cade. I wasn't even sure it was over after Harry. The trouble with your dumb cousin..."

"Quiet," I breathe, forehead laid on hers. "It's been over with Jonas for weeks. That idiot sure as fuck isn't ruining our wedding day. We've had a lot to fret over, sure, but that's over now. Over, beautiful, because I say it is."

I have more than mere words backing it up. I remember the last call I'll probably ever make to my black sheep cousin, after our IT logs caught him red handed. Giselle's confession was the final nail in his coffin. He begged for forgiveness. Promised he'd leave the castle alone if I didn't press charges, and let him ride off into the sunset with his stupid band to fix his battered marriage.

So far, so good. I'll never let my guard down completely. He'll never know how easy he got off thanks to timing. The day after Skittle said she'd marry me, there was no denying the brightness mellowing our world. How could the luckiest man on earth not show a little mercy?

"If you insist," she whispers, flicking her tongue quickly over her lush lips. I smile, loving how her hunger matches mine. "Vinnie can't wait to board tonight. He's never been on a cruise before."

"Long as he's content with his own room," I growl, nipping at her shoulder. My stubble rakes her sweet skin, and her moan puts new fire in my balls.

"Of course. We talked. You're crazy if you think he'd want to be around when we're busy anyway." My tongue lashes her shoulder for a second before I pull away, searching her eyes, hoping she understands how truly busy we'll be for the next two weeks.

"Bullshit. You're just excited for Hadrian's Wall." I've scheduled our layover in England next week just for her, to see her piece of Rome. Then it's on to the rest of Scandinavia, where we're bound to see some castles that'll put this place to shame.

"I love the ancient world to death," she says, her smile getting bigger. Then I feel her hand gliding lower on my shoulder, studying every muscle with her fingertips, calling my cock harder. Skittle leans in, pulsing warm breath in my ear. "But there's nothing I'm looking forward to more than tasting every inch of you, hubby. Tonight."

Sweet fuck.

I crush my lips down on her teasing little mouth furiously. It's the best I can do until we're alone, without a crowd watching our every move, including my folks.

I'll be the good son for the next hour. Mom deserves that much.

Then it's all freak, all night. Man and wife in the most carnal way imaginable, plus some new ones I haven't thought up yet.

"Careful, Mrs. Turnbladt," I whisper, once she's comfortably resting her head on my shoulder. "You tease me like that again and we won't make it to the ship before I peel off that pretty dress."

* * *

SHE LOOKED LIGHTNING hot in the dress just a few short hours ago. Amazing how much hotter she looks out of it, now that it's a crumpled heap on the floor.

It's like I'm conquering her for the first time, even though I've kissed her bare skin all over and spent hours of my life sucking those rosy nipples.

Bigger marvel still how good her ring looks around my cock. "Fuck, yeah, faster. Harder, beautiful. You know what hubby likes."

She's on her knees, eyes big and stormy, teeth tucked into her bottom lip while her hand strokes pure nirvana. Every inch of me throbs, losing pre-come on her fingers. I'm afraid the magma in my balls won't wait when she takes the head of my cock between her sassy lips.

Up. Down. Deep.

I'm grunting, knees buckled, one hand splayed against the wall, holding me up. Tonight my wife's lips have taught me several new levels of love. The chilly North Atlantic laps around outside. We haven't even left port yet, and I couldn't stand a single second more in our suite without her naked.

There's a special devotion in the way she sucks me off tonight. I want to cling to it like mad, but I'm also impatient.

My eyes travel over her sweet curves again and again, imagining how they'll change in my eyes in the years ahead.

Age will give them grace.

Love will renew them.

Our first born will give them battle marks.

Her beauty won't fade. Never, ever in my eyes.

And my desire will never stop me from relishing every opportunity to spread those long legs, push my face between them, and lick her hoarse until she's ready for me.

My mind is fucking racing. It's in meltdown once her little face really finds its rhythm, tasting me over and over, her fingers squeezing my balls.

"Skittle, fuck. Don't stop. I'm –"

Coming? Oh, Christ.

Oh, momma.

Oh, wife.

There's nothing except the sweet, vicious burn of my balls pouring fire in her mouth for what seems like eternity. Her tongue flicks harder, swallowing every pulse of my seed like a champ.

I waste no time rewarding her with a kiss, dumbstruck how fucking good I taste after I've been on her lips.

Then I put my fist in her hair, lead her over to our huge bed, and put her on her back. It's easy to see that shy red blush creeping to her cheeks, like it always does after she's brought me off, and I'm not having it.

"Scream all you want," I say. "We *should* wake the whole damn city tonight. We only get one honeymoon."

Her soft cunt rises to meet my lips. I make every lick count. I tease her lower lips, taste her inner silk, then dive for the swollen nub that leaves her gasping, pleading, exploding.

It takes forty licks to find her first O, and ten more to make her scream.

Ten for the delicious madness sprouting in my heart.

Ten for every wretched hell we've overcome.

Ten for our forever.

Ten more for our promise.

The last ten are for the hungry wolf inside me, desperate to be in her, but addicted to her taste.

"Cade, Cade, oh shit, Cade!" She's going to rip the hell out of those thousand stitch Egyptian sheets. I don't even care. Nothing matters more than the orgasmic frenzy I bring. My mouth smothers her pussy until she's a writhing, breathless, beautiful mess.

I'm harder than steel by the time she goes slack. Except when I stand, I see her eyes aren't closed.

They're fixed on my naked body. Her knees are shaking as her legs pull apart. She touches her teasing cunt and whispers one word.

"Please." One moan, one whimper, one plea. "I really, really need your dick. Cade, now."

Who the fuck am I to deny the other half of my soul on the night we're joined?

The brimstone churning in my balls doesn't give me a second to hesitate. I'm on her, but it isn't just Cade anymore, the loving man she married. It's a beast in full rut.

I've never seen five minutes of pure sweet fuckery go by so fast. They're gone in a blur of piston hips and bed slapping thunder. She goes over the edge again, screaming my name, cotton candy hair tangled in my fingers while my gaze watches her tits swing like pendulums.

I flip her over just before it's too late. My hand sweeps across her ass. I mark her soft flesh with a feral growl bleeding out, the same way she's marked me to my core.

Fist in her hair, ass against me, mounted from behind, we fuck like no tomorrow.

It's filthy. It's rough. It's love.

It's a raw beauty formed by our bodies, and it has no

apologies. Before tonight, we were just two people who'd suffered mightily to get this close, enjoying the best sex of our lives.

Now, I know her like never before. Her heart, her mind, her soul come closer every thrust.

"Skye!" I'm rumbling her name, ordering her to crash her little hips into mine faster and harder. I want her to know how it is when I can't hold back, and I hurl every drop in my balls to the womb I'll own with our kid one fine day.

As soon as we're fucking able, actually.

Her pussy squeezes me blind when her next O hits. Thunder chokes me quiet, rolls my head, and I see stars that have nothing to do with the glorious winter sky over the sea, outside our windows.

I think I see heaven itself, and it speaks its real name: Skye.

It's so much more beautiful than ever before because tonight, it's mine forever.

My spine becomes fire as I thrust one more time, root my cock in her, and blow.

We find our first release as man and wife together, the same way we've done everything else.

Later, I'm giving my dick a few precious minutes to recover. More for her benefit. I could have kept going without getting soft, but damn if just holding her isn't nice, too.

Skye's eyes are half-open, soft grey storms. New hunger builds by the second. I grip her chin, brushing her cheek with my thumb, displacing a few stray locks of that blonde splashed rainbow I love to grip in the thick of our madness.

"How'd I get so lucky?" It comes without a second thought. "Tell me, beautiful."

"You believed when no one else did. You were kind like nobody ever was. You won me over."

Fuck, those lips. So warm, so sweet, and so wise.

Our kiss is a hundred degrees. Pretty amazing onboard a climate controlled ship heading for the North Atlantic in the first week of December.

"Hell of a conquest, then," I tell her, reluctantly breaking away.

"Even the Romans had to put down their swords every so often and build, Cade." Her smile wider, she lays her head on my chest. I stroke that hair through every word. "I'm ready to settle down thanks to you."

"Good thing, too. I want you carrying our first kid after the first dig." A growl catches in my throat. It's not the first time we've talked about this. Now that her dissertation is in, we've agreed she'll go through one more dig in Turkey looking for artifacts next year before my impatient dick doesn't have to wait to breed.

"All in good time," she smiles, tapping me lightly on the chest. "Remember our deal."

I do. "For you, Skittle, anything."

We kiss again, and it's not long before the first one melts into a dozen more. There's no point using words to finish what's meant for our bodies.

Waiting is just fine by me while I'm tasting this sweetness. I'm a patient man – sometimes.

It'll certainly be a very, very, very fucking good wait, too. I knew it since the second I caught my Skye with diamond and branded her torrid smile into my heart.

THANKS!

Want more Nicole Snow? Sign up for my newsletter to hear about new releases, exclusive subscriber giveaways, and more fun stuff!

JOIN THE NICOLE SNOW NEWSLETTER! - http://eep-url.com/HwFW1

Thank you so much for buying this ebook. I hope my romances sweeten your days with pleasure, drama, and all the feels! I tell the stories you want to hear.

If you liked this book, please consider leaving a review and checking out my other romance tales.

Got a comment on my work? Email me at nicole@nicolesnowbooks.com. I love hearing from fans!

Nicole Snow

More Intense Romance by Nicole Snow

CINDERELLA UNDONE

PRINCE WITH BENEFITS: A BILLIONAIRE ROYAL ROMANCE

MARRY ME AGAIN: A BILLIONAIRE SECOND CHANCE ROMANCE

LOVE SCARS: BAD BOY'S BRIDE

MERCILESS LOVE: A DARK ROMANCE

RECKLESSLY HIS: A BAD BOY MAFIA ROMANCE

STEPBROTHER CHARMING: A BILLIONAIRE BAD BOY ROMANCE

STEPBROTHER UNSEALED: A BAD BOY MILITARY ROMANCE

Prairie Devils MC Books

OUTLAW KIND OF LOVE

NOMAD KIND OF LOVE

SAVAGE KIND OF LOVE

WICKED KIND OF LOVE

BITTER KIND OF LOVE

Grizzlies MC Books

OUTLAW'S KISS

OUTLAW'S OBSESSION

OUTLAW'S BRIDE

OUTLAW'S VOW

Deadly Pistols MC Books

NEVER LOVE AN OUTLAW

NEVER KISS AN OUTLAW

NEVER HAVE AN OUTLAW'S BABY

NEVER WED AN OUTLAW

Baby Fever Books

BABY FEVER BRIDE

BABY FEVER PROMISE

BABY FEVER SECRETS

Only Pretend Books

FIANCÉ ON PAPER

SEXY SAMPLES: FIANCÉ ON PAPER

I: Look Who's Back (Maddie)

Something in his makeup made him an utter bastard, but I owed him my life.

It's my heart I refused to give up without a fight. If only I'd known from the very start Calvin Randolph never backs down.

Not in love. Not in business. Not in any corner of his battered existence.

I'll never understand it.

Maybe he's missing the gene that stops a normal man from sinking his hands into the earth and ripping it to messy, screaming shreds until he gets his way.

Perhaps defeat just never made sense in his head.

Or possibly it's because this was just meant to be. There's a natural mischief in every heart that loves bringing together what's complicated, dangerous, and totally incompatible in a blinding impact.

Oh, but I still wish I'd *known,* before our blind collision became love.

We would have prevented so much suffering.

* * *

I'm in no mood to pull a jet black envelope out of my mailbox. Not after an exhausting day dealing with corporate legalese and a language barrier that's like a migraine prescription. Especially when said legalese is a hodge-podge of English and Mandarin bullet points outlining bewildering trade concepts that make me want to pop aspirin like Junior Mints.

But the coal colored envelope isn't what ends me. It's a single word, the one and only scrawled on the front in bright pink, without so much as a return address or a stamp to accompany it.

DOLL.

No one's called me that in years. Seven, to be precise.

I have to steady myself against the mailbox when my heartbeat goes into my ears. For a second I'm afraid I'll faint.

It's incredible how the only man who'd ever call me a name I haven't heard since high school still has a freakish ability to reduce me to a knee-shaking, cement lunged mess so many years later.

My fingernail slides across the seal, digs in, and splits it open. I tear gingerly, like I'm expecting a snake or a tarantula to jump out. There isn't enough room for creepy crawlies, I suppose, though I wonder about the hard lump in the corner, rubbing it against my palm.

The constant noise in the hall of my cramped Beijing flat has faded from a roar to a whisper. It's hard to focus on the slim white note I pluck out when I'm trying to remember how to breathe. There's no mistaking the handwriting.

They're his words. I'd recognize them anywhere, even after so long.

Blunt, mysterious, and taunting as ever. He keeps it short and sweet – assuming there's anything sweet about reaching down inside me, and yanking out a dozen painful memories at once.

It's been too long.
> *You still owe me that favor, doll, and I'm cashing in.*
> *Marry me.*

"Marry me?" I read it again, shaking my head.

If this is a joke, it isn't funny. And I already know it isn't. Cal wouldn't break a seven year silence for a stupid laugh. It's serious, and it's a brand new kind of terrifying.

My eyes trace his three insane sentences four times before my knees give out.

I go down hard, banging my legs on the scuffed tile, dropping the envelope. The object anchored in the corner bounces out with a clatter as loud as a crashing symbol, leaving a haunting echo in my ears.

I look down and mentally start planning my goodbyes. It's a gold ring with a huge rock in the middle, set into a flourish designed to mimic a small rose. I don't need to try it on to know it's probably my size.

I flip the note over in my hands before I lose it. There's a number scrawled on the backside in the same firm, demanding script. CALL ME, says the two words next to it in bold, as if it's the most natural thing in the world to ask for a mail order bride in less than ten words.

As if it hasn't stopped my heart several times over.

I can't believe he's back.

I can't believe he's found me here, on the other side of the Earth, and decided to drag me back to the hell we both left behind.

I really, *really* can't believe what he's asking me to do.

But it's my fault, isn't it? I'm the one who said I'd do *anything,* if he ever needed it.

Without him, I wouldn't have my dream career working trade contracts in China for a prestigious Seattle company. I'd be lucky serving tables with the criminal stain on my record if he hadn't stepped in, and saved me when it seemed hopeless.

There's a lot I don't know.

Like why he's gone emergency bride hunting, for one. Or what he's been doing since the last dark day I saw him, crying while they hauled him off in handcuffs. I don't even know what kind of devils are in the details if I actually agree to this madness – and it's not like I have a choice.

Small town guilt will gnaw at my soul forever if I turn him down.

Oh, but he'll catch up with me again soon, and let me know exactly what new hell awaits. That much, I'm certain.

It won't be long before I'm face-to-face again with the sharp blue eyes that used to make my blood run hot. Twisted up in knots like a gullible seventeen year old with a bad crush and a blind spot for bad people before I know what's hit me. And yes, revisiting every horrible thing that happened at Maynard Academy in ways I haven't since my therapist discharged me with flying colors.

He's right about one thing, the only thing that matters in any of this: I owe him. Big time.

All the unknowns in the world are worthless stacked up against this simple truth.

So I'll wait, I'll shrivel up inside, and I'll chew on the same nagging question some more.

Jesus, Cal. What the hell have you gotten yourself into?

* * *

Seven Years Ago

The beautiful boy with the constant entourage ignored me

271

until my seventh day at the new school.

How my parents thought I'd ever fit into this place, I don't know. They just saw the school's shiny academic track record and absorbed its prestige from Seattle socialites several leagues higher than we'd ever be. A fast track scholarship I won in an essay contest sealed the deal. My old English teacher in Everett submitted it behind my back when I was ready to throw it in the trash, and the rest is history.

Who could blame them for leaping at the chance? They want the absolute best for me. I'm ready to make my family proud, even if it means trading a huge piece of my seventeen year old social life for the best education several states over.

It's not like Maynard Academy has a welcome wagon. The other kids keep their awkward distance since the first day I show up on the seating charts next to them. Almost like they smell the stink of my missing trust fund, or the Mercedes that didn't materialize as soon as I got my license.

I still take the bus. And I'm not sure my parents could ever afford a trust lawyer on their seventy thousand combined income, raising two girls. Their struggle to keep up rent and bills reminds me how lucky I am to get a scholarship to this place.

Turns out the benefactor behind the money at Sterner Corp shares my love for John Steinbeck.

Ever since we moved down to south Seattle, uprooting lives and careers just for this special chance, I'm in another world.

If the black lacquered study desks, the library with the crystal chandeliers and the skylights, or the marble fountain out front hadn't tipped me off the first week, the natural pecking order here certainly does.

My face is stuck in a German textbook when he comes up

to me. He doesn't bother with introductions, just pushes his fingers into my book, and rips it out of my hands.

"Do you ever speak?" His voice is smooth as ice, a rogue smirk tugging at his lips.

"Hey!" I stand up, dropping the rest of my small book stack on the floor, arms folded. "I don't know, don't *you* have any manners?"

"There's never been much point," he tells me, sizing me up with his sky blue eyes.

I hate it, but he isn't wrong. It took all of three days here to notice how everyone hangs on his every word. There are always a couple grinning jocks and puppy-eyed cheerleaders at his shoulder. I think the teachers would love to knock 'Mr. Randolph' down a few marks, if only he didn't keep acing all his tests.

He's too good a student and too big a dick to be worth the trouble.

I've seen the summary sheets tacked to the boards. Every time, every class, Calvin Randolph ranks infuriatingly high. I've heard the gossip going around, too. Just because I like to keep my nose buried in my books doesn't mean I'm deaf.

He's a straight A jerk with money, good looks, and brains behind his predictable God complex.

"Seen you around, Maddie, and you haven't said shit. That's a first for me, being ignored like I'm not worth your time." Oh, he also has a filthy mouth, which makes it doubly ridiculous every woman in our class would kill to have it on hers. "I'd love to know why. Everybody, new or old, wants on my good side if they want off Scourge's bad."

For such cool, calming eyes, they burn like the sun. My cheeks go red, flustered and hot when I jerk my eyes off his. "I don't know who that is," I say. "It's only been a week."

"Interesting. Thought a girl who goes for the librarian look would be a lot more observant than that." I stick out my hand, going for my language book, but he jerks it away like I'm a helpless kitten. His smirk blooms into a cruel smile. "It's okay if you're a slow learner, doll. I'd have my eyes glued to this boring crap all the time too if I didn't have a photographic memory."

He's so full of it he's overflowing.

"Give it back," I snap, looking around to see if there are any teachers walking by. I'm not sure I'd have the courage to ask them to step in. This school isn't any different from an ordinary high school when it comes to attitudes, despite the family income level. Nobody wants to be the class runt who goes crying for help, and suffers the outcast consequences.

"Cal, I'm not playing around. I need to get to class."

The second to last bell of the day sounds over the speaker, adding its emphasis to my words. He clucks his tongue once, his strong jaw tightening. "So, you do know my name."

"What do you *want?*" I whine, trying to keep it together. "I don't have time for games."

I try to snatch my book again. Too slow. He lifts it higher, far above my head. I'm barely up to the neck attached to his broad, vast shoulders. He towers over me, one more way his body tells me how small I am next to him. Even physiology rubs in his superiority.

"I want you to crack a damned smile first," he says, laying a patronizing hand on my shoulder. "Show me something human. I've seen two expressions on your face since the day you showed up, doll. Tell me there's more."

"What happens on my face is *my* business, jerk. Not yours." By some miracle, he relents, letting my German book swing down with my hand the next time I grab it. I stumble a few steps back toward the bench to collect my mess of things.

I've got maybe sixty seconds to make it to class before the next bell if I don't want a tardy slip.

"Jerk? You're adorable." He steps closer, swallowing me in his shadow. A few of the kids racing down the halls slow, watching the tension unfolding between us. "On second thought, fuck the smile. I'd love to see those lips say something nasty a whole lot more than I'd like them right-side up. Fact that you're blushing at the mere suggestion tells me I'm on the right track, doll."

His tone is creeping me out. I stuff a few loose books into my backpack, sling it over my shoulder, and start moving down the hall. Sighing, I decide to waste a few more precious seconds asking him the only question that really interests me.

"Why do you keep calling me that – 'doll?'"

"Christ, do I have to explain *everything?*" His smirk is back, and I decide I don't like it, no matter how much light it adds to his gorgeous face. "Button nose, brown eyes, chestnut hair that looks like it's never seen a real salon. You don't fit the Maynard mold. Must be smart if you made it here in the first place without money, but I can't say I'm impressed. Brains don't matter here. It's my job to make sure you find out how this school works the easy way. You don't want hard."

Hard? I have to stop my brain from going into the gutter, especially when he's looking at me like that. I'm also confused. *What in God's name is he talking about?*

I don't remember being so insulted, and never by a man who uses his good looks like a concealed weapon. "I'm perfectly capable of figuring it out myself. Thanks very much, ass," I yell back over my shoulder, moving my feet to put as much distance between us as quickly as I can.

"Thanks for giving me exactly what I want," he growls back, hands on his hips, his strong arms bulging at his sides. They look more like they belong to a weight lifter in his twenties than a boy who's just a year older than me.

The last class of the day, chemistry, is just a blur. It's one of the few I don't share with Cal this semester, thank God.

He's the lucky one, though. Not me. If I had to sit with his smug, searing blue eyes locked on me for more than another minute, I think I'd rush to find the easiest recipe for a test tube stink bomb that would teach him not to stick his nose where it doesn't belong.

* * *

Okay, so, maybe he's not the biggest dickweed at Maynard after all. It's a couple more weeks before I find out why everyone dreads Scourge. He's gone for my first weeks thanks to a long suspension. Meanwhile, I've aced my language studies, made a few loose friends, and even settled into a study routine blissfully free from Cal's attention.

That changes when the human storm blows in.

There's a commotion in front of our lockers at noon, near lunch, when the kid in the leather jacket rolls in late. He wears mostly black, just like every other coward in a tough guy shell since time began. Chains hang off his sleeves, looking like they were designed for whipping anyone in his path. I don't understand how he gets away with it at first, seeing how it violates every part of the school dress code.

He's every bad school bully stereotype rolled in a cliché. Shaggy dark hair with a black widow red stripe running through the middle, piercings out the wazoo, and a sour scowl dominating his face that makes Cal's smirk look downright angelic. He also has tattoos peaking out his neck-line and crawling along his wrists. Screaming skulls, shooting fire, blood dipped daggers – the scary trifecta for a troubled young man trying his best to look hard.

I've also wondered why there's never anyone using the

locker on my left side. I wrongly concluded it might be a spare.

Oh, sweet Jesus, if only I'd been so lucky.

Alex "Scourge" Palkovich Jr. shows me he means business without uttering a word. The boys and girls in front of him who don't clear a path fast enough get pushed out of his way. I get my first shot of panic when he's still ten feet away, after everybody between us slams their lockers shut and scurries across the hall.

"You." He points. I freeze in my tracks. "Where the fuck's Hugo? You his new girl, or what?"

"Hugo?" I don't know that name.

The psycho has his hands on my shoulders, shaking me like a ragdoll, before I'm able to remember why it sounds so familiar.

I inherited my locker from another student. There's a worn label stuck inside my locker with that name. *Hugo.*

"Don't play dumb with me," he snarls.

"Jeez, look, I don't know him. Honest. I'm not who you're looking –"

"Shut up! Stop covering for his fucking ass, little girl. He put me out for three weeks when his sorry ass got caught smoking what I sold. Nobody does business and then fucks me over, understand? No one!"

My nerves are on needles. His nostrils flare, and the muscular fingers digging into my arms are starting to hurt. "Sorry, I'm new here. I don't think I can help you," I try to tell him, cool as I can manage. "I really don't know Hugo."

He sucks in a long, ragged breath and then shoves me away. He pushes me hard. My shoulder impacts the locker with an *oomph*, and I'm left leaning against it, wide-eyed and staring at the mess of a boy fuming next to me.

Scourge twists the knob on his locker for the combo, nearly rips the door off when he opens it, and slams it with a deafening bang after staring inside for a few breathless seconds. He looks at me. "Consider this your only warning. I find out you lied to me, I'll spend coin getting even, bitch. Already had two suspensions this year. Not afraid of a third, and you look like you're dying for someone to pull up that skirt and throw you against the nearest wall, teach you some fucking respect."

I can't breathe. I can't think. I can't stop my thumping heart from making me light-headed.

"Maddie, come on," Chelle says, tugging at my arm. "Get away from him."

I let her numbly lead me away to the school cafeteria. As soon as we've grabbed lunch and sat down, I start asking questions. It's the best way not to breakdown and cry after one of the scariest encounters of my life.

"What's his deal? Why do they let him stay?" I can't stop thinking how Cal used that name – doll –

as if I'm the misfit at this school. My chicken tenders and chocolate milk comfort me with the slightly-better-than-average charm school cafeteria food has. The academy's selection is nothing amazing, but it's filling and just tasty enough.

"Special protection. Principal Ross wants to run for school council next year, haven't you heard?" Chelle smiles sadly. I shake my head. "Well, guess whose father just happens to be a major shaker in Seattle politics? Ever heard of Alex Palkovich Sr., the councilman?"

"Oh, God." I wrinkle my nose. "You mean *he's* Scourge's dad? He used to show up for fundraisers and inspirational speeches at my dad's company."

"Yep, the apple falls pretty far from the tree this time. It's banged up and rotten."

"Who does he think he's convincing, anyway? I mean, the scary ink, the piercings, the punk bomber jacket...amazing he doesn't get called out for breaking dress code." I look down at my own soft blue blouse and plaid skirt, frowning.

Chelle just laughs. "Girl, you've got a lot to learn about how backs are scratched at Maynard. He's gotten in trouble tons of times. Scourge never gets suspended unless he's done *really* bad. Hugo got caught by his pastor smoking the roaches he bought off that kid. Gave up his source pretty quick, and they had to do something this time because the police were involved."

"Yeah, Hugo, I keep hearing that name. Where the heck is he?"

"You don't get on Scourge's bad side and get away without catching hell," Chelle says, wagging a finger. "Hugo's folks were smart. They pulled him out and transferred to Jackson High the next county over. Heard he *begged* them for it. It's not as good, of course, but it's better than spending the rest of his high school career waiting for the knife in his back."

I'm worried she means it literally. Could it be *that* bad? I knew this boy was bad news, but I didn't know he was a total loon.

"And what's with the name? Scourge?"

Chelle opens her mouth to answer, but another voice cuts her off behind me. "Scourge of God, doll. It's from one of those dumb death metal bands he listens to. He only says it about ten times a week to remind us what hot shit he thinks he is. And don't you know he's got an Uncle in the *fucking Grizzlies?*"

When I spin my chair around, Cal stands there with a twinkle in his blue eyes, his hair tossed in a subtle, delicious mess. He's just come from gym, still wearing his black lacrosse shorts and grey jersey with the school's royal crested M.

"I wasn't asking you." I turn, pointing my nose in the air.

I'm not in any mood for his games after what just went down.

"Heard you had a little run in with our pal. Move over, Emily." He takes her seat without even acknowledging the blonde sophomore next to me who looks like she's just been kissed because he remembers her name.

"I thought the Grizzlies cleaned up their act. That's what mom says, anyway. She used to ride with them sometimes in her wilder days, before she settled down with dad." I'm frowning, trying to figure out why he's decided to give me his precious attention today if it's not for his own amusement.

"They did. The uncle he makes sure everybody knows about has been in jail for years. One of the turds they flushed before the club started making money off clubs and bars from what I hear."

"Always so eloquent," Chelle says, sticking her tongue out.

"Did I invite you to this conversation?" he asks, scorning her with a glance, before turning back to me. "Shame about your mom, though. Good times are underrated. Sure hope the wild streak is hereditary. You look like you could use some fun and take your mind off this crap, doll."

I'm blushing, and I hate it. Especially because it's all too easy to imagine the good times he has in mind.

There's no hope. I'm more like every other girl in my class than I care to admit: smitten, shaken, and yes, completely fascinated by this tactless jerk with an angel's looks. He's bad, thoughtless, and more than a little annoying. But he's safe in a way Scourge isn't, despite how easy his teasing becomes insults.

He also gives everyone on his side a certain amount of protection from what I've gathered. Hugo never got close to Cal, and he became easy prey.

"Seriously, don't be scared of him, doll. *Do* stay out of his way. Tried to warn you when you got here. I can help."

Great. So he's come to impress me by playing hero. No thanks.

I'm also done being a doormat for anyone today. Walking out and giving him the cold shoulder feels like an easy way to replenish the self-esteem I've hemorrhaged with the bully.

"Tell me if you change your mind, doll. We'll work something out." His eyes aren't moving when they lock on, and the flush invading my skin just keeps growing.

I have to get out of here.

It's my turn to do the eye roll. Without saying anything, I pick my tray up, and pause just long enough to share another look with him before the blood rushes to my cheeks. "I'm old enough to take care of myself, thanks. If I ever need your advice, Cal, I'll ask."

He doesn't say a word. But he watches me the entire time as I throw my trash away, drop the tray off, and head out for my evening classes. I resist the urge to turn around until the very end.

Of course, I do. How could I resist?

I'm just in time to see Chelle kick him under the table. He gives her a dirty look, stands, and heads back to his crew of jocks across the cafeteria.

Like I need this weirdo treating me like a damsel in distress, I think to myself, smiling for reasons I can't pin down as I head off to Pre-Calc.

I wish I'd taken more time then to appreciate the smiles we shared, however small. Months later, after the train wreck everyone took to calling 'the incident,' it's a miracle I ever learned to fake smile again.

GET FIANCÉ ON PAPER AT YOUR FAVORITE RETAILER!